ACCLAIM FOR CARL WEBER'S NOVELS

"Weber packs his latest urban soap opera with all seven deadly sins... [To] err is not only human, but a whole lot more fun to read."
—*Publishers Weekly* on *The Man in 3B*

"Contains lots of the drama and tight writing style that has made him a *New York Times* bestselling author, and more importantly, all the surprises and shocks readers won't see coming."
—Examiner.com on *The Man in 3B*

"With his typical flair, Weber brings readers another jaw-dropping tale of African-American life."
—Goodreads.com on *The Family Business*

"Weber's in top form with this fast-paced and oh-so-zany soap opera."
—*Publishers Weekly* on *Big Girls Do Cry*

"After a church member commits suicide, secrets are exposed that could destroy the church and various relationships as Weber successfully explores the multiple megaproblems challenging this church family and scores again with a lively mix of church politics and bedroom follies."

"Weber keeps the pacing brisk and loads the narrative with enough surprise turns to keep readers guessing to the end."

OTHER NOVELS BY CARL WEBER

Lookin' for Luv
Married Men
Baby Momma Drama
Player Haters
The Preacher's Son
So You Call Yourself a Man
The First Lady
Something on the Side
Up to No Good
Big Girls Do Cry
Torn Between Two Lovers
The Choir Director
She Ain't the One with Mary B. Morrison
The Family Business with Eric Pete
The Man in 3B
The Family Business 2 with Treasure Hernandez

the Choir Director 2

Runaway Bride

CARL WEBER

GRAND CENTRAL
PUBLISHING

LARGE PRINT

Copyright © 2014 by Carl Weber
Excerpt from *The Man in 3B* © 2013 by Carl Weber
Discussion Questions © 2014 by Carl Weber

Grand Central Publishing
Hachette Book Group
237 Park Avenue
New York, NY 10017

HachetteBookGroup.com

Printed in the United States of America

RRD-C

First Large Print Edition: August 2014
10 9 8 7 6 5 4 3 2 1

Grand Central Publishing is a division of Hachette Book Group, Inc.
The Grand Central Publishing name and logo is a trademark of Hachette Book Group, Inc.

The Hachette Speakers Bureau provides a wide range of authors for speaking events. To find out more, go to www.hachettespeakersbureau.com or call (866) 376-6591.

The publisher is not responsible for websites (or their content) that are not owned by the publisher.

Library of Congress Cataloging-in-Publication Data
Weber, Carl.
  The choir director 2 : runaway bride / Carl Weber. — First edition.
    pages cm
  Runaway bride
  ISBN 978-1-4555-0521-0 (hardcover) — ISBN 978-1-4555-8430-7 (large print trade) — ISBN 978-1-4789-2536-1 (audiobook) — ISBN 978-1-4789-2537-8 (audio download) — ISBN 978-1-4555-0522-7 (ebook) 1. African American choral conductors—Fiction. 2. African American churches—Fiction. 3. Large type books. I. Title. II. Title: Runaway bride.
  PS3573.E2164C57 2014
  813'.54—dc23
                              2013043032

To my daughter Jasmine, who will be leaving for college this month.
I am very proud of you. You have grown into quite the young lady.
Always remember: Make good choices.

Acknowledgments

Once again, I want to thank my fans for being supportive over the years and having my back. You've been an incredible support system. I pray that each and every one of you has the opportunity to live your dream as I have.

the Choir Director 2

Prologue

I was on my knees, out of breath, drenched in perspiration. My heart felt like it might burst out of my chest. I can't ever remember being that nervous, and to be quite frank, I was scared out of my wits. It felt like I was in the middle of someone else's horrible nightmare that had somehow become my own, which in some strange way was true. Only there was no waking up from this one. This was reality.

"Help me," he murmured, his voice barely audible. "Please help me."

I lifted my head, scanning the room nervously despite the fact that I already knew it was empty. I looked down at his face, sadly taking in the reality of the situation. He was dying. There was no doubt about that. You can always see when death is coming in the eyes. They are a mirror to the soul, and, well, the reflection was grim.

What the hell have I gotten myself into?

"Help me," he murmured again. This time he took hold of my wrist with his trembling hand.

Impulsively, I pulled my arm back to avoid his tightening grip; this consequently slid the nine-inch blade out of his chest. I watched as blood filled the hole the knife had come out of, and within seconds his hold on my wrist became limp.

"Dear God, what have I done?" I thought out loud.

"It looks like you just murdered a man," a voice called out from behind me.

I jumped, startled that I was no longer alone. I turned toward the sound and found two uniformed police officers standing behind me with their guns drawn.

I raised both hands. "This is not what it looks like, officer," I started, unable to keep the pleading tone out of my voice. I was begging them to believe me.

"Really," one of the cops said. "Because it looks like he's dead and you're holding a bloody knife in your hand."

I glanced at the knife, shaking my head. "This really isn't what—"

"Drop the fucking knife! We can see what it is!" his partner shouted, and I froze.

I was in the process of doing as I was told when a tall white man in a cheap suit walked into the room with a black woman. I recognized her right away. Her name was Keisha Anderson, and she was a New

York City police detective. From the way her jaw dropped, I was sure she recognized me too.

"Oh my God!" she muttered.

"Do you know this guy, Anderson?" the plain-clothes cop asked.

"Yes, I know him. Every black person in Queens knows him. He's Bishop TK Wilson. He's the pastor of my church!"

Desiree

1

One month earlier

I'd been staking out the lobby of one of the finest hotels in New York City for almost an hour, and I was pissed. After following new gospel sensation Aaron Mackie and his entourage from Peter Luger's steak house, I'd lost their trail shortly after the limo pulled in front of the hotel. The damn traffic in New York City was so bad that it had taken me almost fifteen minutes to find a parking spot, and by the time I reached the lobby, they were nowhere to be found. I checked out the hotel's restaurant, bar, and private conference rooms, all to no avail. I even used the house phone and pretended I was Aaron's mother trying to get in touch with him, but there was no room registered in his name, so I was stuck. I did, however, know they were still in the building somewhere, thanks to the fifty-dollar bill I'd slipped the bellman, so I stayed put.

I finally caught a break when four very out-of-place black women, each wearing six-inch heels and clothes that screamed "I'm a stripper!" entered the lobby, followed by two gorilla-size brothers who were obviously either bodyguards or pimps. They stood out from the clientele of the hotel about as much as Ray J would at Kim Kardashian and Kanye West's wedding. The four misfits didn't ask any questions or stop at the front desk to register, like most people I'd seen enter the hotel. Nope, they headed straight for the elevator. It didn't take much effort to figure out where they were going.

The thought entered my mind to follow them onto the elevator, but I decided that wasn't necessary. The beauty of this hotel was that the elevators were made of glass, and I was able to watch them travel up and step off on the tenth floor. With that information, I headed straight for my car to retrieve my bag then went back to the elevator. I'd had the bag packed just for this occasion. Ever since I read the announcement in *Jet* magazine's online edition last week, I knew that this opportunity to be near Aaron would present itself.

As I exited the elevator, I spotted one of the two gorillas who'd been following the girls. He was standing guard outside a row of rooms I assumed were suites. I made sure to flash my best smile as I approached him, knowing that the yellow dress I was wearing displayed all of my assets at their best in a classy way, unlike the strippers he'd been following. Not many men could resist what I had to offer.

"Excuse me. Is Aaron Mackie in there?" I pointed at the door behind him.

"Private party," he barked at me, answering my question without answering my question.

"Yes, I know. I'm here to work," I assured him in my most flirtatious manner. "This is Aaron Mackie's bachelor party, isn't it?"

"Yeah, but you're not one of my girls." He slid his eyes over my body, unable to hide a hint of interest. "You're not even a stripper. What are you, a groupie? I heard these gospel cats had groupies. Church girls gone wild." He laughed.

"No, I'm not a groupie. I'm a fan," I purred, trying to avoid eye contact. "But today I'd like to be a stripper, if that's what it takes to get in that room with Mr. Mackie. I even have the outfit." I tapped my bag.

"Sorry. We're already full." He looked away, dismissing me.

"Are you sure? Because I'm willing to make it worth your while."

He turned his gaze to my lower half, suddenly interested again. "Oh yeah? And how is that?" He reached an arm around my waist, and I allowed his beefy hand to palm my ass.

"You let me work this party, and I give you this."

I reached in my bag and pulled out two one-hundred dollar bills. I'd much rather Benjamin go down his pants than me have to let this gorilla in mine. But don't get it twisted: I was prepared to do whatever I needed to do in order to be on the other side of that door.

He smiled at the money. "You know, me and my boy, we got a reputation to uphold. We're known for having some of the best talent in NYC. Do you have any idea what a stripper does at one of these parties?"

I swallowed hard, reluctantly placing my hand between his legs. I massaged his manhood and asked, "Would you like me to show you?"

He shook his head, releasing my ass from his grip. This caused me concern, until I noticed he was staring at the money. Even the straightest man will sometimes choose a dude over pussy—as long as that dude is big-face Benji. "No, I think you get the idea. But you better add three more hundreds to that if you think you're getting into this party. And I don't want any funny business, or I will throw your ass off the balcony myself. You get that?"

I didn't reply. I just reached in my bag and pulled out three more hundred dollar bills, thanking the Lord as I did it that his nasty ass hadn't said yes to my erotic suggestion. He took the bills then opened the door.

"You can change in here. The party's in the adjoining suite. And like I said before, I don't want any funny business."

Three strippers were in the room, getting dressed for the party. I could feel the tension the second I walked in. For the first time since I arrived in New York on this crusade to meet Aaron Mackie, I was nervous.

"Damn, how many girls they got coming up in here tonight?" a tall, very pretty, dark-skinned sister with a blond wig and thigh-high boots whined.

"I'm the last one," I assured her.

"Good, 'cause we barely about to make any money in here in the first place," a short, half-black, half-Asian spinner snapped. "And I ain't here for my health."

"Why aren't we going to make any money?" I asked, curious about the profession I was pretending to be a part of.

"I can answer that in one word," the dark-skinned sister replied.

All three of them said in unison, "Niggas!"

"Niggas," I repeated.

"That's right," the half-Asian girl replied. "Cheap-ass niggas. When I first heard this bachelor party was here, I thought I was gonna get paid, but as soon as I found out the party was for a brother, I knew it was gonna be a whole lot of work for a little bit of money."

"I don't understand. Those men in there are rich, aren't they? This place has to be five, six hundred a night."

She laughed at me. "You ain't been in this business long, have you?"

"No, I haven't," I replied, thinking *Am I that obvious?*

"I didn't think so, otherwise you would have known that these cheap-ass black motherfuckers never tip that good at bachelor parties. That's why I like doing the white parties. Brothers think that your shit is supposed to be free. They don't like to pay for pussy, especially not from black women. But don't take my word for it. You'll see."

"Wow." I commiserated with them as I opened the bag and pulled out my costume. "Well, I don't care how much money they pay me as long as I get to fuck the groom. That's all I care about."

"What makes you think I'm willing to let you do that?" A high yellow girl with green eyes and a big booty sucked her teeth. "Giving the groom his last piece of ass is the only thing these cheap-ass fools are willing to pony up for."

"Because I'm willing to give you two hundred dollars as insurance that I get what I want," I offered.

"That's two hundred dollars each, right?" the half-Asian chick asked.

"Yes, two hundred each." I looked around to see if there were any more objections.

"Hell, I'm willing to do it as long as I get my money up front." Miss High Yellow laughed as they all high-fived her.

"We cool?" Every girl nodded, just like I thought they would. They had no idea, but if she had asked for four hundred dollars each I would have given it to them.

Five minutes later, I was dressed in a black lace bustier, matching garter, thong, and six-inch heels. I put on my last accessory and stood up to survey my outfit.

"Whoa, what the hell is that, a mask?" one of them blurted out.

"Mm-hmm. It's all part of my act. Men love mystery, and this is mysterious. The groom gets to be the only one to see all of me, if you get what I'm saying."

"Damn, that shit is tight." Blondie laughed as she headed for the door. "I might have to get me a mask."

The moment we stepped into the room, hands were grabbing for us. One guy attached himself to me and tried to pull me down onto his lap. His paws were all over my ass. I felt like turning around and slapping the shit outta him.

"No, no, no!" I scolded, pushing him back.

"What do you mean, no? I'm a paying customer!" This fool had the nerve to be waving a dollar at me like it was a hundred dollar bill. Now I was starting to see what the other girls were talking about, because this dude with his dollar wasn't giving up easily. His hands were still moving a hundred miles an hour.

I responded in a voice loud enough for everybody in the room to hear. "Not to me you're not! I'm here for one person and one person only—the groom-to-be." I served them all notice in my most authoritative tone. "If you're not him, step aside, because when I'm finished with him, he's going to think twice about getting married tomorrow. Now, where is he?" I was doing my Beyoncé stallion walk through that piece like I was about to perform at the Super Bowl.

I heard a lot of "Oh, shit!" and "Day-um!" as the men moved aside, parting into a path for me to follow. There at the end of it, sitting in a chair and holding a beer, was Aaron Mackie. He was even better-looking up close and personal than viewing him from afar in my car. I was glad I was wearing a mask, because I was sure my face would have given away my emotions.

"You looking for me?" he flirted, taking a sip of his beer before tossing the empty can to the side for effect, like we were in some movie. That set his friends off into a testosterone-filled frenzy, and the room filled with shouts of encouragement to spur the two of us on.

I held my breath for a second, during which I actually thought about what the hell I was doing and whether it was worth it. I'd come a long way to have sex with Aaron Mackie and done a lot of things a girl like me shouldn't, but was this how I really wanted to do it? I took one more look at him and came to my conclusion: Of course it was worth it! I'd been waiting for this day ever since that Sunday morning two years ago, when I turned on my TV and saw him being introduced as the director of the First Jamaica Ministries choir. From that moment on, I'd followed his career on Google alerts to make sure I saw any and everything that was posted about him. I didn't even want to think about how much money I'd spent following him around the country to gospel festivals and shows. I wouldn't regret one dime of it if this night went as planned.

I sashayed over to him. "Yeah, I'm looking for you. Me and you got a date in that bedroom over there." I nodded toward the door like I owned the place. "That is, if you think you can handle this." I rubbed my hands over my breasts and thighs, trying to imitate Beyoncé when she did that stripper imitation on the Grammys. This sent his friends into a frenzy again.

"I guess we'll just have to see," he replied, full of self-assured swagger.

"I guess we will." I took hold of his loosened tie, tugging it until he stood up. Using it like a chain on a dog, I led him into the empty room, where he sat on the bed.

I began to perform the kind of striptease that could make a priest have to take confession. My hips were moving from side to side as I released my breasts from the top of my bustier. I leaned over and shoved them in his face, ready for him to succumb to my seduction. Then I turned around, lowering my ass onto his lap and grinding around like I was about to orgasm any minute.

I imagined he was into it, until he said, "Stop," and gave me a slight shove. Undeterred, I kept trying to back it on up. "Hey, I said stop!" he protested, pushing me off of him a little harder this time.

I turned around to face him, unable to believe he was resisting this. "Um, did you say stop?"

"Yeah, I did. I can't do this." He straightened up his shirt and tie, looking every bit as serious as he sounded. "I have an amazing woman that I'm about to marry tomorrow. No disrespect, but I'm not going to cheapen it by being with you."

My jaw just about dropped to the floor. "Are you for real?" I threw the whole Beyoncé demeanor out the window and replaced it with some ol' hands-on-hips Nicki Minaj shit.

"Yes, I'm very much for real." He stood up.

"Look, did I do something wrong? Whatever it is, I won't do it again. I promise." He shook his head, but I didn't believe him. I had to have done something wrong. No way was a man going to just say no to a body like mine. "What about your friends? They paid for—"

"What about them? If they don't understand that I'm getting married and don't want to sleep with a prostitute, then they don't really know me and they're not my friends." He walked out the door, leaving me half-naked and very confused.

"Fuck." I stood there for about five seconds, stunned and on the verge of tears. Somehow, I had just blown the opportunity of a lifetime. I glanced at my reflection in the mirror above the dresser. Dammit, I looked good. How the hell could he have turned this down? Maybe it was the mask, I thought.

Part of me wanted to just give up and go back home to Virginia, but I couldn't. I'd come too far and wasted way too much money not to see this thing through. I would just have to be more creative if I was going to end up with what I wanted.

There was a knock on the door, and then a tall, well-built, brown-skinned brother walked in the room. "Uh, what the hell just happened?" he asked.

"I don't know. I guess he doesn't like women," I snapped in frustration.

He laughed, eyeing me from head to toe. "Maybe not, but his best man sure does."

Aaron

2

My stomach was full of butterflies when I poked my head into the sanctuary from the side door. The church was packed from wall to wall with folks dressed in their Sunday best, and Bishop TK Wilson stood at the altar with Bible in hand. It wouldn't be long before the bishop gave the church organist the signal to play and we'd be heading out to the pulpit ourselves. In all honesty, I couldn't believe how nervous I was. I mean, technically this should all be a cinch. It wasn't like we hadn't practiced and gone over the whole thing last night. Besides, I'd mounted that pulpit hundreds of times before as the choir director. But none of that could stop my nervousness.

I glanced over at my mother and my aunt, Bertha, sitting in the front-row pews. They'd traveled all the way from Virginia to be here for this very special occasion, and the look of pride on my momma's face was priceless. I don't think she had a clue just how much I loved her.

I pulled my head back into the room feeling like I was going to pass out from the anxiety. The butterflies in my stomach had morphed into bats. I turned to Ross Parker, my lifelong friend and the newly appointed business manager for our church choir. He was sitting on the small, worn-out sofa about three feet away from me.

"You okay? You don't look so hot," he said, gazing down at my trembling hands.

I took a deep breath, as if I could exhale my nervousness. I tasted bile at the back of my throat. "I feel like I'm gonna be sick," I said.

Ross stood up and closed the short distance between us. "Dude, you're getting married in about five minutes. It's a big step. Everyone has last-minute jitters before they get married. I bet Tia's out there thinking the same thing." He reached over to the table and picked up a can of Sprite. "Here, take a sip of this. It will calm your stomach."

I did what I was told, my hands shaking as I tipped the can up to my lips. "I don't know, man. I don't think I've ever been this nervous. Am I doing the right thing?"

Ross took the soda from me, placed it back where it had come from, and then turned to me. As he straightened my collar and adjusted my tie, he looked me dead in the eye and asked, "Do you love her? I mean, do you *really* love Tia?"

I looked back into my friend's dark eyes and nodded. "Yeah, man. I love her more than anything in this world. If any woman is my soul mate, it's Tia."

"Well, if that's the case, what are you worried about?"

I made a gesture in the direction of the sanctuary, where so many people were waiting for the opulent ceremony to begin. "I didn't want all this," I said. "I didn't want a huge wedding. As far as I was concerned, we could have gone down to City Hall and gotten married by the justice of the peace."

"Oh, that would have worked out well," Ross said with a laugh. "Besides the fact that you're the choir director in this church and Bishop Wilson would have killed you, every woman wants a big wedding, man. They want that day. You know that." He patted my shoulder. "Besides, when that music starts playing, all this nervousness is gonna go away."

No sooner had he spoken the words than the sound of the organ music filled my ears, signaling that it was time.

I looked at Ross and told him, "You were wrong. It hasn't gone away."

He shrugged his shoulders. "Aaron, you'll be fine."

I dropped my hands to my sides and shook my head. "I'm still nervous. I don't think I can go through with it."

"Man, if you don't get your behind out there..."

He pointed at the door. "Do you know how beautiful she must look right now, standing outside the church waiting for your black ass?"

He'd finally said the right thing. An image of Tia flashed through my mind, and I knew there was no way that I could leave her at the altar. I really did love her and wanted to marry her. I exhaled loudly and shook my arms to release the tension, announcing, "Okay, let's do this."

Ross gave me a final once-over to make sure nothing was out of place, then he patted my shoulder. "You look good. You ready to get married?"

I nodded, straightened my shoulders resolutely, and walked out the door into the sanctuary. I stopped momentarily before ascending the steps in front of the altar, and I felt Ross's hand on my back.

"We out here now, bro," he said. "Ain't no turning back."

I looked at him over my shoulder and said, "Wasn't trying to turn back, my man. Just stopping to pinch myself to make sure this is not a dream."

"Oh, it's real a'ight. Now get your ass up there."

I continued up the steps on wobbly knees and didn't stop until I was in position next to Bishop Wilson.

"You all right, son?" he asked.

"Yes, sir, Bishop. I'm good to go." I nodded nervously as I looked out at the crowd.

The bishop studied me momentarily then said, "I've never met a man who wasn't nervous on his wedding day, including myself."

Ross said with a chuckle, "He's fine for now, Bishop. Let's just speed this up a little before he changes his mind."

"Well then, let's do that, Brother Parker." Bishop Wilson turned and nodded to the organist again. On cue, the music changed and another, more majestic song began.

I stood at attention, still nervous but with a feeling of excitement, too, as I looked toward the doors at the back of the sanctuary. Every head in the church turned to see the first of four women being escorted down the aisle and into their positions at the altar. Each wore a form-fitting blue dress with white trim. They were being escorted by my groomsmen, who wore black tuxedos and blue vests.

The last bridesmaid was being led by John Nixon, or Pippie, as we called him. Pippie was one of my childhood friends from Virginia. He wasn't the most attractive brother, but he'd been there for me when no one else was, including Ross. That's one of the reasons why I'd asked the bishop to give him a job upon his recent release from prison. Being the janitor at First Jamaica wasn't what I would call a high-achieving job, but Pippie was grateful.

Once everyone had taken their places in the front,

all eyes were on the matron of honor, who happened to be none other than First Lady Monique Wilson, wife of the bishop. It was no surprise that Tia chose her to be the matron of honor. She'd been a good friend to both me and my wife-to-be.

To distinguish her from the bridesmaids, Monique wore a hat made out of the same material as her dress—which was custom made to accentuate her very large breasts and rather grand rear. If she were anyone else, I would have sworn she was trying to upstage Tia, but I knew Monique well enough to understand that she wasn't doing anything but being herself. She was definitely not like any other first lady I'd ever met.

Monique took her place across from Ross, and then I knew the time had come. The flower girl had dropped her last petal, and the doors to the church sanctuary had closed. I glanced over at my mother, who blew me a kiss as she stood with the rest of the guests when the first strains of the "Wedding March" began.

So far, everything had gone just as I expected, and the butterflies in my stomach had settled—that is, until the time stretched on into a second and third repeat of the "Wedding March," and still no sign of my bride. I felt the butterflies taking up flight again.

I glanced at the bishop, who was looking at me

with raised eyebrows. I shrugged. Bishop turned to Ross, who also shrugged.

We all looked to the first lady.

"Where is she? I thought she was going to ride in the limo with you guys," I whispered to Monique.

"She did," Monique whispered back. "It was a little chilly outside, so she stayed in the limo with her brother when we got out. I sent the driver back to get them right before I came through the doors."

"Then where is she?"

I looked over at my mother and then at the crowd. People were starting to get restless, some sitting back down and others mumbling their confusion to each other, swiveling their heads around as if they'd find the bride somewhere other than coming down the main aisle. I was sure everyone was wondering the same thing I was: Where was my bride?

God, this cannot be happening. Tia wouldn't leave me at the altar, would she?

"Everybody just relax," Ross said to the group assembled in front. "You know how women are. She'll make her grand entrance and get the reaction she's hoping for. Just chill."

I tried to buy into his confidence. "Yeah, man. Yeah, you're right," I said, loosening up my shoulders and then cracking my neck.

Once again I turned my attention to the closed

sanctuary doors. After a brief, confused pause the organist started on her fifth repetition of the "Wedding March."

Finally, the sanctuary doors opened. I felt a momentary rush of relief when I spotted Tia's brother, Kareem. She'd asked him to escort her down the aisle to give her away.

I heard my mother let out a pronounced, "Thank you, Jesus!"

There was a collective sigh of relief from the crowd, and my heartbeat slowed down a little, but only for the few seconds it took to register that Kareem was striding toward the front—alone. The noise from the guests in attendance was no longer a whisper, but more like a frenzied buzzing. The organist stopped playing altogether.

As Kareem got closer, I could see the expression on his face, and I knew it meant nothing good.

He came up the steps and stood in front of me. "Look, Aaron, man, I'm sorry." Dude could barely look me in the eyes. "I'm really sorry."

"Sorry about what?" I gave a nervous laugh.

"It's Tia. She's gone," Kareem said.

"What do you mean, she's gone?" Bishop's voice was barely above a whisper, but he was still clearly taking charge of the situation. I was glad for that, because I sure couldn't. As weak as my knees felt, I was lucky I was still standing.

"She's gone, Bishop, as in 'she's not here,'" Kareem answered.

I looked to Monique, whose expression told me she was as confused as I was.

"What—where...?" I couldn't even finish my sentence. I felt a splitting headache coming on.

"I don't know, man. Once Monique got out of the limo, Tia burst into tears. Then she told me she couldn't go through with it and asked me to tell everyone."

"What the hell are you talking about? Where is she, Kareem?" I snatched him by the collar, but Ross quickly pulled me off of him.

"Stop, Aaron! This isn't his fault."

"Then whose fault is it?" I was on the verge of tears. "Somebody tell me something."

"I don't know what to tell you, Aaron," Kareem said, sounding apologetic.

I stared off at nothing in particular. "Tell me she's coming back. That's what you can tell me. I thought she loved me. I thought she wanted to marry me." What was I supposed to do now?

Ross

3

All hell had broken loose at First Jamaica Ministries with Tia not showing up for the wedding. As Aaron's manager, it was my job to do damage control, which was part of the reason I shuttled everyone from the groom's side of the wedding party into the bishop's office to regroup. I wanted Aaron as far away from all the gossips, cameras, and press as I could get him. I knew it would only be a matter of time before the entire borough of Queens knew about our runaway bride. I was also sure that the local news would be on the story as well. I could already hear the anchors of the six o'clock local news: *In a sad local story, First Jamaica Ministries' award-winning singer, songwriter, and choir director, Aaron Mackie, was left at the altar by his bride this afternoon.* I could only pray that the story didn't get picked up by the national media, but with Aaron's rising stardom on the gospel circuit, I didn't have much faith in my prayers being answered. Representatives from *Ebony* and *Essence* magazines were already in attendance, so I figured it was just a matter of time before we'd get a call from TMZ.

Still, the bishop always said "Be thankful for what you have," so at the moment I was giving thanks for the fact that we were in the safe confines of his office. It was time for me to stop acting like a manager and more like a best friend. My poor buddy looked like he was about to break down and cry.

"You okay?" I asked, placing my hand on Aaron's shoulder. He was sitting in a chair in the far corner of the room with his head hung low, and didn't bother to answer me. A few of his groomsmen stood by helplessly.

"Did you two have a fight?" the bishop questioned from his seat behind a large mahogany desk.

"No, everything was great. I thought we were the happiest people on the face of the earth. This whole thing doesn't make any sense, Bishop." Aaron shook his head rapidly as if it might wake him up from this nightmare.

"No, it doesn't, son," the bishop reassured him. "It doesn't make any sense at all."

"I never much liked that heifer anyway," Aaron's mother blurted out in her characteristic fashion. I'd known Mrs. Mackie for years. She was a sweet old woman—except when it came to her son. She'd go gangsta in a minute if she thought someone was doing him wrong. If you crossed him, you crossed her, no matter what the circumstances. "If you ask me, you were too good for her trifling behind. I'm sure you're better off without her."

"No, Ma, I'm not!" Aaron protested. "I'm a much better man with her than without her. I just don't know what happened. I thought we were happy." The look on his face was one of pure devastation. "I just want to find her so she can tell me what I did wrong."

"Ha! You say you wanna find her? If I could get my hands on her, I'd wring her skinny little neck!" His mother's voice shook with rage, and although I loved Tia, I imagine I would have felt the same thing if it had been my son Tia left at the altar.

"Sister Mackie, we just have to give God time. We may not know it today, but there is always a reason," Bishop preached. "We need to trust that God has a plan."

I could see from her eyes Mrs. Mackie was about to say something to the bishop that wasn't very Christian-like. She was looking for a scapegoat for her anger, and the bishop seemed to be directly in her crosshairs. Luckily, her sister spoke up before she could do any damage.

"Emma, why don't we get on out of here and head over to the reception hall. We got a lot of family from outta town to see, and they're going to want some answers."

"I'm not leaving my baby," Mrs. Mackie protested.

"Aaron is in capable hands. He'll be okay. Besides, in times like these, men need to be with men. You don't want them to think Aaron's some kind of momma's boy or a sissy, do you?" Mrs. Mackie snapped her head toward her sister and they shared a long, hard stare before she nodded, conceding to her sister's request.

A few minutes later, after hugging her son like he was a little boy, Aaron's mother excused herself and left the room with her sister.

Silence overtook the office, each of us lost in our own sense of disbelief over the day's events. A strong knock on the door jolted us back to the moment.

"Come in," Bishop called.

The door opened and a tall, well-dressed man, probably in his late forties, walked into the room. I had no idea who he was, and from the looks on their faces, neither did anyone else. Whoever he was, he was a confident SOB, striding in like he owned the place. It was as if the dude's feet weren't even touching the floor. He just floated inside.

"Can I help you?" Bishop asked. He stood from his chair to greet the man.

Instead of acknowledging the bishop and stating

his business the way most people would, this guy didn't even look in the bishop's direction as he walked past him.

"No, you can't help me, but he can." He stopped directly in front of Aaron, staring down at him over his designer glasses. This had suddenly become really interesting. Who was this guy and what did he want with Aaron? I hoped he wasn't a process server, because that was the last thing Aaron needed.

"Hello, Aaron. Can I call you Aaron?" he asked, continuing to speak without waiting for an answer. "My name is Jackson Young. I'm with the Johnson Morris Agency in Manhattan. I'm sure you've heard of us. We're one of the most prestigious agencies in the world. I realize that this is not the most opportune time, but I really would like to speak to you about your career. We're very impressed with your talent, and I think we could take your career to the next level."

Of course Aaron knew what the Johnson Morris Agency was, and so did I. Jackson Young wasn't lying. An agency like that could take him and the choir to new heights.

"You're right, Mr. Young, this is not the most opportune time. I kind of have other things on my mind." Aaron gave the man a withering look, but his tone remained polite. "If you have any business with me or the choir, you should talk to our manager, Ross Parker."

He motioned toward me. I stepped up, eager to take the guy's card. I had no idea how he ended up in the bishop's office today of all days. Maybe his timing was a little off, but I still wanted to hear what he was offering. Young, however, held on to the card, eyeing me up and down like I was some kind of joke. He finally let it go with a little chuckle, but he'd officially put himself on my personal shit list.

"I'll give you a call on Monday," I said.

"You would want to. It's in your best interests," he said, stepping closer to me. He turned back to Aaron. "I hope everything works out for you. I always found that working takes my mind off my problems. I'll be in touch." Without another word, he headed for the door, only to run into First Lady Monique Wilson as she entered the office. She'd been in the sanctuary, trying to calm some of the chaos and inviting everyone to the reception hall for lunch. The food was already paid for, and it was the least we could do considering how far some people had traveled to be at the wedding.

"Why, hellooooo, pretty lady." Jackson grinned, eyeing the first lady provocatively.

Before any of us realized what was happening, he reached down and took her hand to kiss it. First

Lady Wilson's cheeks flushed bright red, and to be quite honest, I wasn't sure if it was because she was flustered or because she was flattered. Whichever it was, her husband's loud "Ahem!" helped bring her back to reality. He clearly wasn't happy, but the man carried himself with so much dignity that he didn't show it for long.

"I have got to start spending more time in Queens. This borough is full of surprises." Jackson kissed her hand again. "I mean, who knew there were real live queens here?" He was slopping the syrup on First Lady as if she were a stack of pancakes.

"Um, hello, I'm First Lady Monique Wilson," she said, forcing the formality into her tone.

"Pleasure to meet you, Monique. You certainly are a beauty. Are you by chance an actress?" He was grinning at her like she was the only person in the room.

Her cheeks were still red, and I swear she looked like she was about to start fanning herself. "No. What would make you think that?" she asked, sounding on the verge of giddiness.

"Sorry, your beauty has me so mesmerized, I forgot my manners. I'm Jackson Young. I'm a talent agent at the Johnson Morris Agency."

"Oh, really? What exactly does a talent agent do?"

"We make beautiful women like you into stars."

That fool was smiling so hard you could see every one of his teeth, including his molars.

"Well, no, I'm not an actress, but I have acted a little in plays here at the church." By this time it was pretty obvious that she was falling prey to his game.

"Oh, I bet you were the star of the show," Jackson said, reaching into his pocket for a business card. "We should have dinner tonight and discuss me being your agent."

Out of the corner of my eye I saw the bishop rising from behind his desk. Dignified or not, no man could sit by and watch some other dude hit on his wife without speaking up.

First Lady Wilson didn't seem to notice her husband at all. "Are you serious? You'd like to represent me?"

"I'd love to represent you. I think I can make you a star."

She looked like she was about to burst wide open with glee, but then the bishop stepped up to stand beside her, and her whole demeanor changed. "I'd have to talk this over with my husband, of course." She gestured soberly toward the bishop. "Have you met my husband, Bishop TK Wilson?"

Jackson glanced over at the bishop then back to the first lady. "No, I haven't, but he's really not relevant to this conversation. I'm not interested in making him a star. My interest is totally in you, so please give me a call so we can have dinner." He reached out for her hand again, leaning down to kiss it for the third time. "Monique, we have so much to talk about. You have something. Even a blind man can see it. I just hope you allow me to help you reach your full potential as an actress."

Bishop Wilson finally spoke up. "She's not interested."

"I wasn't talking to you," Jackson replied.

"But *I* was talking to *you*," the bishop snapped back.

"TK!" the first lady scolded her husband.

The groomsmen, who'd been standing in the corner leaned against the wall, were suddenly standing at attention. We were all gearing up to break up a fight.

"I didn't marry any actress. You are plenty busy around here being first lady of this church," Bishop insisted. His eyes were focused on Jackson. "Mr. Young was just leaving when you came in. I think it's time he left."

Jackson shook his head and shot the bishop a look of pure arrogance. "You know, it's a shame when a man tries to hold back a woman just to coddle his own ego. I guess it's true what they say about all you preachers."

"And what exactly is that?" the bishop growled.

"You all wear panties under your robes." While

Jackson was laughing at his own joke, the bishop lunged after him. Before he could get a good grip, Aaron and I grabbed him. He struggled, out of control. Pippie pulled Jackson toward the door.

"Monique, you have my number. Please give me a call. Anytime." Jackson left the room looking every bit as confident as he had when he entered.

Tia

4

It was supposed to be the best day of my life, but sometimes things don't turn out the way you plan. Breaking up with anyone was tough, but this breakup was especially hard considering the amount of time we had both invested. Still, I'd promised myself that I wouldn't second-guess my decision to walk away—not today, not tomorrow, not ever—so instead of sitting around wallowing in self-pity, my girl Kenya and I headed over to this new club in Long Island City to see what kind of trouble we could get into. I'd never heard of the place, but Kenya told me they'd recently been featured in both *Vibe* and *XXL* magazines as one of the hottest dance clubs in the country.

It looked like the club was going to live up to its reputation when we showed up and saw that the line to get in was snaked around the block. Kenya seemed to know everybody, and judging by the fact that no one complained when she grabbed my wrist and led me straight to the front of the line, they all knew her too.

"Kenya, how's it going?" the doorman, a big bruiser of a white guy, asked as he leaned down to kiss her on the cheek. My girl Kenya has this petite body and these big huge tits that seem to drive white guys crazy.

"Much better, Paulie, now that I've seen you," Kenya flirted.

"Who's your friend? I thought you rolled solo." He gave me the once-over but didn't seem impressed. I have a dynamite ass, but I'm lacking in the breast department.

"I usually do, but this is my girl, Tia. She just broke up with her man. We're celebrating the end of an era and the beginning of a new one. I'm about to get her drunk and laid."

I joined in with her laughter, although I was only agreeing to the getting drunk part. The getting laid part I wasn't so sure about. Kenya was the slut, not me, which was why my ex had always made it his business to keep us apart.

"Well, you brought her to the right place to do it." His eyes were feasting on Kenya's cleavage as he opened the rope and allowed us to enter the club. "Hey, Kenya, save me a dance, will you?"

She turned around and smiled. "I'll save you more than that if that girlfriend of yours isn't around tonight to block it."

There was no doubt in my mind that she was serious. If she had a chance, she'd be screwing that white boy later that night.

"She's here. I'll take a rain check on that and settle for a dance," he said with a wink.

Kenya squeezed my hand and led me into the crowded club, which was already jumping. I had to stop myself from displaying a wide-eyed, gaping-mouth expression, because I'd never been to a club like this. There were raised platforms with half-naked dancers simulating sex acts. On the dance floor, hot, sweaty bodies were pressed up against each other, grinding to the beat as the DJ served it up.

We got lucky and found seats at one of the bars when a couple got up to dance. Five minutes later, Kenya was on the dance floor with some guy she'd obviously been screwing, and I was left sitting there by myself, nursing my drink. Justin Timberlake's "Suit & Tie" hit the turntable, and I felt my body swaying to the beat when I noticed a really hot white guy leaning against a pole, giving me the eye. He wasn't trying to hide the fact that he was looking, either. I gave him a smile when our eyes met then turned away to order a drink. Before I could get the bartender's attention he had slipped into Kenya's seat.

"I'm sorry, but that's my friend's seat," I shouted over the music.

"Your boyfriend?" he shouted back, looking dis-appointed.

I shook my head, pointing at Kenya on the dance floor. "No, my friend!"

"It's okay. I'll keep it safe until she gets back. Can I buy you a drink?" He flashed a flawless smile at me. I wanted to say no, but I had to admit he was easy on the eyes and, well, one glance at Kenya told me that she had no plans of coming back to her seat anytime soon.

"Sure. You can buy me a drink." I tried to play it cool, but inside I was nervous as hell. After all, less than twenty-four hours ago I wasn't even single.

Now, normally white boys weren't on my radar, but this one was all kinds of fine: green eyes, dark hair, and a body his tailored shirt couldn't hide. Be-sides, maybe after what had happened this afternoon with my ex it was time for a change. "I'll have an ap-pletini."

"Appletini it is." He moved in closer so he wouldn't have to shout. "My name's Michael."

My first thought was to give him a fake name, but my mouth betrayed my brain and I told him, "My name's Tia." I looked over at Kenya on the dance floor, wishing she would come over and rescue me before I said something stupid to this fine specimen of a man. She was grinding all over the guy on the dance floor, though, so I would have to fly solo.

"Tia. That's a very pretty name," he said with a charming smile that made me want to melt in my seat.

Michael flagged down the bartender, and three drinks later we were still sitting there talking—or, rather, I was talking. Maybe it was the alcohol loosening my tongue, or the fact that I had just broken up with a man who never seemed to shut up and let me get a word in edgewise. Whichever it was, it was working for us. I talked about the death of my parents and how my brother Kareem had pretty much raised me since I was thirteen—things I normally didn't like to talk about, but this guy was such a good listener. As time passed, I realized I wouldn't mind seeing him again.

Somewhere around one in the morning he asked me to dance, and when we hit the floor, that white boy put me to shame. He had moves on top of moves, and my stiff behind could barely keep up. I mean, he could really freakin' dance. After I made a fool out of myself for about twenty minutes next to this John Travolta clone, the DJ slowed the tempo down and put on a slow jam. I was about to walk off the floor in shame, but Michael took my hand and pulled me in close. I didn't resist. It felt good to wrap my arms around his broad shoulders and lean my head on his chest.

This trip to the club had been the perfect way

to take my mind off of the day's events. I was really enjoying myself. I glanced up at Michael and smiled, and to my pleasant surprise, he leaned down and kissed me, ever so gently pressing his soft lips against mine. As his tongue slipped into my mouth, I could feel an electric current going through me, as if our bodies were meant to connect this way. When our lips parted, I returned my head to his chest, holding on to him even tighter as I savored our first kiss.

When the music changed back to a more up-tempo beat, Michael leaned in close, whispering in my ear, "Hey, you wanna get out of here? Go for a drive?" The feeling of his breath against my neck sent a shiver of arousal between my legs.

I looked around for Kenya, who was nowhere to be found. I'd be violating every rule in the girl-friend handbook if I left without telling her first, but knowing her, she was probably off with some guy in the bathroom or something. Technically, she had left me first, I reasoned. I was not about to miss the opportunity to spend time with Michael just because I couldn't find Kenya's ass. I was really feeling a connection to him, and if that first kiss was any indication of what was to come, this guy had the skills to make me forget all about my ex.

"Yeah, I'd love to go for a ride with you," I said with a smile.

He wasted no time leading me out of the club, holding the door open like a perfect gentleman. At his car, a beautiful Porsche 911, he rushed over to the passenger-side door and helped me in. I slid into the leather seat thinking, *Damn, I could get used to this.*

Before we pulled away from the curb, he leaned over and kissed me again. To be very frank, it was that kiss that convinced me I wanted to sleep with him, and I think he knew it.

We drove around for a while, listening to music and holding hands. There was very little conversation, but I didn't mind. After the banging bass in the club, it was a nice break.

After a while he said, "Do you smoke weed? I've got some really good hydro back at my place. You wanna go back there and smoke?"

I laughed, but not because he asked if I smoked weed. I wasn't a big pot smoker, but I had been known to indulge from time to time. I was laughing because it was a pretty slick-ass way of getting me to his apartment.

"Sure." I turned my head toward his so he could kiss me again. At that moment, we both knew where this little joyride was going to end up. There was an undeniable chemistry between us. Even if it only ended up being a one-night stand, I wanted to be with this guy.

Twenty-five minutes later we pulled up in front of a house. I'd been so busy daydreaming about the two of us making love I hadn't paid much attention to the route he took. "Where are we?"

"My house," he said.

I glanced up at the two-story colonial. "Your house as in 'you own it,' or your house as in 'you stay here with your momma'?"

Michael chuckled. "It's my house. I bought it, but I do have roommates."

I looked at the large house again, impressed. "You own this place?"

"Yes," he said as he opened his door to get out.

I'd only slept with four guys in my life, but there was no doubt he was going to be number five—and my first white boy. I still couldn't believe my luck. He was cute, ambitious, and owned his own home. I must have died and gone to heaven, because I didn't know anyone our age who owned a house. Heck, I didn't know many people of any age who owned their own homes after the recession.

I turned away, imagining him reading my dirty thoughts.

Once again he walked around the car and opened my door. He held my hand as we entered the quaint house. His roommates, two black guys who looked like athletes, were playing on an Xbox in the living room. I could tell they were in the middle of some heavy competition since they barely acknowledged us. That was fine with me, because all my attention was on Michael, who quickly guided me past them, up the stairs and into his bedroom.

I was even more impressed by Michael when I saw his room. It was far from the typical messy, mattress-on-the-floor, twentysomething-year-old male's room. His room had style and taste and, surprisingly, it was neat. Everything was in the right place, and the covers were smoothed over the big-ass water bed that dominated the room. I couldn't control my grin. Sure, I'd seen water beds on television and always thought they were cheesy, but now that I was standing in front of one, it was actually intriguing. This was about to be a long series of firsts, I thought as a laugh escaped my lips.

"What's so funny?" Michael asked as he leaned in and kissed the back of my neck.

"Before you came along I thought today was going to be the worst day of my life," I confessed.

He walked over to the dresser and pulled out his weed and started rolling a blunt. "Really? Well, the day's not over, and you have no idea what I have planned for you."

I couldn't help but blush. "I can't wait to find out."

Michael took a hit, leaned in, and blew the smoke into my mouth before he planted a deep, passionate kiss on my lips. I held in the smoke as I enjoyed the feel of his body pressing against mine. When he broke our kiss, I exhaled then took the blunt from him, drawing on it until my lungs were full. I exhaled, and he kissed me again, exploring my mouth with his tongue. I had no idea one kiss could make my body tingle like that, but I definitely didn't want him to stop.

He sat down on the bed and patted the spot next to him. I plopped down beside him and nearly fell backward from the motion of the water bed mattress. He caught me in his arms and held me close as I tried to control a sudden case of the giggles. Whatever we'd been smoking was some really good shit, because there was no doubt I was high now.

I usually wasn't the aggressor in sex, but the combination of the alcohol I'd had earlier, the powerful weed, and Michael's sexiness had me hornier than I could ever remember. When he leaned in for another kiss, I pushed him back on the bed and crawled on top of him. Our lips locked in the most deliciously lustful kiss.

He moved his hand slowly up my thigh, raising my skirt and causing my pussy to throb in anticipation. As he reached a finger into my thong and skimmed it over my short hairs, I felt my juices begin to flow. Slowly but surely he worked my clothes off, turning me on with every touch and every kiss.

Michael rolled his body on top of me, and I felt a big, thick, rock-hard dick pressing against my thigh. This boy killed all the stereotypes about white men. He felt like a true Mandingo. I arched my back, feeling sexy and horny. My legs opened, inviting, anxious for him to take me, but without any warning, he stopped.

I opened my eyes and looked up at him in confusion. "What's the matter?" Was he not feeling this the way I was?

"Condom. I need to go get a condom," he told me, and I nodded, relieved and impressed. I'd been on the patch for almost a year, but we all know a patch can't keep you from catching a disease. At least he was thinking responsibly. Yeah, I had scored with this one.

As he walked out, I lay there in his bed wanting to pinch myself. I couldn't believe I was about to have sex with this man and had absolutely no regrets. I had gone from zero to ho in no time flat, and I didn't care one bit. If the way Michael moved on the dance floor was any indication of how good he'd be in bed, all I could say was *holla*! I giggled at the thought of all the nasty sex we'd be having, imagining him inside of me as we rode the waves of his water bed.

I heard the bedroom door swing open and looked

toward it eagerly, only to get the fright of my life. One of his roommates was standing in the door-way—totally naked.

"Oh my God! What the fuck are you doing? Michael! Help!" I called out just before the room-mate lunged toward me. The motion of the water bed made it impossible for me to get up quickly, so he was on top of me in no time.

I heard Michael's voice when he came to the room, but I was confused because rather than sounding upset or angry, he said "Yo, dude!" like he was on the verge of laughter. Although I was pinned under this huge man, I managed to move my head and catch sight of Michael. What I saw made me want to vomit.

Michael was in the doorway, also buck naked, and he held a video camera, capturing everything that was happening to me. His roommates were nearby, and no one was wearing a stitch of clothing.

"Happy birthday!" Michael said with a laugh, still pointing his camera at me. "You did say it was your twenty-first birthday, didn't you? Well, we're here for the party."

I was suddenly stone-cold sober, as I realized that these guys were about to gang-rape me. With tears blurring my vision, I struggled to get free. The huge guy on top of me deadened his weight, making it impossible for me to move.

I looked up at Michael, pleading, "Please don't let them do this to me."

His defiant laugh told me that my request had fallen on deaf ears. I was living every woman's worst nightmare, and there was no escape.

"Me first," I heard one of them demand.

"No, you were first last time," the man on top of me shouted.

"Let him go. He's already on top of her," Michael reasoned. That's when I felt them grab my legs, spreading me apart like a wishbone.

"No! Oh, God! Please, no! Somebody help me! Somebody please help me!" I screamed until my throat was raw, but no one came to help as the first man had his way with me. Soon the sounds of their laughter changed, becoming an incessant pounding. I kept shouting, but nothing I did would make it stop.

That's when I shot up in my bed, waking from the recurring nightmare I'd been having for six years now, ever since I was raped on my twenty-first birthday. I was still trembling and sweating as I realized that the pounding sound was someone banging on my door, and they obviously weren't going away.

Monique
5

While everyone else was speculating about what could have made Tia leave Aaron at the altar, I was determined to find out the truth from the horse's mouth. It had taken me a day to locate the limo driver who had driven Tia away, but by 7 o'clock the next night, I was sitting down for a little pow-wow with him and his boss. At first he had refused to give me any information about Tia's where-abouts—until I informed his boss that I was the first lady of the largest black church in Queens. If he withheld Tia's location, I told him, I would make sure that none of our members ever patronized his business again. With the threat of unemployment dangling over his head, the driver suddenly saw the light and told me what I needed to know.

It turned out that Tia was hiding in plain sight, not fifteen minutes from the church in the Marriott hotel by LaGuardia Airport. She'd checked into the honeymoon suite where she and Aaron were sup-posed to have spent their first couple of nights, before heading to the Bahamas for their honey-moon.

So there I was, knocking on the door, when I heard Tia's terrified screams. I was so afraid for her that I started pounding with both fists, but still the screaming continued. I was just about to get security when the screaming stopped and the door was flung open.

"Monique, what are you doing here?" Tia looked disheveled, still clothed in her wrinkled wedding dress, with her hair all over the place and makeup streaked across her tear-stained face.

"I should be asking you that question." I forced my way past her, wanting to see who or what had caused her terrified screams. "You all right?"

"I'm fine," she said, though her tone left me un-convinced.

"You sure? You don't look fine," I said as I peeked into the bathroom. "Is someone here? I heard you screaming."

"It was nothing. Just a nightmare."

"A nightmare? What kind of nightmares make you scream like that?"

"The kind I don't wish on anyone," Tia said with a sigh, casting her eyes to the floor. "How'd you find me?"

"I'm the first lady of the only black megachurch in Queens. You'd be surprised by the resources I have at my disposal." I folded my arms, suddenly feeling less worried and more impatient with her. "We've all been worried sick about you, Tia. You could have at least called. Nobody knew if you were dead or alive."

"Look, no disrespect, First Lady, but as you can see, I'm very much alive and right now, I just want to be left alone."

Now she'd pushed the wrong button and any sympathy I might have had for her was gone. I certainly didn't come all the way over here to be dismissed by Tia. If that was the case, I could have just stayed home to deal with my own issues. TK had let me know in no uncertain terms that he didn't appreciate the way I had "entertained" Jackson Young, as he put it. I didn't understand what his problem was. I mean, who wouldn't listen when she was being offered the chance of a lifetime? My husband was standing right next to me, for goodness' sake. It wasn't like I was flirting with the man. But TK saw it differently, and I had no doubt he would be harassing me about it later. With that problem in the back of my mind, I was in no mood to be disrespected by the girl who had our whole church in a tizzy right now.

"No disrespect? That's a joke, right?" I said, moving closer to her. "This little visit of mine isn't a social call, Tia. It's a damn intervention. You should be glad I didn't bring the bishop and the rest of the Holy Rollers with me." She looked at me with wide eyes, probably horrified at the thought of anyone else seeing her in her current state. "Now, I want to know what's going on."

"Well, I don't need an intervention, First Lady, and I definitely don't need you all up in my business. I know what I'm doing." Her voice had taken on a defiant tone I'd never heard before, and for a moment I was so confused by her transformation that I didn't know how to respond. In my silence, she had the nerve to glance at the door as if she was waiting for me to walk through it and leave her alone.

"Do you really think you can just shoo me away? After all the money I spent on your ass, buying that dress and putting together your wedding shower?" I placed my purse on the desk then took a few attitude-driven steps toward her. "Now, I don't give a damn if you talk to anyone else, but you're gonna tell me something."

"I don't know what to tell you." This time her voice shook when she spoke, revealing her truly fragile emotional state. She retreated back to the bed and sat down, holding her knees with her arms in upright fetal position. She looked so lost, so sad.

"Tell me something, Tia," I said, sitting down next to her.

"I couldn't do it, Monique. I just couldn't do it,

all right?" The dam burst, and tears began pouring down her face. She was a mess, but I still felt like I'd made some headway, because she'd called me by my first name instead of my title.

I put a hand on her shoulder. "I thought you loved Aaron."

She flinched at the mention of his name. "I do. I really do, but I can't marry him," she cried. I pulled her close, allowing her a safe place to put her sadness. "I can't marry him, Monique. As much as I love him, I can't marry him."

"Tia, Aaron loves you. I'm sure that whatever this is about, you're just blowing it out of proportion. It's always worse in our imagination," I said, attempting to reassure her.

"What kind of wife would I be to Aaron? I can't even give him the one basic thing that solidifies a marriage."

She'd just lost me. I had no idea what that was supposed to mean. "What are you talking about? A marriage is solidified by love. You just said you love Aaron, and I know he loves you."

"Monique, I can't have sex with him," she said flatly, lifting her head. She appeared ready to break down again. "And he's waited so long."

As hard as I tried to stay neutral, my tone rose with the shock of her revelation. "Wait. You and Aaron haven't had sex yet?" I might be a first lady, but I'm a realist, and I know that very few folks actually wait until their wedding day anymore. Even the bishop and I had slipped once and gave in to our passions before he married me.

She shook her head as she wiped away her tears.

I had an inkling of what the problem might be: Tia was afraid that she wouldn't be able to perform. Poor girl.

"Okay, I think I understand the problem," I said. "First, let's get you into a nice warm bath."

She didn't protest as I led her to the bathroom and ran the water then helped her out of her wrinkled gown. I found a small bottle of bath gel and poured it in, creating a foamy bubble bath where Tia could soak away some of her anxiety.

"I'm sorry you had to find me like this," Tia said a while later when she came back into the bedroom wearing a bathrobe. She looked much better, but no amount of soap and water could disguise her dark circles and red, puffy eyes.

"You don't have to apologize to me. I'm your friend. I'm here to help you." I'd ordered her some food from room service, which she promptly started devouring. It was probably the first thing she'd eaten since before she ran away from the church.

Her cell phone rang while she was eating, but she didn't move to answer it. We shared a look that said we both knew it was Aaron.

"I wish he'd just stop," she said. "Can't he see I'm not going to answer?"

"You have to talk to him at some point. He's not just going to go away. He loves you." I could see from the look on her face that she knew I was right, but she still resisted.

"I don't want him to love me."

"Well, it's not that easy. You don't just stop loving someone, do you?"

She picked up her phone and began typing. I felt better, thinking that she was reaching out to him, making the first step toward working things out. Oh, how wrong I was.

"There. It's done." She placed the phone next to her plate and picked up her fork, shoving some food in her mouth.

"Good for you. Did you tell him where you were?"

"No," she replied bluntly. "I told him to go fuck himself and move on with his life, because that's what I'm doing."

My jaw dropped and I had to resist the urge to slap her. "You did what? Don't you understand that man loves you? Why would you do something so hurtful?"

Her whole body seemed to deflate, and her tears had started again. "I don't want him to love me anymore."

"Tia, you don't have to go to these extremes. Plenty of people have problems in the bedroom. You're not the first woman who was nervous about making love to her husband. I have a few techniques I can teach you. Or if you'd prefer, I have a friend who—"

"Stop! This is not about sex. This is about *him*."

"Girl, what the hell are you talking about?" She was making absolutely no sense.

"I saw him, Monique," she said quietly, her voice cracking. "I saw him, and just like that, it changed every damn thing."

"Jesus, Lord, don't tell me you snuck into that man's bachelor party. I told you not to do that, Tia. When you go looking for a mess, you find a mess." I put my hand on hers and waited for her to make eye contact. "So you saw him with a stripper?"

"No."

I didn't want to imagine what could be worse than that. "A church member?" I asked, praying I was wrong.

She shook her head vehemently. "Aaron didn't do anything wrong, Monique. Hell, I wish he had. Then I wouldn't feel so bad."

This girl had my head spinning. It didn't look like I was going to get to the bottom of things soon enough to go take care of my own home. "Then what? Who could make you leave a man you profess to love?"

Other than perhaps another man you love, I thought.

Tia began sobbing. Looking up at me through her tears, she cried, "It was my rapist, Monique. I saw one of my rapists the other night."

I held her as she released her pain, wailing and shaking. When she calmed down enough to speak, she told me, "Just the sight of him brought it all back. I'll never forget his face, and that hot, nasty breath of his kissing my neck as he…" All I could do was stare at her as the magnitude of her words sank in and tears fell from my own eyes. "It was like it was happening to me all over again. I still can't shake the feeling. I don't think I ever will."

"Oh, no. Sweetheart, I'm so sorry." I rubbed her back, making a futile attempt to comfort her. "Why didn't you tell me?"

"I'm a rape counselor. I tell women every day to be strong, to fight through it, not to let them win. I was hoping that if I could just get in the church and see Aaron I'd be all right, but I couldn't," she said, finally giving me the explanation I'd come for. Sadly, her reality was much more tragic than any reason I could have imagined for her disappearance that morning. "The closer I got to stepping out of that limo, the more ashamed I felt."

"You have no reason to be ashamed," I told her. "This was not your fault."

"Really? Because it sure as hell doesn't feel that way. I met this guy, and I probably drank too much, but I had already made up my mind that I was gonna end my birthday in his bed."

I listened in stunned silence as she shared details of that night that she'd never told me before. Actually, I realized, other than admitting that she'd been raped, Tia never said anything else about it. Now I understood that her reticence did not mean she had healed.

"Monique, I wasn't a good girl back then. I went to his house and got high. Heck, I was planning on sleeping with him, and we'd just met. But he and his roommates had other plans. They gang-raped me over and over and over until I passed out. I woke up in a Dumpster somewhere near the Staten Island ferry."

My stomach churned at the thought of her ordeal. What type of men could do that to another human being? "Those bastards. I hope the judge made them rot in jail for a good long time."

She shook her head and whispered, "I never went to the police. I was too ashamed."

"You never went to the police? But it wasn't your fault."

"I never should have been at his house. I was

afraid they would just tell me I asked for it by going home with a stranger."

As she broke down in tears again, I knew that nothing I said would really comfort her. So I did the only thing I could; I held her as she cried.

After a while, I asked, "When did you see him?"

"At my bachelorette party, after we left the rehearsal dinner," she told me.

"But it was a private room. How could he possibly have gotten in?"

"He was the bartender out front," she said. "I'd recognize him anywhere. I'd recognize all of them anywhere. It was him, Monique. It was him." She clutched onto me, burying her head in my sweater as she trembled with tears.

I rubbed her back again and tried to soothe her. "Come on, Tia. Don't let him take your life away from you. You've worked so hard to build a good life. Don't let these bastards hold you back. You can make it through this. What about therapy?"

"I thought I could." She stood up, separating herself from me. "That's what I kept telling myself over and over, that I could get through this. But then on the limo ride to the church, I just kept seeing his face. I could feel him. I could smell him. I could feel his sweat dripping off his skin onto mine. I could hear his body smacking against mine, using and abusing me as if I wasn't even human." She shuddered, a look of pure disgust on her face. "I felt dirty and violated all over again. The last thing I could do was allow Aaron to touch me. We couldn't start our lives together like that."

"We've got to tell Aaron about this, Tia. He needs to—"

"No! I can't. I can't go back to Aaron, and I can't go back to the church."

I closed my eyes and said a quick prayer for guidance in this situation that felt impossible.

Bishop
6

The stress of the past couple of days had caught up to me, and it felt really good to be lying in my bed doing nothing now. I couldn't remember ever being this worn out. I was definitely feeling my age.

With Aaron's recent celebrity status, Tia's disappearance had turned my church into a three-ring circus, with me in the middle circle as the ringmaster. We had media parked outside the sanctuary, cameras flashing during Sunday service, and a congregation that was overrun with gossip and speculation about things that had absolutely nothing to do with them. We'd had our share of touch-and-go moments the past few years at First Jamaica Ministries, and media scrutiny pretty much came with the territory of being pastor of a large church, but this time around felt particularly stressful to me.

It wasn't helping matters much that my wife and I seemed to be on different wavelengths. Her sudden disappearance without even a phone call on a Sunday afternoon caused my anxiety to skyrocket.

Normally I wouldn't worry about Monique; we had a tight bond and a strong marriage, but I couldn't shake the nagging feeling that she might be out somewhere with Jackson Young. I wasn't usually prone to jealousy, but something about the way she had lit up when he started paying her compliments just didn't sit right with me. That was one shady character, and I was really struggling to understand why my normally confident and self-possessed wife had turned into a giggling, blushing girl in his presence.

When I heard the front door open and Monique called out my name, I felt a mixture of annoyance and relief. I wasn't about to let her know it, but I was glad she was home.

"In the bedroom!" I hollered. A moment later she entered our bedroom, waving as she made a beeline for the bathroom and quickly shut the door behind her.

"TK?" she called out from behind the door.

"Yeah, honey?"

"I saw Tia tonight."

"What did you say?" I sat up in the bed but resisted the urge to go into the bathroom. Married or not, I'd always believed in giving her privacy in the bathroom. I preferred to see the finished product and not the things that went on behind the curtain.

Monique peeked her head out of the door. "I saw

Tia," she said solemnly. The troubled expression on her face erased any lingering feelings of anger I'd held about her disappearance that afternoon.

"When? How? Where?" I rattled off, my head spinning with possible scenarios. Could this mean they were headed for a reconciliation? I certainly hoped so. Maybe it was a bit selfish of me to be thinking this way, but their presence as a couple in the church was inspiring to the young people. It made them consider slowing down, taking time with a relationship rather than simply "hooking up," to steal the phrase they so often used to describe their encounters with the opposite sex.

She stepped out of the bathroom and approached me. "TK, if I tell you this," she started, "you can't tell anyone, especially not Aaron." It wasn't like Monique to issue a warning when she shared information with me, so I immediately understood the seriousness of whatever she had to say. As much as I wanted to put Aaron out of his pain by sharing Tia's location with him, I knew that I couldn't betray my wife.

"I won't. I promise," I said, lifting my right hand as if taking an oath.

"I'm serious," Monique emphasized. "She made me swear not to tell anyone. Not even you. So you can't say anything to anyone else."

"Monique, I'm a man of the cloth. Keeping people's secrets is something I'm asked to do on a daily basis, and you know I take that responsibility seriously. Now, tell me what's going on with Tia."

Her eyes welled up, and a single tear fell as she leaned against her dresser. "Tia saw one of her rapists."

"Dear Lord, that poor girl." Tia had been working as the church secretary for almost four years now, but she wasn't just an employee. She'd found her way into our hearts. We knew she'd been raped a couple years before joining our congregation, but Tia had an uncommon resolve. Rather than falling apart after such an atrocity, she found a way to battle her demons by helping others with the same problem. She ran a rape crisis and counseling ministry out of the basement of the church that not only helped her heal, but hundreds of others.

"Is she going to be okay?" I asked.

"I don't know. I hope so." Monique had a faraway look in her eyes, as if picturing the state she'd found Tia in. "She was still wearing her wedding dress this afternoon when I found her. Whatever those men did to her, it has all come back. She's an absolute wreck."

"You do know we need to tell Aaron." The daggers from her eyes told me I should have kept the suggestion to myself.

"You gave me your word, TK Wilson," she

snapped angrily. "I expect you to honor it. We're not telling Aaron anything right now." I'd heard this hard tone in her voice before, but never directed at me.

"I'm not going to tell him," I said, backing off a little, "but he deserves to know."

"Not when she's like this."

"That man loves her. He can help her," I insisted.

"You didn't see her, TK. You bring Aaron within ten feet of that girl and we may never see her again. She can't feel good about him until she feels good about herself, and right now, she's not in a very good place."

"Well, we've got to do something. Maybe we should call the police?" I understood my wife's point, but I still couldn't imagine sitting back and doing nothing.

"No, it's too late for that. Besides, Tia doesn't want to have to deal with them."

"What's that supposed to mean?" I found myself getting irritated. Men and women dealt with things differently, that was for sure. I could not relate to this apparent desire to just drop it. Part of me wanted to step up and take charge, to defend Tia, but I had to remind myself that I was not her father. I was her spiritual adviser, and as such, it was my job to back off and let God handle things, as difficult as that would be in this case.

"She's got to get through this her own way, in her own time," Monique said.

"Well, when is she coming back to work? Maybe I can talk to her then."

Monique's eyes welled up with tears again. This experience was really causing her a lot of pain. Even though we didn't have children of our own, we certainly loved Aaron and Tia like family.

"She said she's not coming back."

"What do you mean she's not coming back? That church is more than a job to her. She has to come back at some point."

"I tried to talk some sense into her, but there was no changing her mind. She said it has to be this way." Monique shook her head sadly. "I don't know, TK. I can't pretend to understand what it feels like to go through what she did. I didn't feel right pressuring her."

"But what about Aaron? This doesn't sound like Tia. She's always been so responsible. She has to come back and deal with him, because he's hurting too. Is she going to at least do that?"

"I don't think so. If it happens, it's not going to be anytime soon."

"I communicated with him today. This information would help him." I stepped across that line again. Sometimes you had to look past what people thought they wanted and do what was right, and I felt at my core that revealing this to Aaron was absolutely the right thing to do. My wife, on the other hand, thought differently, and it was my job to try to convince her to change her mind.

"You promised not to say anything."

"But I had no idea what I was promising," I argued.

"TK, that girl is fragile and she needs to be able to trust someone. Right now, that someone is me. I can't destroy her faith in me without risking losing her forever."

"But what about Aaron's faith in me and the church? This isn't right."

"Right or wrong, we are not playing God. You made me a promise, and you need to keep your word."

"And I'm supposed to stand by and watch Aaron suffer? He's like a son to me."

"And Tia is like a daughter to me. Unless you want me to start keeping secrets, you will keep your word." With that, she headed into her walk-in closet.

Honesty had been at the foundation of our relationship. Without it, everything else would fall apart, so I knew what she was threatening and the ramifications it would have on our relationship. Whether I agreed or not, I had to step back and leave this situation up to God.

When Monique came back into the room, I was struck speechless by the sight of her in a white negligee.

"You look amazing," I said. "Did I buy you that? If so, I have excellent taste—in my woman and in gifts."

"Yes," she said with a laugh. "Last Valentine's Day. And I suggest that we stop worrying about Tia and Aaron and start thinking about ourselves."

"Well, I can certainly do that." I couldn't stop staring at this beautiful woman I was lucky enough to marry.

She sat down on the bed next to me, and I went in for some loving kisses.

"Somebody's in a frisky mood tonight," she joked when I finally released her.

"What did you expect to happen with you wearing that?"

"This is exactly what I *hoped* would happen," she said.

I couldn't keep my hands off of her. There was nothing like the feel of a real woman, I mean one that felt like a woman in your arms, soft and warm.

She started to kiss me on my face, neck, and chest, and then she kept moving to my stomach. It was a wonder I didn't up and die from the kind of happiness this woman gave me.

"Does that feel good?" she whispered as she offered more warm kisses all over my body. I was grateful that she was my wife because it felt so good it was almost sinful. There was a reason I was a bishop and not a priest, I thought. I could never understand signing on for a lifetime of celibacy when I could praise God and still have a healthy, happy marriage.

She started rubbing me in all the right places. All the lethargy I'd been feeling earlier was completely gone now. I lay back down, ready to enjoy the sensations as my wife worked her magic.

"TK?"

"Yeah, baby?" I murmured, anxious for her to continue. This woman knew how to rev my engine from zero to one hundred when she wanted, and from the looks of things, that was her plan.

"You still think that I look like a younger version of Jackée from *227*?"

"Yeah, except you're finer than her," I said, and I wasn't kidding. I married her because I fell in love with her, but I also couldn't stand the idea of any other man going near her. I was a red-blooded, old-fashioned man, and I didn't care if that dated me. On the contrary, I had no issue with appearing territorial. I was a one-woman man, and this amazing woman was it for me.

"I mean, am I that sexy?"

"Sexier," I assured her, ready to have more of her.

"You think I could be on television?" she flirted, looking for a compliment that I was more than happy to give. This was looking like the beginning of a great night.

"Oh yeah, you could definitely be on TV," I answered emphatically.

She rose up on her haunches. "Then how come you're against me being an actress?"

Monique might as well have doused water on the flame that had ignited between us, because suddenly the last thing on my mind was making love to my wife. I wanted to shake some sense into her.

"Are you serious? We're in the midst of making love and you want to talk about being an actress?"

"It's important to me." She pulled away from me and crossed her arms over her chest, letting me know that we were in the beginning of a cold war.

"We both know that you're too busy being first lady to mess around with any showbiz nonsense."

"So you don't support me?" She sounded like a child who had just found out that she wasn't going to get the toy she had been hoping for, instead of a sensible adult having a conversation with her overtaxed husband.

"I support you in anything that I know is good for us," I reasoned. And anything that involved Jackson Young was definitely not good for us, I thought.

"Well, I never told this to anyone, but I've always wanted to be an actress. It wasn't until I saw Jackée on *227* that I realized a well-endowed woman could be an actress and a sex symbol."

I reached out and took her hand gently. "This is crazy. You have a life already. It's not like you're a young girl anymore."

"So now you're calling me old? Or is it that you don't think I have any talent to act?" she cried, taking my comment completely out of context.

"Of course not. To be quite frank, this acting thing is my second problem. My real issue is with that agent," I said, refusing to speak his name out loud. "I don't like him."

"Is it that you don't like him, or you don't like that he finds me beautiful?" she asked.

"That's right," I said, realizing there was no point in denying the truth. "And it's not worth talking about, because you are not doing it."

As soon as I said the words, she was up and on her feet.

"Monique?" No response. "Monique? Dammit!" The door slammed behind her as she stormed out of the room.

Aaron

7

When I pulled up to a red light on the way to the airport, I grabbed my phone to steal a glance at the picture of Tia that I used as a screen saver. In the passenger seat, my mother sucked her teeth, letting her displeasure be heard loud and clear.

"That heifer don't deserve you," she said.

Maybe she was right, but it didn't change the way I felt. I loved Tia more than any other person in the world—including my mother.

"Dammit, Ma, don't call her that." I wasn't trying to be disrespectful, but this wasn't a conversation I wanted to continue all the way to the airport. Both my mother and aunt had already done their share of Tia bashing.

Unfortunately, Ma didn't intend on stopping her assault on the woman I loved. "Why?" she said. "I ain't lying. Any woman crazy enough to leave my baby standing at the altar got a whole lot worse names coming when I see her black ass. Isn't that right, sister?"

"You sure got that right, Emma," my aunt Rita cosigned from the backseat. She didn't have any children of her own so she was like my second mother.

"Auntie, please don't encourage her," I pleaded.

"I'm sorry, Aaron, but she ain't wrong this time," Aunt Rita stated simply.

"What you need to do is get yourself back out there," my mother continued with her unsolicited advice. "You know what they say: You fall off one horse, you get back on another."

"Mm-hmm, I know that's right," my aunt agreed. "I pity the rat who only has one hole."

"Auntie! What is wrong with y'all?" I couldn't believe what I was hearing.

"What? You don't need to be sitting home all pitiful and pining over some ungrateful woman. She should be kissing your ass for talking to her."

"What your mother is trying to say," Aunt Rita said in a tone a little less indignant than Ma's, "is any woman would be happy to have you."

"And, matter o' fact, I just happen to have a few names." My mother reached in her bag and pulled out a clump of torn papers.

I pulled over to the shoulder, bringing the car to a screeching halt. "Those are not what I think they are!"

As cool as can be, my mother smiled and said, "If you think they're women's phone numbers, then yes, they are absolutely what you think they are."

"No." I shook my head in shame, wondering if I'd ever be able to set foot in the church again. "You two did not go soliciting women's phone numbers for me."

"'Soliciting' is a rather strong word, but yes, we talked to several young ladies on your behalf at the reception," my aunt said.

"Two in particular were very interested in you taking them out," Ma said, sounding proud of her accomplishment. "What were their names, sister?"

"I don't remember."

Ma started riffling through the papers as I pulled back into traffic. I could not get to the airport fast enough to drop these two off before they made me insane.

"Here they are!" she announced, waving a paper in front of my face. "Tiffany and Keisha."

I brushed her hand away so I could see the road. "Tiffany Johnson and Keisha Holland?" I asked.

"Yeah, you know them? They were more than happy to give me their numbers too." She shoved the whole stack of papers and business cards in my direction, but I kept both hands on the wheel. "One of them is a doctor's assistant," Ma continued, undeterred. "Now, she could be the prescription to help you heal."

"I know that's right!" Aunt Rita reached over the seat to give my mother a fist bump.

"Not interested." It was all I could manage to say as I gratefully pulled up to the terminal.

"I'ma leave these numbers in the cup holder, and when you're ready, you can use them," my mother stated confidently as she got out of the car. "Don't wait too long."

It was the first time I was glad to be saying good-bye to my mother and aunt, as I helped them with their bags and watched them head into the airport.

Back in my car, the silence and solitude gave me too much time to think about the mess that was my life, and I was hit with a wave of sadness and longing. I pulled over again on the side of the road and took out my phone, sending yet another text to Tia.

I'M GOING OUT OF MY MIND WORRYING ABOUT YOU. PLEASE ANSWER ME. I stared down at the screen, knowing it would continue to be a one-sided conversation. I'd left so many texts and voice messages that all went unanswered.

AARON PLEASE, PLEASE LOSE MY NUMBER. Her response shocked me. I sent back a quick reply.

WHAT DID I DO WRONG?

Her next text hit me right in the solar plexus:

WILL YOU PLEASE JUST LEAVE ME THE FUCK ALONE! WHAT PART OF NOT FUCKING INTERESTED DO YOU NOT UNDERSTAND?

I think it was the word "fuck" that sent me over the edge. Such a simple word, but it screamed at me with such blatant disrespect from the woman who was supposed to be my soul mate.

I threw the phone on the passenger seat and started driving again, but I didn't get far before it started ringing. I grabbed it, thinking maybe Tia had come to her senses and wanted to apologize.

A quick glance at the caller ID revealed that it was not Tia, but Ross. He had been calling me three or four times a day to check on me, but I definitely wasn't in the mood for one of his pep talks about how I should go back to work to take things off my mind. He just didn't get it. I needed some time away from everybody. I ignored the call and kept on driving, not knowing where I was going until I pulled up in front of the flashing neon sign: BENNY'S BAR AND GRILL.

Benny's was located in a questionable neighborhood in Jamaica, Queens. Ross, Pippie, and I had adopted the joint as our own personal watering hole right about the time Pippie moved up from Virginia. Benny's was a hole-in-the-wall, but the drinks were cheap, they had a pool table that took quarters, and quiet as it's kept, their cook made the best cheeseburgers in New York.

I sat down at a booth in the corner. I'd walked in with the intention of having a drink to dull my senses; however, the smell of those greasy burgers from the kitchen reminded me that I hadn't really eaten since the night of my bachelor party.

Not long after I sat down, Jewel, the barmaid, came over to take my order.

"Your boys have been looking for you." Jewel smiled, whipping out a notepad.

"Yeah, well, if you see them again, don't tell them I was here, okay."

"Your secret is good with me," she said with a wink. "Now, what can I get you to drink?"

"I'll take a Jack and Coke. And can you bring me a cheeseburger and fries?"

"Sure thing." She stepped away to place the order but then turned back. "Um, Aaron, I heard about you and that girl you was supposed to marry. If there's anything I can do to help—and I mean anything—just holla," she said.

Well, it didn't take a rocket scientist to figure out what that meant. I'd never really paid much attention to Jewel in the past. Not only was I in a relationship with Tia, but Jewel had a reputation for being pretty loose, and I wasn't normally into women like that. But with her overly friendly gesture and my need for some comforting, she definitely had my attention now.

I'm not going to lie; the thought of what she was offering was tempting. It had been almost eighteen months since I'd made love, and I can't emphasize enough how taxing that can be on a man. I truly missed that physical intimacy. Waiting for our wedding day was worth it, I thought, but seeing as how Tia never made it down the aisle, I sort of felt like I'd been played for a fool. Jewel's offer was appreciated, not necessarily because she was this superhot woman that I couldn't resist, but because it was comforting to think that someone was interested in me. I'd been pretty down on myself ever since Tia's rejection.

I smiled my thanks then gave her a very flat "I'll let you know."

"Please do." I watched her sashay away to the bar, purposely throwing a little extra something in her hips for my benefit. Like I said, I'd never really paid attention to her in the past, but now that I got a good look, I had to admit she had a really nice figure and an exceptionally nice ass.

By the time I finished my burger and downed two Jack and Cokes, Jewel's shift was over and she had taken up permanent residence in the seat next to me, holding two shot glasses and a bottle of tequila. She placed one glass in front of me and poured a shot. "You're not going to let me drink alone, are you?"

She picked up her glass, daring me to join her. I never was one to refuse a dare, so I downed the tequila without a second thought, and a drinking contest ensued. As we drank, Jewel let me know that she had just broken up with her boyfriend and, in her own words, wasn't looking for anything complicated.

"That's fine," I said, slurring my words a bit as the tequila did its job, "because I'm not looking for anything at all."

I thought that would be the end of it. Evidently I was wrong.

"That's even better. Men who are looking for things usually end up spending more than one night," she said.

"Whoa, girl. Slow down," I warned her. "I'm not sure I'm ready for all that."

"Why? You don't want me to be too fast? From everything you've told me, I'm thinking that you need just the opposite. You know what they say: If you fall off a horse, you have to get right back on another one." She laughed.

"Funny, my momma said something just like that earlier today."

"Well, we wouldn't want your momma to be a liar, would we?" She gave me a devilish smile as she slid closer to me. Next thing I knew, Jewel had unbuttoned my pants and had my jewels in her hands, massaging them like a pro. Girl had serious skills. I looked around at the other patrons, none of whom seemed to notice what was going on under our table. Thank God I'd chosen a booth in the corner.

"Mmm!" I murmured, feeling my excitement grow. It had been so long and her hands felt so good. I felt like I might explode right then and there. "Maybe we should—"

"Slow down?" She laughed. "We're way past that." I thought about kissing her, but before I could lean toward her, she did something unexpected. Jewel slid down under the table.

"Uh, aren't you afraid someone will see you? I mean, you do work here," I asked, though I didn't make a move to stop her.

"Ain't nobody paying attention to us. They're all at the bar watching the game." She slurped my entire dick into her wet mouth and I shut up.

I leaned my head back and closed my eyes for a few seconds, enjoying the sensation, until I heard someone say, "Hey, man."

My eyes popped open, and I saw Pippie and Ross standing beside the booth. Shit! I reached my hand under the table to stop Jewel, but I think she was trying to mess with my head, because I swear she started sucking me like a damn vacuum cleaner.

"Where you been?" Ross asked.

"Oh, you know, I been around," I said, trying to act nonchalant.

"Four shots?" Pippie said, noticing the tequila and glasses on the table.

"Man, that's a lot of alcohol for one person. Aren't you usually a lightweight?" Of course Ross had to stick his nose in it.

"They're not all mine," I said. "I'm drinking with someone, so maybe you two can just go away now, huh?"

"Aw, hell no," Pippie said. "We been looking for you everywhere and we finally found you. We ain't going nowhere." He slid into the booth before I could protest. I knew the second he bumped into Jewel, because she pulled her mouth off me in a hurry.

"Ow!" she said from under the table.

"What the—?" He leaned down and peered under there, his face screwed up in confusion for a second when he spotted Jewel.

Jewel, in the meantime, was unfazed by the whole thing. She calmly put my penis back in my pants and zipped them up, then climbed back up into the seat next to me. "Sorry, baby. I'll have to finish you off some other time. Your friend here was kicking me under the table." She shot an indignant look at Ross and Pippie and then left us alone.

As soon as she was gone, Pippie said, "What the fuck is wrong with you, Aaron? Have some respect for Tia if you don't have any for yourself." He looked like he wanted to wring my neck.

Ross, on the other hand, was pissed for other reasons. "Do you realize someone could have seen you? Or even worse, they could have recorded you? This could be a PR nightmare," he lectured. I reached for the bottle of tequila, but Pippie snatched it away.

"I think you've had enough, man," he said. "Look, I know you're hurting over Tia, but this is out of control."

"I can't believe you two," I said. "Weren't you the ones who told me I needed to cheer up and move on, stop wallowing in my sorrow? Now I'm out here having a little fun and y'all are acting all high and mighty." I turned to Ross, who had some nerve to be talking about my behavior considering he wasn't exactly a choirboy himself. "Aren't you the one who said there's no such thing as bad publicity?"

"It was a figure of speech. I was trying to make light of a bad situation when the wedding didn't go as planned. It certainly doesn't apply to you getting a blow job under the table in a bar."

I looked across the room and saw that Jewel was standing by the bar, watching us. When I made eye contact with her, she raised her eyebrows and then tilted her head toward the door. She was offering to go home with me.

"Well, gentlemen," I said, "it's been fun, but it looks like Jewel and I are going to continue our party somewhere a little more private. You two are welcome to the rest of the tequila." I stood up to leave, but Pippie put a hand on my arm.

"Aaron, don't do this. There's still a chance you can work things out with Tia," he said in an attempt to change my mind.

I yanked my arm away from him. "Tia sent me a text and told me, and I quote, she's 'not fucking interested.' Does that sound like there's a chance to you, Pippie?"

"Come on, man," Ross said, trying a different approach. "Don't do something you'll regret." He looked over at Jewel, who waved at me. "That chick's a cokehead, man. All she's going to do is spend your money on drugs and alcohol."

"You forgot one thing," I said. "She's also going to screw my brains out, and considering I haven't had any in over a year and a half, there ain't nothing you could say to change my mind."

"Aaron." Ross stood up to try to block my exit.

"If you don't get out my way, we really are going

to have a PR nightmare," I warned him. With a final exasperated sigh, he stepped aside and let me pass. I grabbed Jewel and headed for the door. "Oh, and for the record, the old Aaron Mackie is back and he's planning on making up for lost time."

Ross

8

"Damn, I expected a lot of BS, but that?" Pippie served me a look as he opened the passenger door, shaking his head like he was trying to get the image of Jewel being freaky under the table out of his mind. Now, I'm not gonna pretend her body wasn't on point, from her porn star–size breasts bursting out of her blouse to the taut, whittled waist to the full-size sister girl cake being held up by incredibly long legs. Still, Aaron should have had the good sense to turn her ass down. Aaron was the kind of guy who'd always had a nonstop pussy parade in his honor, with women eighteen to eighty, married, blind, crippled, and crazy ready to give up the kitty cat. Frankly, though, I thought he had moved past sex as a contact sport, especially after he rejected that big-booty stripper at his bachelor party.

"I can't believe him!" This kind of behavior in public frustrated me as his manager, but it also had me scared for my friend. My boy had tripped over to

the dark side. Over the years, I'd seen enough people on the precipice of success and then suddenly
one bad decision sidelines their dreams for life. His
out-of-control behavior threatened to ruin his
saintly image. I could just see the headline on Bos-
sip, the leading black gossip site: *Choir director has
his knob slobbed in public.*

"Our boy is in trouble," Pippie lamented, never
afraid to overstate the obvious.

"It's not just him. He's the captain of the whole
thing. He goes down, so does the choir, the bishop,
and me. I have to figure out some way to get him
back on track, and I don't care what it takes."

"I don't know, man. You know how Aaron can
be. He's stubborn as hell, and I'm telling you he
ain't getting in that choir loft anytime soon." His
words tightened the knot in my stomach, because as
painful as they were to hear, they were true.

"Not unless I give him something bigger than his
pain."

"Tia? How you gonna do that?" Pippie asked.

I shook my head. "No, I don't think I could pull
that off. No one even knows where she is. I'm thinking that I should meet with that Johnson Morris
agent, Jackson Young. Put our heads together and
come up with a strategy to elevate his career to the
next level." As much as I despised this guy on sight,
even more so after he opened his mouth, I was will-

ing to make a deal with the devil if it meant saving us all.

I pulled up to Pippie's place. "Do what you gotta do," he said, fist-bumping me before he got out of the car.

I really wished there were some other options, but no one else of Jackson's stature had come calling before. If I could get him a deal, I could refocus Aaron's attention on his work, the one area of his life where he actually had some control. As much as Jackson Young bugged me, I had to put Aaron's needs first and set up a meeting.

When I pulled into the driveway behind Selena's car, I was glad to be home, though I wasn't sure what awaited me behind the front door. Things had been a little intense lately, partly because my wife was pregnant and partly the normal stress of being married. I hadn't always been the most well-behaved husband. Even though we'd been to therapy and I'd turned over a new leaf, there were still days that Selena liked to remind me of the dog I used to be. Right now, I was seriously hoping for a reprieve.

I took a deep breath and got myself together before I approached the door. To my surprise, I entered to find my wife in a sexy lace negligee and high heels, just like I like it. Damn, she made pregnancy appear appetizing. She wore a huge smile as she lifted her dress to give me a flash of her sheer white thong.

"I made you oxtails and pineapple upside-down cake," she purred.

"What? Why?" I couldn't hide my surprise. It had been a long time since Selena had initiated anything sexual between us. And throwing in a meal too? Man, she certainly knew how to keep a brother guessing.

"I kept thinking about Tia and Aaron," she explained. "It made me realize how lucky I am, and how I haven't been such a good wife to you lately."

I admit that it was nice not to hear her blaming everything on me for once, but I couldn't let her accept all the responsibility for our marital issues. "No. Honey, you're pregnant. It's got to be hard giving your body over to a little alien."

"Having a baby is no reason to forget that I got a good man, and I need to make him feel appreciated. And that's exactly what I plan to do from now on. Women need compliments, and men need sex. I want us to make it, not just because we're married, but because we belong together." She leaned in and gave me a kiss that let me know she meant business.

In a perfect world, my body would have responded immediately to her touch, but unfortunately, I was so stressed and exhausted from worrying about Aaron that things weren't working the way they should.

Selena looked down at my unresponsive member then looked up into my eyes. "What's wrong, baby?"

"I'm just worried about Aaron. I'm afraid he's going off the deep end."

She led me to the couch and sat down next to me. Taking my hand, she said, "Baby, he'll be okay. He just needs some time to heal."

"I don't know, Selena. If he keeps going in the direction he is now, his music career will be over. He'll be left with nothing—and so will we."

Her eyes opened a little wider. She had given up her job to get ready for the baby, and if I lost my biggest client, we could be in a really bad situation.

"Babe, what are you going to do? You have to get Aaron back on track," she said.

"I'm working on it," I said, then told her about my idea to meet with Jackson Young.

"So, you really think this guy can take Aaron to the next level?"

"I do. He might be just what Aaron needs to take his mind off Tia."

She gave me a hug. "I'm proud of you, honey. If anyone can get Aaron back to work, it's you. Everything is going to be fine. I just know it."

Her confidence in me felt good. If things with

work were a little crazy right now, at least my home life was improved. Slowly but surely, the tension was leaving my body.

Selena noticed it, and gave me a devilish smile. "Looks like you're feeling better. Let's see if I can help you relax some more," she said as she slid to her knees and reached for my zipper.

Damn, I love this woman, I thought, grateful as hell. Yep, despite how it had started, this turned out to be a great day for me.

Tia

9

"Thank God," I said, standing up to wipe the sweat off my forehead.

I'd been picking up rocks in my brother Kareem's garden for almost ten minutes before I finally found the one that hid the key to his house. It was the same house we'd grown up in, and until a few years ago, we'd lived there together, big brother taking care of little sister. After he kicked his last girlfriend to the curb, he'd changed the locks. Luckily, he always left a key hidden in the garden just in case I needed to come home.

"Kareem!" I called out to him as I walked through the door. The silence that followed was welcome, letting me know that I had the entire place to myself.

I stood there in the foyer and looked around at this place that had always been my refuge, my safe haven; but not anymore, not since I saw *him* in the bar that night. Now, no place and no one felt safe—not this house, not Kareem, not even Aaron. I felt so raw inside, so violated. The image of his face invaded my thoughts almost constantly.

I forced thoughts of the rapist out of my head as I checked my watch and realized I only had two hours to do what I needed to do and get out of there. I wanted to be gone before Kareem got home. I loved my brother, but I really wasn't ready to play twenty questions with him about my whereabouts and my reasons for bolting from the wedding. He'd been nice enough to give me the benefit of the doubt when I told him I couldn't go in the church and go through with the wedding; however, he'd been blowing up my phone almost as much as Aaron. I just couldn't bring myself to face him, because I knew I'd be forced to lie, and I wanted to avoid that for as long as I could. My brother and I had always been close, and there was a good chance he'd see right through me.

I headed down the hall to my old bedroom and opened the bottom dresser drawer, which still held some old jeans I hadn't bothered to throw out when I left. I reached underneath the piles of pants expecting to find what I'd come for, but it wasn't there. I pulled everything out of the drawer and threw it on the ground, and still I came up empty-handed. A search of the other drawers had the same result.

What the fuck! Where the hell is it?

Trying to remain calm, I turned to the closet and

started pulling shoe boxes off the shelves. Maybe I'd put it in the closet and forgotten. There was nothing in the boxes, though, except for shoes I no longer wore. Leaving everything in total disarray, I headed for Kareem's room, thinking that since he'd been the one to give it to me in the first place, maybe he'd taken it back.

Stepping over piles of dirty clothes on his floor, I made a mental note to suggest to Kareem that he should get a cleaning lady. The mess in his room was ridiculous. I'd told him once that I couldn't believe he had the nerve to bring women into this pit, but he just laughed. "Shit!" he'd said. "They ain't coming to see how clean my place is." And sure enough, that boy kept a steady stream of women, and none of them seemed to care what a pigsty he lived in.

In spite of the mess, I was desperate to find what I'd come for, so I dove in and started digging through the clutter. I went through his dresser, searched under his bed, and pulled everything out of his closet. Nothing there.

I stood in the middle of his room, which was now in even worse shape than before, wondering what the hell I was supposed to do now. Kicking a pair of sneakers in frustration, I watched them land in the corner. That's when I remembered the loose floorboard.

I ran to the corner and dropped to my knees. Slipping my fingers along the edge, I was able to pry up the loose board. I was flooded with relief when I spotted the black box I'd been looking for hidden beneath the floor.

The metal box required a three-digit combination to open the lock, so I put in the code I'd used to set it the last time I locked the box.

"What the hell!" I shouted when the lock didn't budge. Not only had the box been moved, but the combination had been changed. I was about two seconds away from going to find a hammer and busting the damn thing open. The contents inside were way too important to me.

I leaned back against the wall, racking my brain to think of what Kareem could have changed the combination to. Taking a stab in the dark, I put in 317, and to my great relief, the box unlocked. "Of course he used Momma's birthday," I said out loud with a laugh. My brother was a straight-up momma's boy. That was why he still hadn't moved out of the last place we'd lived with our mother.

For a second, I stared at the contents of the box—a .38 handgun my brother had given me a long time ago. Black Beauty. I picked it up and held it in my hand, feeling a sense of power and, even more important, a feeling of safety I hadn't had ever since the night I saw *him*. I shoved the gun in my purse then closed the box and put it back under the floor. It was time to put the house back together. The trick would be to leave it no cleaner than I had found it. That would be a dead giveaway.

I'd torn up the place so bad that cleaning it took longer than I expected. By the time I finished, it was too late to get out of there undetected. I heard keys in the door, and Kareem entered carrying a bag of groceries.

"Hey!" He sounded happy to see me. "Where the hell you been?" He set the bag on the counter and gave me a hug.

"I been around."

"What? You don't know how to call?" he scolded. I hated it when he acted like my daddy instead of my brother.

"I just needed to get away from it all, Kareem."

"And that included me." I could tell by his tone that he was hurt. "I'm not those church people, Tia. I'm your family. Your only real family."

As much as I wanted to reassure him, I just couldn't tell him anything. Not yet. There was nothing he could say or do to make things better for me, so there was no use telling him anything.

"Kareem, sometimes I have to deal with things by myself. You can't protect me from everything, you know."

"Protect you? Did Aaron put his hands on you?" His eyes flashed with rage.

"No, of course not," I said.

"Then what? He cheated on you?"

"No, it's nothing like that. Aaron didn't do anything. He's a good man. This is all about me."

I could see he wasn't buying my excuse. "Little sister, what aren't you telling me?"

"A lot," I said truthfully. "But you can't save me from it. I gotta save myself."

He looked like he wanted to say more, and I knew he was frustrated with me, but thankfully he dropped the conversation. I gave him a quick kiss and hug then headed to the door before he could try to press further.

"If you need anything, you know where to find me," he said with a look that told me my big brother was willing to do anything for me.

I squeezed my bag, felt the cold, hard steel of Black Beauty. "I got everything I need," I said, and for the first time in days, I believed it was true.

Desiree
10

As I entered the church office, I quickly assessed the people in the room. Bishop TK Wilson stood much taller than I had expected based on his photo on the church website. The first lady's photo also painted an entirely different image than she projected in person. The hoochie-mama crop top and body-hugging pants would have been enough to get her tossed out of my church back home.

They were deep in conversation, so I had a few moments to observe the dynamics between them before they noticed me. I still couldn't believe that I was standing in the church where Aaron Mackie worked.

"Hello. May I help you?" The bishop moved toward me, causing his wife to swivel around and check me out. I lowered my eyes, attempting to appear shy and submissive. I could tell just from the few moments I'd spent observing him that he would feel protective of me if I came across as a nice Southern Christian girl.

"I'm new to the area," I said as demurely as I could, "and I've heard so many amazing things about First Jamaica Ministries. I'm looking for a new church family…and a job." I forced myself to wince when I said the word "job," as if it were too big a dream to imagine.

"Where you from?" Monique took a few steps closer to her husband. Game recognized game, so I was well aware she was about to lift her leg and piss on her territory if I didn't play my part right. And of course I would play it right. The last thing I wanted was for Miss Thing to be my enemy.

"I'm from Virginia," I said quietly.

"What part of Virginia you from? That's my home state," Bishop Wilson said, telling me something I already knew. I had done my homework.

"Petersburg. I'm a member of Bishop Thomas's church, Mount Calvary."

"I know that place. He's a good man."

"I've also seen your choir on television," I raved. "We don't have anything like that in Petersburg."

"Best choir in the world. We just won the championship," Monique announced, beaming at her husband.

"If he's around, I'd love to meet your choir director. I grew up singing in my church choir. My grandmother told me that there's no better way to feel like a part of the community than to join a church choir."

"He's taking a little time off," Monique said, giving me the once-over. Maybe I had come across as too eager. I should pull back a little, I decided.

While she looked ready to give me the brush-off, Bishop Wilson was still welcoming. "Well," he said, "you might not be able to join the choir right away, but it just so happens we are in need of a church secretary. Since you're looking for a job, I may be able to help you out."

I saw a tense look pass between him and his wife. Clearly they were not of one mind when it came to hiring me.

"Wow," I said, "it looks like I came along at the right time. Must be divine intervention or something."

The bishop raised his eyebrows at his wife as if reminding her who was boss. After a beat, she turned to me with a fake smile.

"Do you type?" she asked, though it was obvious that she really couldn't care less about my office skills. "Of course, I must tell you that this would only be a temporary position."

Since the demure Southern-girl thing wasn't working on her, I decided to change it up a little. Based on the way she dressed, it was clear that the first lady didn't give a damn what anyone thought of her, so strong and independent was probably my best bet for bonding with her—which I still intended to accomplish, even though she obviously had no interest in me right now.

"Yes, ma'am. I helped put myself through college working as a secretary," I answered. It didn't seem to change her demeanor at all.

"Mm-hmm," was all she said.

"Where you staying, child?" the bishop asked. Obviously he was more impressed by my country-girl innocent act. It was beginning to feel like I would have to be two totally different people around them.

"I have a room at the Y." I saw him flinch. "It's clean," I insisted.

Bishop Wilson shook his head. "Oh, no. That will not do. We'll figure something out... What's your name?"

"Oh, yes. We've been so rude," the first lady said, seeming halfway sincere. Either she was softening a little, or she was just giving up the fight for now. Whether I could get her on my side would remain to be seen.

"My name is Desiree Jones," I answered.

"Well, Desiree, let my wife show you where you'll be working," Bishop Wilson said, and I followed her out of the office, trying not to burst into a smile. I had been hoping to get my foot in the door at the church, but to have them offer me a job on the spot was almost too good to be true. Fate was definitely on my side.

Bishop Wilson stuck his head out the door and said, "By the way, Monique, we still need to finish our other conversation."

"But I'll be busy training Desiree here," she answered with a little bit of attitude.

"I won't let up until you tell me where Tia has been," he said.

She shrugged her shoulders but didn't answer him.

"Don't worry. I know where you live," he joked as he headed back into his office.

I had no idea what they were talking about, but I was too busy marveling at my good luck to really care. The first lady led me to a small, neat desk. It was obvious that someone else worked there because of the personal belongings on top.

I spotted a framed photo on the desk and my heart started beating faster. I picked it up, asking, "Who's the happy couple?"

The first lady looked at the picture and sighed. "Oh, that's Tia, our permanent secretary. The man is Aaron Mackie, our choir director, and also her former fiancé."

Her use of the word "former" confused me. I was just at the man's bachelor party not too long ago, and he sure as hell acted like he was ready to get married the next morning.

"Very nice. I guess they're married now, then?" I asked, trying to sound casual as I pressed for more information.

She sighed again. Whatever it was, something had her surely vexed. "Well, if you're working here you'll find out sooner or later, so I might as well tell you. She left him standing at the altar last weekend. That's why she's not here."

"Oh, my. That's terrible." I shook my head, staring at the man in the photo. "How could anyone do that to him?"

She snatched the picture out of my hand and placed it in the bottom drawer of the desk. "You shouldn't judge someone that you don't know," she said in a tone that let me believe Tia was off-limits as a subject of gossip.

"Oh, no, ma'am. I'm not judging," I said, regretting my slipup. I did not want to get on this woman's bad side. "It's just sad. They look so happy together."

"Yeah, it is sad," she said, then promptly changed the subject. "So, we have two phone lines here..."

She proceeded to tell me how to field certain calls; which ones I should patch through to the bishop right away, and which ones I should just politely take a message.

She was still explaining when the phone rang. A quick glance at the caller ID made my heart skip a beat, and when I looked at the first lady, I saw that she was a little uncomfortable herself.

"It's Aaron," she said, her hand hovering over the receiver like she couldn't decide if she wanted to answer the call. I gave her an out.

"It's my job, First Lady. Shouldn't I answer it?" I asked. She pulled her hand back, looking relieved that she didn't have to pick it up.

"Hello, First Jamaica Ministries, this is Desiree. How can I help you?" I glanced at Monique and she nodded her approval, so I guess my voice hadn't betrayed my nerves.

"This is Aaron Mackie. I was calling to see if there were any messages for me." His voice sent a little chill through me. It was sexy but sad.

"Um, just a minute, please." I covered the phone and whispered his question to the first lady. She shook her head.

"No, I'm sorry. No messages, Mr. Mackie." After a quick thank-you, he hung up.

I placed the phone on the receiver, my heart still racing. I turned to the first lady hoping she couldn't see how flustered I was, but she seemed pretty distracted by her own thoughts. I wasn't really sure what was going on, but it must have been something big, because Aaron Mackie's wedding never happened, and the first lady appeared to be pretty freaked out by a simple phone call.

Given her quick reaction when I spoke about the runaway bride before, I knew enough not to comment on the fact that I had just spoken to the jilted groom. I must have played it correctly, because she seemed to warm up to me after that. She got back to my training as if the call had never happened.

"So, your day starts at nine a.m. and usually ends at five," she said.

As I listened to her drone on about the particulars of my secretarial duties, I didn't have a moment to process my feelings. I was so close to achieving my dream of getting near Aaron Mackie, but I had to remain cool.

Then, as if things weren't already going well enough for me, Monique made an offer that sweetened the deal. "You know, the church owns a small apartment building not too far from here, and we do have a vacancy at the moment. It needs work, but if you like, I can talk to the bishop about letting you stay there."

"Really, are you sure?" Everything was falling into place even better than I could have hoped for. Someone was watching over me, for sure.

"I'm sure he wouldn't have it any other way," she said. "At least now he won't be worrying about you." She gave me a small smile that appeared to be genuine, and I felt a sense of victory. "Come on, let's tell him."

I followed her back into the office. Bishop Wilson was sitting behind his desk, going over some paperwork.

"We're going to give Desiree that apartment that was just vacated," she announced as we walked in. I wanted to laugh out loud. She had told me she was going to talk to him about it, but here she was *telling* him what he was going to do. This sista was not meek by any stretch of the imagination. *I could take a few lessons from her*, I thought.

"Fantastic," he beamed, not bothered in the least that his wife was making decisions in his church.

A knock caused him to look up toward the doorway. "Pippie, come on in here," he said.

I turned around to see a man in a blue janitor's uniform with a big, easygoing grin on his face. I recognized him instantly; he was one of the guys I saw at Aaron's bachelor party.

He stepped into the office and said, "I fixed those gutters, so the next time it rains there won't be any problem."

"Thank you," the bishop said, but then a look of concern crossed his face. His mind was obviously not on the gutter situation. "Pippie, I was wondering if you'd seen Aaron," he said.

Wow, there was his name coming up again.

Either the failed wedding had everyone around here pretty upset, or they were all as obsessed with the choir director as I was.

Pippie shook his head. "Me and Ross saw him the other night when his momma left town. I offered to take him fishing this weekend, but he just wants to be left alone. He'll be all right, though. We'll figure something out to help take his mind off of everything."

"Well, as long as he has good, loyal friends like you and continues to love the Lord, ain't nothing the devil can do," the bishop responded.

"Amen," I chimed in. They all turned toward me, looking as if they'd forgotten I was even in the room. "Oh, I'm sorry. I don't mean to intrude," I said. "Your words just reminded me of something my father used to say all the time: There's nothing in the world that can stand up against your faith."

Bishop Wilson nodded. He seemed pleased once again by my good-Christian-girl act.

"Have I met you?" Pippie asked, sizing me up. Thank God I'd been smart enough to wear a mask the night of the bachelor party.

"This is Desiree Jones," Bishop Wilson said. "She just moved to New York. She's going to be helping out until Tia gets back."

"Nice to meet you, Miss Jones. I hope you stay in our little community," he said, and I realized I wasn't the only actor in the room. This guy's polite greeting was a far cry from the lecherous partygoer he'd been the other night. In fact, he was the one trying to play grab-ass with me for a dollar.

"Now that I'm here, I can't imagine ever leaving," I said.

"You'll love being church secretary. It puts you in a position to know everything that's going on," Pippie informed me.

I smiled at the group of people watching me. Yeah, this was exactly where I wanted to be. Things couldn't have worked better for me if I had hit the lottery.

Bishop

11

I woke up with a sick feeling in the pit of my stomach, the kind that demands immediate action around it. Although Monique still wouldn't tell me where Tia was, I did feel we were working toward the same goal: helping Aaron and Tia fix their problems and possibly getting them back together. Unfortunately, we weren't getting very far. Last night, Monique had tried calling Tia and I had reached out to Aaron, but neither of us had any luck contacting either of them. Aaron's voice mail was full, so I couldn't even leave him a message.

As I drove to the church to start my day, I was determined that I would make some headway with Aaron. If he didn't answer my calls, then I would go find him. He shouldn't be alone during a time like this.

When I pulled into my reserved spot in the church parking lot, I saw Pippie and Ross seated on the church steps, deep in conversation. As I got out of the car and walked toward them, Pippie tapped

Ross and they shut up in a hurry. Now, that's not totally unusual when the pastor of the church shows up, because people have a tendency not to want me to see or hear them in any negative light. It comes with the job. However, these two weren't those type of churchgoers; they were also my friends.

"Gentlemen, I'm going to assume you weren't out here talking about football, so what's on your minds?"

"We're a little worried about Aaron," Pippie admitted.

"No, Bishop, we're a lot worried about Aaron. I was hoping you could talk him into coming back to work," Ross added, sounding as worried as I felt. "Aaron's always depended on the church and choir to help him through tough times, but not with this."

"I've reached out to him several times," I said, "but his phone keeps going straight to voice mail, and that's full."

"Maybe you should stop by his place," Pippie suggested. Ross gave him a quick elbow in the ribs, which was clearly meant to end the conversation, but I wasn't about to let that happen.

"Gentlemen, what's going on?" I asked, knowing that these were good men and neither would feel comfortable lying to me. "I want the truth."

There was an awkward moment of silence.

"I can't help him if I don't know what's going on," I advised them.

Pippie spoke up hesitantly. "We just left Aaron's place. We tried to talk some sense into him, but he wouldn't even let us in. I smelled alcohol on his breath." He shook his head sadly. "Bishop, he was drunk at nine o'clock in the morning."

"You don't know that for sure," Ross snapped protectively.

"I know what alcohol smells like, Ross," Pippie replied, not holding back now. "And I know what I saw the other night."

Ross remained silent, frowning at Pippie for what he probably saw as a betrayal of Aaron. I could understand it, I suppose. As his manager, Ross had an instinct to protect Aaron's image, but it was misguided loyalty at the moment.

"Ross, whether you know it or not, we are the three best friends Aaron has, and this is not the time to protect him. We need transparency in order to really help him," I counseled.

Fortunately, Pippie saw things my way and kept talking. "He was at a bar the other night, women all over him, getting drunk. It was like he wasn't himself."

It took longer for Ross to come around, but Pippie just stared him down until he relented. "Yeah," Ross started. "When we tried to talk some sense into him, he lost it. He basically told us to screw ourselves and leave him alone. He's in real trouble, Bishop. It's like he don't care about nothing. The barmaid he was with the other night is a real coke-head."

Pippie asked the question that had us all worried at the moment: "I know he got hit hard, but it's not like him to be self-destructive. What if he goes someplace that he can't come back from?"

"It's up to us to make sure that doesn't happen." They both nodded their agreement. "And with that, gentlemen, I think it's time I paid our choir director a visit."

I hated the idea of just popping up on Aaron without notice, but by the time I parked, I realized it was my only choice. Aaron's car stood out because it was alternate side of the street parking, and judging by the number of tickets on his windshield, he hadn't bothered to move the car in three or four days.

He lived in a second-floor walkup, and I could hear loud music thumping from his apartment as I ascended the staircase. If I didn't know about the heartache he was going through, I would think he was having a party up there.

I rang the doorbell several times but got no answer. For a split second I thought about walking away, but that was probably just what he was hoping

I'd do. I couldn't let him off the hook that easily, especially if he was as bad as Pippie and Ross said. I started banging on the door, intent on pounding until he finally opened it. I had no concern about waking anybody else in the building, because it was half past ten in the morning—and there was no way anyone was sleeping with Aaron's music blasting the way it was. After a few committed moments, my efforts paid off.

"Who the fuck is—?" Aaron, wearing only underwear and a robe, flung open the door like a wild man. The alcohol on his breath nearly knocked me over.

"Bishop? What are you doing here?" As drunk as he sounded, he was still alert enough to pull his robe closed to cover himself.

"I came to see my choir director. You still are the church's choir director, aren't you?"

It took him a second to answer. "Yeah, I guess."

"Good, 'cause it's time for you to get back to work." I pushed past him, getting a whiff of his unshowered body as I entered the apartment. What I found inside was even more distressing than his disheveled appearance. "What the hell is this?"

I was looking at the remnants of a wild party. Marijuana and empty liquor bottles littered the table. The only glimmer of hope was the fact that there was no evidence of cocaine in the room. But if I thought weed and alcohol were the extent of his debauchery, I soon learned I was mistaken as my eyes rested on a trail of shiny thongs, bras, and six-inch heels leading to the bedroom. I turned back to Aaron, who was looking a little wobbly.

"Bishop, this isn't a good time," he said, leaning against the wall for support. "Why don't I take a shower and meet you down at the church?" He cast his eyes downward, avoiding my angry glare.

I wasn't about to let him dismiss me. This boy was in serious spiritual trouble. I made a beeline for the bedroom.

"Seriously, this isn't a good time!" he called out in a panic.

"The hell it isn't," I said as I reached for the doorknob.

"Bishop, no!"

I flung the door open, expecting to find a woman in the room, but what I saw was much, much worse. Not one, but two naked women were in Aaron's bed, their limbs entwined as they slept. What took things over the top was the fact that I recognized both women. Tiffany Johnson and Keisha Holland had both grown up in my church.

I turned away from them, flipped on the light switch, and pounded my fist on the wall, causing the women to stir.

"What?" Tiffany said groggily, squinting her eyes

against the bright light. "We can't be doing this all night, Aaron. You got to let a sister get some sleep."

"You ladies should be ashamed of yourselves!" I yelled.

"Oh my God! Bishop!" Keisha was the first one to realize I was in the room. She grabbed the covers and shoved Tiffany's legs off of her as she covered herself as best she could.

I glared at Aaron, who looked like he wanted to fall through the floor and disappear.

"Now, I just know that both of those young ladies were not raised to be up here in all this foolishness," I said, so disappointed in all three of them.

"Bishop, we're sorry." Tiffany started to cry.

"We are," Keisha agreed, though she didn't look the least bit embarrassed.

"Get up and get your clothes on now!" I grabbed Aaron's arm and pulled him into the hallway with me.

"Bishop, look, you weren't supposed to see that."

"That's the best you can do?" I said. "You don't even sound sorry, Aaron."

"I'm not."

My mouth dropped open; he'd actually left me speechless. I felt like I was talking to a stranger. The Aaron I knew would not disregard the church's teachings so blatantly.

"What do I have to be sorry about?" he continued. "I'm a grown man and they're both consenting adults."

"What about Tia, Aaron? How do you think she'd feel if she knew you were doing this?"

He laughed. "Tia treated me worse than a dog. She dumped me like I meant absolutely nothing to her. Tell me, how am I supposed to feel after that?"

"I know she hurt you, but that young lady loves you," I insisted.

"No disrespect, Bishop, but after what she did to me, she can eat rocks for all I care. You need to step off and let me just be."

"I can't do that. Especially not when you're making such bad choices right now. You have to believe me when I tell you that Tia loves you. There is still a chance for the two of you."

"Yeah, well, I don't believe you. Actions speak louder than words, and her leaving me at the altar let me know loud and clear how she really feels."

"You're wrong. Not only does she love you, but she's going to need you to be there for her," I said, coming dangerously close to breaking my promise to Monique.

"Be there for her!" he yelled indignantly "Tia don't give a shit about me, Bishop. Why should I care about her?"

We were interrupted by Keisha and Tiffany, who stepped out of the room to do their walk of shame.

"Bishop, please don't—" Keisha's face was pleading.

"Don't what? Say anything to your parents? Don't tell your friends? Don't mention this to any other church members?" I scolded. "It would serve you right if I did. But you two are grown, and *you* have to decide if how you're living is the way that God intended for you."

They stared at me with wide eyes, accepting my lecture as penance for their transgressions.

"This is not right, and you both know it," I said, shaking my head in disappointment.

"But we're sorry. We really are, we got caught up in the moment," Tiffany insisted. She sounded like a teenager, much too young to be involved in the debauchery I'd just witnessed. "Please don't be mad," she said, practically begging.

"Lord help you, child, if you think I'm the one you need to be worried about right now. You better get home and get down on your knees and pray for forgiveness from the one who really matters."

"Yes, Bishop," they replied together then headed past us, heads hung low.

"And I want to see both of you in my office after services next Sunday. We'll be setting up some volunteer hours for you so you can spend your time in service to the Lord, not frolicking on the devil's playground with the choir director," I called out to them just before they shut the front door.

"This isn't their fault. I invited them over here," Aaron admitted.

"I haven't begun to assess blame yet. But you think I don't know those girls' reputations?"

I turned back to Aaron, whose soul needed saving too. Apparently he wasn't ready to hear the message yet, though.

"Bishop, you have to leave too," he said.

"I'm not leaving you like this."

He scowled at me. "Look, I can take care of myself," he said. "Why don't you go help those two say their prayers or something?"

"I'll deal with those two in my own time, but right now I need to be here with you." I reached out and put a hand on his shoulder. "You're in trouble, man. I'm worried about you."

He shook my hand off. "I just need you to go!" he yelled.

"I'm not leaving you like this," I said, standing my ground. "Get some clothes on. We're going to have a talk."

Aaron's shoulders slumped, and I knew that he had finally accepted defeat. "I'll put on a pot of coffee," I told him as I headed toward the kitchen. He went into the bedroom and shut the door behind him.

As I waited for Aaron, I thought about what I was preparing to do. I had promised Monique that I wouldn't betray Tia's confidence, and I didn't normally break my promises. This situation was anything but normal, though. Aaron was in a desperate downward spiral, and there was only one way I knew to snap him out of it.

He started to speak as he entered the room. "Bishop, you don't under—"

"Tia saw one of her rapists. At her bachelorette party," I blurted out.

"What?" Aaron reacted as if he'd been punched in the gut.

"That's why she didn't show up at the wedding. She said she was too ashamed to face you."

"Why?" he said, collapsing onto the couch. "I don't understand. Why didn't she just tell me?" He dropped his head into his hands and I gave him a few minutes to process the horrendous news.

When he finally lifted his head and looked at me, his eyes were searching mine for an answer on how to proceed. "Son, you need to get up and get yourself together," I said. "Then you need to go out there and find your woman. You understand?"

"Yes," he said, and I could see the old Aaron returning. He stood up and started cleaning up the remnants of his party. He was ready to take action.

"Thank you, Bishop. I'm going to make things right."

I patted him on the back. "That's just what I wanted to hear," I said as I headed for the front door.

"Just one more thing," I said before I exited.

"Anything."

"If First Lady ever finds out that I told you, it will cost me my marriage."

"That won't happen," Aaron assured me. I left knowing that I had done the right thing.

Ross

12

Despite the fact that the bishop had spoken to Aaron and gotten him to go back to work, he was still moody as hell. Yes, he'd stopped his hard partying, but he still didn't seem like himself. He was distracted most of the time, and "sullen" and "brooding" had become the best words to describe my once outgoing friend. He'd gone from the good guy on the straight and narrow to Mr. I-Don't-Give-a-Fuck in no time flat, and it had me truly worried. Not just for him personally, but for his career. It was the reason I'd arranged for us to meet with Jackson Young. I hoped that a meeting about his career would remind Aaron how much he had to lose if he didn't shape up soon.

I was relieved when I saw Pippie's car pull into the parking lot and Aaron climbed out of the passenger side. It had taken a lot of convincing to get him to agree to the meeting, and until now, I'd had my doubts about whether he'd actually show up.

"Hey, man, thanks for coming." I attempted a brotherly hug, but he left me hanging.

"Fifteen minutes and I'm out of here," Aaron replied.

"What's up?" Pippie fist-pounded me in greeting. He rolled his eyes in Aaron's direction, letting me know he'd put up with the same kind of attitude on the drive over here.

"Aaron, this is a really important meeting. This man could take your career to the next level. I think we owe him more than fifteen minutes."

"Right now, Ross, I've got a lot on my mind and very little patience. You're supposed to be my manager, so manage. I trust you," Aaron said as we stepped inside the Red River Restaurant. Jackson had picked a high-end establishment for our meeting. Either he had money to burn, or he was really trying to impress Aaron, I thought, as the maître d' led us to the best table in the house.

Jackson stood up and reached out to shake Aaron's hand. "Mr. Mackie, it's good to see you again. Please, have a seat."

Once we were all at the table, Jackson got right down to business. "So, can I get you gentlemen anything? Drinks? Food? An agent?" he joked.

"Water is fine," Aaron responded without any hint of humor in his voice.

"Heineken," Pippie said.

"I'm good," I said from my seat between Aaron and Jackson. Jackson made it apparent that as far as he was concerned, what I wanted didn't really matter anyway.

"Aaron, I'm going to cut to the chase. I think you are being poorly managed," Jackson said, as if I weren't even there. "I've looked into how things are being handled for you, and I have to say, not only am I unimpressed, I'm disappointed."

"Excuse me? What the hell did you just say?" I said, leaning close and glowering at him. It was a good thing we were in such a fancy restaurant, because I was about two seconds from putting my foot in his ass. Who the hell did he think I was, some punk who would sit on the sidelines while he ripped apart the hard work I'd put in for my friend and client? I may have been dressed in a suit, but I was more than capable of getting hood if need be.

"Ross, no." Pippie shot me a look warning me to keep it calm. It wasn't really necessary, though, because I looked at Aaron and realized he was barely paying attention to Jackson. Aaron's mind was somewhere else, so there was no reason for me to let this jackass get me all riled up.

Jackson gave me a smug look and a fake apology. "Hey, I'm not trying to offend anyone. I'm just speaking the truth. Aaron, I know that you have a good career in gospel, but frankly, you have an R&B voice."

Aaron didn't answer. He looked at his watch, probably checking to see if his fifteen minutes were up yet.

"He wants to be a gospel singer and a choir director," I answered for Aaron. "This is what God put him on earth to do."

"Is that right?" Jackson asked Aaron directly.

Aaron finally spoke. "It's true. I've always loved singing in the church and giving back to God, who has given me so much," he responded, with the stock answer that he usually gave for radio interviews. He was clearly not trying to be here longer than his promised time.

"All this talk about God. What did God do for you on your wedding day?" Jackson asked boldly. This guy had a lot of balls bringing up the worst day of Aaron's life as part of his sales pitch. "I can make you rich," he said. "I'm talking about the kind of money where you can buy your mother a house and let her retire so that she never has to work again. Send her on cruises around the world. I'm talking real money. That's the kind of rich I can make you."

He waved a dismissive hand in my direction. "See, unlike your current situation, where you are regrettably being mishandled, I will look out for you."

"What the hell are you talking about?" Whether or not Aaron was paying attention, I had to stop this guy from running his mouth.

"Are you the manager of Aaron Mackie, or Aaron Mackie and the First Jamaica Ministries choir?" he challenged.

"What the f—" I stopped myself from cursing as a waitress approached the table. Jackson shot her a look. She got the hint and backed away without asking for our orders.

"Can you really look out for both Aaron *and* the church choir? And honestly, tell us, how many pieces are being cut from his pie? And once that pie is cut, how many pieces go directly into your pocket?"

"You gotta be kidding me with this bullshit. I'm a good manager," I said, feeling more defensive by the minute. All the while, Aaron's eyes wandered around the restaurant like he was totally bored by the whole conversation.

"So you say?" Jackson pushed on. "Let's be honest. Who do you work for? Bishop TK Wilson signs your check, doesn't he?"

"This isn't about the church."

"Exactly my point. You work for the church, so who is working for Aaron?" He turned to Aaron and said, "I'm not just an agent. I will make sure your every need is met. I look out for clients, because when they're happy, I'm happy. That's how this works."

I pounded my fist on the table. "You saying I don't look out for Aaron? Man, you have no idea what the hell you're talking about." I was so close to going upside the dude's head, but he didn't know it, because he didn't even look in my direction.

"Be honest with me, Aaron. You love singing gospel, but haven't you ever thought about being a pop star? You have the voice for it." Aaron didn't answer, but the look in his eyes said enough to let Jackson know he had his attention. "I work with people like Clive Davis, Quincy Jones, Jay-Z. I put someone with your talent with the right people and you become an overnight sensation. Has anyone even offered you the opportunity to work with people like that?"

Aaron looked at me, and for a second I thought he was going to ask me why he'd ever let me manage him. Instead, he said, "Mr. Young, I'm late for a meeting with Bishop Wilson. I trust Ross to handle my business, so you two can stay and continue this conversation without me." With that, he stood up, shook Jackson's hand, and said, "Pippie, let's go. I don't want to be late."

Not even loudmouth Jackson had time to protest before Aaron was out of there.

Jackson and I sat eyeing each other for a minute

like two warriors about to do battle. I imagined myself reaching across the table and wrapping my hands around his neck.

"What the fuck was that about?" I hissed, leaning toward him. "You're trying to steal my client, who also happens to be my best friend? What kind of snake are you?"

Jackson smirked. "If he's your best friend, then you better make sure you sign with me, or you're gonna lose him."

If I hadn't realized it that day in the bishop's office, I sure as hell did now: This guy was beyond arrogant. The fact that he would come for another person's client in front of their face told me he was either stupid or dangerous.

"Aaron's not leaving me. Like I said, we're tight, and our business relationship works."

"This ain't called show *friendship*. It's called show *business*." He pulled out a legal pad, ripped off the first page, and handed it to me. "That's a list of things I'm going to need you to get Aaron to agree to if you still want to be his manager. You've got forty-eight hours to get him to sign off on it."

"And if I don't?"

He laughed. "If you don't, then I'll walk into First Jamaica Ministries with Clive Davis, and when we walk out, I can promise Aaron will be with us, and you'll be out of a job."

"I don't know who the hell you think you are, but I'm gonna do whatever is best for my client, so don't threaten me."

"For the record, I'm Jackson Young, superagent to the stars, and I don't make threats. Consider it a promise."

I picked up the paper and turned to leave, almost crashing right into Monique Wilson as she approached the table.

"First Lady?" I didn't disguise the surprise in my voice.

"Ross," she said, sounding like she was less than happy to have run into me. "I didn't know that you were going to be here."

"I was just leaving," I said, looking with disgust at Jackson. Once again he ignored me as he turned on the charm for the first lady.

"Monique, I was just finishing up this meeting. I ordered us a very expensive bottle of champagne."

She looked at me and quickly tried to explain. "I'm meeting Jackson to talk about my acting career. As you know he's a—" I raised my hands, stopping her mid-sentence. It was information I neither needed nor believed.

"None of my business, First Lady. None of my business," I said before getting the hell out of there.

Monique

13

"How do you like the champagne, Monique?" Jackson's voice snapped me out of my worried daze. From the moment I'd arrived at the restaurant, I was distracted with thoughts of Ross and what he might have done after he left the restaurant. Lord knows, I wanted to trust his "none of my business" comment, but the way things had been going in my life lately, I couldn't be sure this meeting would remain secret. For all I knew, Ross had already told Pippie, and who knows where the news would go after that? God forbid TK discovered my whereabouts.

I hated the idea of being untruthful to TK, but his jealousy was making him entirely unreasonable. If Jackson had been a woman, TK wouldn't have had a problem with this meeting or with me taking up an acting career. I couldn't let that stop me from agreeing to meet Jackson when he called, though, because if I hadn't taken this meeting, I would have spent my life wondering, "What if?"

"I'm sorry. Did you say something?" I looked up to see Jackson gazing at me across the table, and it gave me a jolt. Even if this visit was strictly business, I had to admit he was a handsome man.

"You seem a little distracted. Is everything okay?" he asked.

I sighed and answered honestly, "I didn't tell my husband about this meeting. I'm afraid Ross will."

"I wouldn't worry about Ross Parker right now. He's got plenty of other things on his mind," he said with a smirk. "So, back to my question: How's your champagne?"

I glanced down at the nearly empty glass I was holding. "I like it. I'm sensing a mixture of a few things," I said as I finished off the last of the champagne.

He gave me an appreciative nod. "You're very perceptive. It's nice to meet a woman with a sophisticated palate."

"So what exactly is it called?"

"Armand de Brignac Ace of Spades rosé. Jay-Z made it famous when he featured it in his video 'Show Me What You Got.'"

"Well," I said with a smile, "I can't say I watch too many Jay-Z videos, but I know when I like something, and this is some of the best champagne I've ever tasted."

"I'll have a case sent over to your house," he said nonchalantly.

"A case? This must be a two-hundred-fifty-dollar bottle of champagne."

"Four fifty, to be exact, but when you're talking about good champagne like this, who's thinking about price?"

"My husband." I chuckled. "I don't think he'd approve of me spending that kind of money on champagne."

"Who said anything about you paying for it? I'm making it a gift. I like giving gifts." He poured me another glass then sat back and watched me take a sip. Something in his eyes made me feel like it was best to take the conversation back in the direction of business.

"So, Mr. Young, why exactly am I here?" I asked.

"You're here because we both know you have what it takes to become famous. We could be a formidable team. I can make you a star. The real question is: Are you going to let your husband stop us?"

"What makes you think he would do that?" I asked, though we both knew the answer.

Jackson didn't bother to entertain me with an answer to my question. "This is not a business for the faint of heart. It takes time, dedication, and a great work ethic," he said. "But it's a great opportunity for you, Monique. What neither of us can afford is your husband running around all half-cocked, having tantrums because you're not around to make him eggs in the morning." He leaned back and crossed his arms over his chest, challenging me with, "So, if you can't control him, we might as well end this meeting and forget the whole thing now."

"Mr. Young," I started, but he raised his hand to stop me.

"Please, call me Jackson."

"Okay, Jackson. You don't have to worry about my husband. I'll take care of him," I said. Jackson looked satisfied with that; I, on the other hand, wasn't even sure I could do that. Given his feelings about Jackson Young, getting TK on board might prove to be impossible.

"I can't wait to get those beautiful eyes of yours in front of the camera," Jackson said.

I couldn't help blushing.

"You really believe it's possible?" I hated to sound insecure, but this was new territory for me, and as exciting as it was, it also felt scary.

"Give me six months," he said with confidence. "Now, we're going to have to get you acting lessons, but that's just standard. Don't worry; I know a great coach. He's worked with Angela Bassett, Goldie Hawn, and Madonna, although he insists she wouldn't take any of his direction."

"Really?" This went beyond even my biggest dreams.

Jackson leaned in closer and spoke dramatically. "I'll tell you a secret. A friend of mine is doing his next film based on a book I'm sure you've read. Can't tell you the title, but you would be perfect for one of the leads. It's about a group of four best friends. Blows *Waiting to Exhale* away. You'll wind up on the cover of *Essence* magazine for sure."

I stared at him, wide-eyed with excitement.

"I believe in celebrating a sure thing." Jackson lifted the bottle and poured me another glass of champagne. He raised his glass and waited until I picked up mine. "Here's to the beginning of a great career."

I couldn't stop grinning as we drank to my success. I had heard that both Morgan Freeman's and Samuel L. Jackson's careers didn't take off until after they were forty, so why couldn't it happen for me?

As we finished off the bottle of champagne, Jackson gave me the inside scoop on the business and how he saw it working for me. I loved hearing all the plans he already had for my career.

"You're going to be the next Angela Bassett," he raved as he ordered a second bottle.

I didn't know how TK would react once I shared

Jackson's vision for my career, but at that moment, fueled with alcohol and visions of my new life dancing in my head, I didn't even care. When the time was right, I would set TK straight about his opinion of Jackson. TK had been totally wrong about him. Jackson had remained a complete gentleman during this meeting. Not once had he made a suggestive or disrespectful comment. In fact, I was starting to feel a little insulted that he hadn't. I mean, a woman like me does like her compliments, you know. Why else would God have given me a figure like this? But all Jackson did was keep pouring me glasses of that fabulous champagne as he plotted a course for my future.

"I'm so excited to begin," I gushed. "Just let me know what I have to do."

"Hell, why not just jump right in?" he said, then sat back and waited for my response.

"You mean now?" I asked, glancing at my watch. I was surprised to see I'd already been with him for two hours.

"Nah, never mind," he said when he caught me checking the time. "We'll just wait until next week and then set you up with an acting coach."

"No, wait. We *can* start right now," I blurted out, wanting him to understand that I wasn't taking this opportunity lightly.

He didn't answer right away. It was obvious he

was toying with me a little as he sat back and let me squirm for a minute. Jackson was obviously very good at what he did. He gave off an air that wasn't totally unfamiliar to me. Some people might call it arrogance, but to me it was an aura of confidence that transcended looks or money. It was the swagger of influence, and the mark of a very powerful man. To a woman who understood it, it could be intoxicating. My husband had it to an extent, but not quite like Jackson, whose aura was on steroids. One thing was for sure: It could get a woman into a lot of trouble if she wasn't careful.

When he finally spoke, he said, "John Legend is a client at the agency, and tonight he's gonna do a surprise late-night show. He's performing his new material at a small venue in the Village. I'd love for you to be my guest."

"John Legend? He's my favorite. He's so smooth." For a hot second I was envisioning myself in the club listening to John Legend croon, but then reality hit in the form of my husband. A brief afternoon meeting was one thing, but how would I explain being out late at night?

"I can't go," I admitted, feeling annoyed with TK and then ashamed for feeling that way.

"That's a shame," Jackson said, "'cause I wanted to introduce you around. Robert De Niro will be

there, along with my good friend Laurence Fish-
burne. I hear that Jay-Z and Beyoncé will be making
an appearance."

"You're kidding me, right?" I got so excited my
hands started shaking.

"That's what I'm talking about. It's important for
you to meet people like this, especially in a social
setting. People like to work with people that they
know and like. It's not just what you know in show
business. It's also *who* you know."

There was no way I could miss this. If Chaka
Khan was giving a concert and TK had five minutes to decide to attend, there was no way he'd
miss it, so why should I be denied the same kind
of opportunity? TK would just have to understand.

"You know what? I think I will—"

Before I could finish, my phone started vibrat-
ing. I felt like a child who'd just been caught
red-handed, even though I wasn't doing anything
wrong. I was sure it was TK. Maybe word had gotten back to him about my meeting with Jackson.
I truly didn't want to answer and hear TK going
off on me, but I knew it would be a lot worse to
ignore him and let his imagination slip into over-
drive.

"Excuse me a minute," I said, stepping away
from the table as I pulled the phone out of my

purse. When I looked down at the caller ID, I was relieved to see it wasn't TK's number on the screen.

"Hello?"

"Monique." It was Tia, and she sounded distressed. "I followed him, Monique. I followed him from the bar to his house."

"Followed who?" Before she even answered the question, I understood who she meant: She had followed her rapist.

"Where are you?" I shouted, suddenly feeling panicked. Rushing back over to the table to get my things, I tried to keep the conversation going with Tia. I wanted to understand what was happening, and I had to talk some sense into her.

"I'm in Hollis Gardens on Murdock. I just watched the bastard walk into his house," she said with pure hatred in her voice. "Me and him are about to have a talk."

"Don't do anything stupid, Tia. I'm on my way." I knew that my words fell on deaf ears.

I held my hand over the phone and whispered to Jackson. "Look, I'm sorry, I know meeting people is important, but I have a friend who is in a lot of trouble, so I have to cut this evening short." I didn't even give him a chance to reply before I hurried away, listening to Tia ramble on almost incoherently.

"Please, Tia, just go home," I pleaded with her. "Promise me you're going to go home."

"I can't promise you that."

"Tia! Dammit!" I yelled as I realized she had hung up on me. A hand on my shoulder caused me to almost jump out of my skin.

"It's just me." I'd been so distracted by the call that I hadn't realized Jackson was on my heels. "Monique, talk to me. What's going on?" he questioned, looking genuinely concerned.

"I can't talk right now. My friend's in trouble and I have to get to her before something bad happens." My voice was shaking I was so concerned.

I tried to step away, but he put a hand on my arm to stop me.

"You've had too much champagne to drive. Can't someone else help her?" he asked.

"The man she's about to confront is her rapist!" Maybe he was right about me having too much alcohol, because the words just spilled out, in spite of the fact that I'd promised Tia not to tell anyone about her problem.

"I can't let you go there by yourself," Jackson said. "It could be dangerous."

"But I have to help her," I insisted.

"Then we'll go together." The look on his face told me he wasn't going to accept anything except my complete submission, so I stopped protesting and let him lead me over to his Mercedes. All my thoughts were on Tia as he pulled out of the parking lot. I prayed that she was all right and hadn't done anything crazy.

Desiree

14

Part of my new job as the church secretary was to collect and sort the day's mail, and I was continually amazed by the amount of fan mail that Aaron received. I wasn't supposed to open it, just leave it in a pile for him, which he would collect whenever he came back to work. That pile of perfume-laced envelopes had me more than curious, though. I just knew they contained some wild letters. One day I gave in to temptation and opened a couple, and I was blown away by what I saw. Talk about steamy. These sisters made my obsession with Aaron look tame. One woman even sent a naked selfie, her legs spread-eagled and her pubic hair shaved to look like a cross. The caption written in red ink read: BAPTIZE ME. How crazy is that? I filed that one in the trash can in a hurry.

I was in the process of sorting the latest mail delivery when my cell phone rang. I answered it without even thinking. "First Jamaica Ministries."

"What? Jamaica who?"

"Oh my God, Lynn, I'm so sorry," I whispered into the phone. "I thought I was answering my work phone."

"Work? You got a job?" she shouted. "When the hell did that happen?"

Lynn was my best friend and roommate down in Virginia. She was in the army and had gone out into the field on a training mission right before I made the trip up to New York. She'd known about my plan to seduce Aaron, and if her training exercise hadn't interfered, I would have asked her to make the trip along with me.

This was my first time talking to her since I'd left Virginia, so we had a lot of catching up to do. Lynn did not like being out of the loop.

"Yeah, I got a job. Can you believe it?"

"No, I can't. What kind of job you got?"

"I'm the new secretary at First Jamaica Ministries." Saying it out loud made me want to get up and do a little dance. I still couldn't believe how the job had just fallen into my lap.

"But you're not a secretary!" Lynn said.

"I am now," I said, chuckling.

"Wait! Roll that back a second for me. You said you're a secretary...for First Jamaica Ministries?"

"That's right." I thought she'd be proud of my accomplishment, so I was surprised when she started yelling at me.

"Girl, are you out your fucking mind? The plan was for you to go up there and fuck the man, not work at his damn church!"

"I know, but the plan had to change," I protested. "Don't be mad at me."

"What do you mean it had to change?"

"I didn't get the chance to sleep with him at his bachelor party."

"Well, I'm sorry about that, but you need to come home. Aren't you supposed to be going to the doctor?"

I rolled my eyes. Lynn had the annoying habit of trying to parent me sometimes.

"I'm seeing a doctor up here," I told her.

"Well, I'm worried about you. With everything going on, you need someone to look after you."

"I know you are, Lynn, and I appreciate that, but I still have a chance to see this plan through, and I'm going to stick with it. I mean, the way things are falling into place for me, I feel like I'm meant to succeed."

"Desiree, I know it feels like that, but—"

"No, it's more than just the job, Lynn. I mean *everything* is falling into place. Aaron's wedding didn't even end up taking place. His fiancée stood him up at the altar, and then I ended up getting her job. Can you believe my luck?"

"Holy shit! Are you kidding me?"

"Nope. That will tell you what can happen when God is on your side," I said confidently. "I still haven't met Aaron yet, but today's supposed to be his first day back to work."

There was a lull in the conversation as Lynn processed everything I'd told her. "Wait," she said. "Does your taking this job mean that you're not coming back to Virginia?"

"Kinda," I said hesitantly. I hated to think that my friend was sad, but I wasn't about to give up this opportunity. I had the perfect solution. "I'd love for you to come to New York and hang out with me."

"Serious business?" she hollered in my ear, her mood suddenly lighter.

"Of course I'm serious. You know you're my girl."

She definitely liked the idea, because she started singing "Empire State of Mind." I held the phone away until I was certain that she was done. Lynn had a lot of talents, but singing wasn't one of them. "I always wanted to go to New York! You want me to come up for the weekend?"

"No, I want you to come up for the *duration*." I knew what the gravity of my words would be on her. I didn't make a habit of needing anyone, and she knew it. "I need you here Lynn."

She hesitated for a minute. I was sure she understood that this wouldn't be just a fun "girls in the city" kind of trip. I was recruiting her to help me fulfill a once-in-a-lifetime dream.

"Okay," she finally said. "I'm there till the end."

"What about Uncle Sam?"

"I have some time coming to me before I go TDY to Afghanistan. Now's as good a time as any to take it. I'll tell them my mom is sick or something." Just like I expected, Lynn had my back in whatever way I needed. I could hear the unmistakable sound of excitement in her voice.

"Hey, Lynn," I said, changing the subject. "Did you get the mail? Did my check come?"

"Yep, I got it right here."

"Well, then you need to get your ass up here as soon as possible." As much as I didn't mind trying to exist on this measly salary for show, in my real life I liked money and everything that it could buy. I'd waited a long time for this check, and it was going to provide for me in a way that this job could not.

"Done. I have some loose ends to tie up with my CO, but then I'll be there on the first thing smoking tomorrow."

"Perfect. I can't wait," I told her. As much as I had come to like living in New York, it was really lonely. It would be nice to have someone to hang with, because spending every night with books and television as my company was getting old fast.

"Me neither. You need me to bring you anything else?" she asked.

"Nope. Just bring me my check, girl," I said, eager to get my hands on that money.

"You sure?" she persisted. "Have you filled that prescription yet?"

I sighed. "Lynn, I am fine. Would you stop worrying about me for once?"

"I would if I thought you were doing what you were supposed to and taking your medicine," she said. "This is nothing to play around with. You're acting way too casual about your health, and that shit ain't funny."

"Look, someone just went to get my prescription filled up here today," I said. "I promise I'll take a pill as soon as I get it, okay?"

"Don't make me FaceTime you to prove it," she threatened. I imagined her tapping her foot like a drill sergeant with an I-mean-business look on her face. It was the same look my father used to give me when I was in trouble.

"I will text you as soon as it gets here and I take it, okay?"

"As long as you're clear that this is not something you can mess around with," she said. "I don't know what I would do if anything happened to you."

"I'm sitting pretty up here. Don't waste a good worry on me," I assured her. "Look, I got to get off this phone and get back to work, okay? Text me when you make your travel arrangements."

"All right, girl. I love you."

"I love you too. I'll see you *and my check* real soon," I said, then hung up.

No sooner had I put away my phone than Pippie came strolling into the office. "Here's your prescription," he said, handing me a small paper bag.

"Thank you so much. I told you I could have gotten it myself." Pippie had been coming by the office quite a bit ever since I started working. It was obvious he was interested, and even though I had no plans of giving him any, I didn't want to push him away. I knew he was a friend of Aaron's, and he could turn out to be a good source of information at some point.

"No problem. It was on my way," he said with a smile.

Just as I'd promised Lynn I would, I opened the bottle of pills and poured one into my hand. Before I had time to blink, he handed me a bottle of water.

"Thanks again, Pippie," I said after I swallowed the pill.

Waving his hand, he said, "Please, that's how we do around here for each other. I would've had it to you sooner if I didn't have to chauffeur Aaron around. It took a little longer than I thought."

"So the choir director is back, huh?"

"Yep, he's down in the chapel talking to the bishop as we speak. Who knows? Maybe this place will finally get back to normal."

"Do you think that girl Tia's coming back for her job too? I hate to swim in other people's misery, but I need this job."

"I think you're good. From what I hear, she's trying to stay as far away from this place as she can. So I wouldn't worry about it." He gestured toward the bottle of pills. "Is everything all right?"

I resisted the urge to snap at him for being a nosy-ass. Fortunately, it was a pretty common pill prescribed for many different illnesses, so most likely he had no idea what my problem was. If I reacted harshly, he might sense that I had something to hide.

"I hope so," I said casually. "I probably should have filled this a while ago, but now that I got this, I'm gonna be perfectly fine." I made sure to add a little extra Southern lilt to my voice. It was the quickest way to divert a man's attention away from whatever you didn't want him focusing on.

"Good." He smiled at me, and I looked down at my desk, hoping he would get the hint and let me get back to work. He didn't.

"Can I ask you something?" he said, still hovering over my desk.

I looked up at him and nodded, waiting for him to continue.

"Are you doing anything this evening?"

"This evening?" Oh Lord, I thought, this man was about to ask me out. I would have to figure out a way to let him down easy, so I didn't alienate him. No need to have Aaron's friend talking bad about me just as Mr. Mackie was coming back to work. "No, I haven't made any plans," I said. "I've been pretty much a homebody ever since I moved here."

"You like Alicia Keys?"

"Yeah, that's my girl!" I said, dropping my guard just a little. I didn't just like Alicia Keys; I loved her. Just thinking about her music had me moving my head to the imaginary beat of one of her jams. I couldn't stop myself from singing a few bars. "You and me together, through the days and nights; I don't worry 'cause everything's gonna be all right."

I realized I had gone a little overboard when I saw the look in Pippie's eyes. It was the one men get when they've settled on their next target. I should've shut the heck up.

"Damn, girl, you can blow! You have got to join the choir."

"Yeah, I'm thinking about it."

"Well, Aaron is back. I can't wait to tell him about you," he said. "He's going to love having you in the choir."

He can have me anywhere he wants, I thought as I gave Pippie a modest smile.

"So, one of the church members hooked me up with prime seats to Alicia's concert at Madison Square Garden. Since you're not doing anything…"

"Pippie," I started, "that's really kind of you to offer, but I don't want to lead you on. I'm not looking to date anyone right now. Maybe you want to use those tickets for someone who's available."

He looked crestfallen for a split second, but then he covered it with a smile. "Oh, no. It's not like that. We can go as friends."

Given the amount of time he'd spent hanging around my desk recently, it was obvious he was hoping for more than friendship, but hell, if that's the way he wanted to play it, who was I to pass up tickets to see my girl Alicia?

"Oh, what the heck," I said. "Why not?" Between now and Friday I was sure I could come up with a plan to make sure that Pippie kept his hands to himself now that we were "just friends."

Tia

15

"I can't promise you that," I told Monique then ended the call.

How could I promise her anything when I didn't have a clue what was going to happen next myself? It wasn't like I planned on being in front of his house. Hell, I hadn't planned much of anything since the night of my bachelorette party. Ever since I saw my rapist, I had sunk into a pit of despair. I was full of so much hatred and rage that I barely recognized myself. All the counseling of other rape victims that I had done at the church felt like wasted time now, because I couldn't even take my own advice. I had told so many women to rely on their faith, to pray for emotional healing, but I couldn't do that for myself. Instead, I was stalking the guy, entertaining revenge fantasies all the while.

For three days I had been sitting in and around the restaurant where he worked, content with just watching and hating him. At one point I gathered the nerve to sit at the bar and order a drink from him, and that's when my anger boiled over. He looked me in the face and took my order, as calm as can be. The guy had no clue that he was looking at a woman whose life he had destroyed. As if that wasn't bad enough, he tried to flirt and make small talk with me for a minute, until my dead stare told him I wasn't interested.

I left the bar before he even came back with my drink, and I sat in my car, trembling with fury. Part of me wanted to go back in there and confront him immediately, but I couldn't do what I really wanted to do in a crowded restaurant. So I waited until his shift was over, and then I followed him back to his apartment. This bastard was going to know who I was, dammit, and he was going to apologize for ruining the last six years of my life—years I could never get back.

I watched him enter the building as I considered my next move. Reaching into my purse, I rested my hand on Black Beauty, which I'd been carrying everywhere ever since I picked it up from Kareem's house. The gun gave me a sense of security, and now it gave me a sense of power that propelled me to step out of the car and head toward the apartment building.

Not long after he walked in, a light came on in the third-floor window, so I knew where I would find him. Approaching the building, I planned on pushing buttons until someone buzzed me in, but it turned out that wasn't even necessary. He lived in such a crappy building that the front door lock was busted and I was able to go right in.

I headed up to the third floor, where there were two doors, and I knocked on the one facing the front of the building, where I had seen the light come on. My heart was pounding as I wondered briefly what I would do if somehow this was the wrong apartment. What would I say to whoever opened the door? Then I heard him say, "Who is it?" and I knew I had the right place. The sound of his voice had been seared into my memory, filling my nightmares ever since the night he raped me.

"It's me," I said, resting my hand on my purse to gain confidence from Black Beauty. "Open the door."

I saw a shadow pass over the peephole, and then I heard him taking the chain off his door. He pulled it open and my knees began to wobble as he stood before me, wearing only boxers and an unbuttoned shirt. Taking a swig of the beer he held in his hand, he looked me up and down then said, "You look familiar."

"Yeah, you gonna let me in?" I asked, trying to maintain my calm, at least until I gained access to his apartment.

His eyes wandered down to my chest again, and

then he shrugged. "Why not?" He stepped aside, and I rushed in before I could lose my nerve.

"What's up?" he asked casually, like an unexpected visit from someone he thought was a stranger was nothing new to him.

"You alone?" I asked, looking around the small, dirty apartment.

"Nobody here but you and me," he said, rubbing a hand over his exposed chest in what he probably thought was a seductive move. "So what's up?" he asked again. "Somebody sent you here?" The guy was acting like he'd just gotten a pussy delivery, and I had to wonder if it was something he and his other rapist friends did for each other—sent random women over for them to use and abuse.

"Do you even remember me?" I asked, sliding my hand into my purse.

"Aw, don't get mad, sweetheart," he joked. "I was probably drunk the last time we met."

I pulled Black Beauty out of my purse and aimed at the middle of his chest. "Oh, you were definitely drunk," I snarled, "but that still wasn't an excuse for you to rape me."

He took a step backward, his demeanor going from arrogant to freaked the fuck out. Now instead of staring at my chest, his eyes were locked on my gun.

"Who—I don't even know what you're talking

about. I didn't rape you or anyone else," he said in a shaky voice.

"You fucking liar!" I shoved the gun into his chest, backing him further into the apartment. "You and your friends raped me like I was a worthless piece of shit."

"Look, you've got the wrong guy. Now please put down that gun before someone gets hurt," he pleaded, raising his hands.

"Sit down!" I demanded.

"Sure, sure, just stop pointing that gun at me."

He fell back on the sofa, staring up at me with fear in his eyes. Keeping the gun aimed at him, I glanced down at his laptop, which was open on the coffee table. His Facebook account was on the screen.

"Vinnie Taylor. So that's your name, huh?" I said. "Sounds like a pretty average name for a fucking monster, wouldn't you say?"

He was still watching the gun until I said, "So if I look through your friends list, will I find your old roommate Michael?" Then his eyes left the gun and he took a good look at my face. I could see recognition dawning.

"Oh . . ." he said. "You're that chick . . ."

As I watched a smirk form on his face, I realized that the event that was burned into my brain as the worst night of my life was for him a pleasant memory. My vision became blurry with tears, and just like that, I lost the upper hand. I'd shown my weakness, and he was no longer scared, in spite of the gun in my hand.

He leaned back on the couch and took another swig of his beer. "I got to give it to you. You are one bold bitch coming up in here like this. Now, let's just say I did rape you...and I'm not saying I did..." he said, with a big grin on his face that told me he was, in fact, proudly admitting that he'd been involved. My stomach turned and I tasted bile in the back of my throat.

"You bastard," I shouted. "Just admit it! You raped me. You and your filthy friends."

He took another swig of beer, wiped his mouth, and said, "Sure. Why not? I'll admit it. I probably did rape you. There were so many I barely remember. But so what? It ain't like you the only bitch who had one too many and then had to pay the price. Get over it already."

The tears escaped and began running down my cheeks.

"Why'd you bother to come here with your weak ass anyway? You got me to admit it, but what the fuck you gonna do about it now? You think the cops are really gonna believe you this many years later?"

"Who said anything about cops?" I said, trying to sound tough even as I struggled to keep myself together. "Did you forget I have a gun?"

He laughed at me. "You mean the gun you can't even hold straight because you're shaking so bad?"

I took a step toward him, hoping it would intimidate him enough to make him shut up, but it was a big mistake on my part. Once I was within reach, he grabbed my wrist and knocked Black Beauty out of my hands. Within seconds, he had the upper hand, and I was pinned to the floor, with him sitting on my midsection.

"You dumb bitch," he said as he pressed his hands on my shoulders to keep me from struggling. "You come into my place with a gun, threatening me? I should shoot your ass right now and be done with you. Wouldn't do a day in jail for shooting a deranged psychopath who broke into my place because she mistook me for someone else," he said, sounding like he was enjoying himself. "But I don't think I'll kill you right away. I think first we'll play around a little. You know, take a trip down Memory Lane." I could feel his penis begin to harden against me. "You had some pretty good pussy if I remember correctly."

He raised up on his knees and pulled down his boxer shorts, and in the split second that he released his grip on my shoulders, I began flailing like a wild animal. "Noooooooooo!" I screamed. "You're not going to rape me again!"

"That's it bitch, fight me, that just makes it better!" he laughed, and I could see the pleasure on his face.

As I scrambled to try to regain control, I swung my leg and it connected with his groin. He yelled out in agony and fell to the floor, grabbing his balls and curling into a ball. I jumped up and grabbed the nearest object, a lamp on the table beside the couch. Acting on survival instinct, I raised the lamp up high then brought its heavy ceramic base down on his head. I swung it one more time. His body jerked, and then he lay totally still.

I dropped the lamp and stood looking over the unconscious, bleeding body of my rapist for a few seconds then calmly walked over to pick up my gun from the spot where it had fallen during the scuffle. It felt good to have Black Beauty in my hands again. I could feel the power it wielded come back to me.

Monique

16

"Stop!" I shouted when we passed a blue Honda Civic. "That's her car!"

Jackson said, "You sure? There's a lot of blue—" but stopped when I pointed out the red-and-white I SUPPORT AARON MACKIE AND THE FIRST JAMAICA MINISTRIES CHOIR bumper sticker on the car.

"The car's empty," Jackson said, stating the obvious. "You think she went after him?"

"I hope not," I replied, though I didn't hold out much hope. She'd sounded pretty agitated on the phone, and I worried what she was capable of in that state.

With so many apartment buildings on the street, it would be impossible to know which one Tia might have gone into.

"Jackson, let me out here. I'm going to check in her car to see if there's anything that will help me figure out where she is," I said.

"I'll go find a parking space and be right back," he said.

Surprisingly, Tia had left her car door unlocked—not a good sign. I climbed into the passenger seat and opened the glove compartment. As I
was pulling out papers to check for a clue, Tia came
racing out of a building across the street. My relief
at seeing her was short-lived as she climbed into the
car, spotted me, and started talking crazy.

"Monique! Oh my God, oh my God, oh my God!
I gotta get out of here! I didn't mean for it to happen! I just wanted him to apologize."

I put a hand on her shoulder to calm her down
and she flinched. I could feel her trembling beneath
my touch.

"Tia, slow down. What happened?"

She looked at me and burst into tears. "I don't
know what happened. One minute I was calling
him a rapist and the next he had me on the ground.
He was gonna rape me again." She sounded so frail
and broken. I wrapped my arms around her and she
sobbed against my shoulder.

"Where is he now? How did you get away?" I
asked.

She pushed away from me and wiped the tears off
her face. "I hit him over the head with a lamp. As
soon as he hit the floor I ran."

"And you're sure that he's alive?" We both turned
to stare at the person who had spoken. I had forgotten about Jackson.

"Who is this?" she shouted at me, tensing up as if she thought he, too, was there to hurt her. She was clearly traumatized.

"It's okay," I said, speaking softly. "He's with me. We were in a meeting when you called, and he saw that I was upset and refused to let me come by myself." I couldn't tell her that while she was fighting for her life I was talking about becoming an actress.

"I wanted to make sure that you were okay," Jackson explained, though he kept his distance so as not to make her any more frightened than she already was. "I thought you two could use a man in case he got violent or something."

"He did," Tia said and started crying again. After a minute she looked up at me and said, "Oh my God. Do you think he's really hurt? He wasn't moving."

This was bad. Really bad. What if she had gravely injured the guy, or even worse, what if he was dead? I didn't know what to say. I was worried about Tia, but I was equally worried about the church. I could picture the headlines now: FORMER CHURCH SECRETARY ARRESTED FOR MURDER.

Jackson spoke up. "I'll go check on him. Which building is it?"

"Are you sure?" I asked, though I was relieved and grateful he was offering to do it, because I was pretty much paralyzed with worry at the moment.

"Yes, I'm sure. I wanna go up there and handle this guy myself. If he's conscious, I want to knock him out for what he did to Tia."

Tia looked at him and then at me. For a second I thought she was going to curse me out for telling Jackson about her rape, but instead I watched the tension leave her shoulders as she whispered "Thank you" to Jackson.

After Tia told him the location of the apartment, Jackson turned to me and said, "Monique, you need to get her out of here."

I nodded, and he cautiously reached over to open the driver's-side door. Tia allowed him to help her out with no resistance. He guided her to the other side of the car and settled her into the passenger seat.

Getting into the driver's seat, I took the keys from Tia and started the engine. I looked at Jackson and mouthed the words, "Thank you."

He nodded and told me, "Take her someplace safe. I'll call you later." With that, he headed across the street toward the apartment building.

I knew just where I would go with Tia. When I married TK, I had kept the house that I owned. Recently, the tenant had left after a long dispute over unpaid rent. Just like that, a situation that had caused me frustration turned out to be a blessing, because now the house was empty for me to take Tia there.

"I don't know who he is, but he's a really nice guy," Tia said as I pulled away from the curb.

"Yeah," I answered. "He's one of the good ones."

Tia's eyes filled with tears again, and I wondered if my comment made her think of Aaron. "Monique, what have I done?" she asked, sounding so sad and lost. No matter what happened, I knew that I had to protect her.

I reached out and covered her hand with mine. "You're going to be okay, Tia. I promise."

Desiree

17

"In New York…" With my earbuds in and my iPhone cranked all the way up, I was singing along full volume with Alicia Keys. Flipping through the concert program, I smiled, wishing I could be back at the concert, not at my desk at the church. I was so caught up in the memories of the night before that I didn't even notice the bishop come in until he tapped me on the shoulder. I nearly jumped out of my skin.

I pulled the earbuds out and turned off the music in a hurry. "Oh, Bishop, I'm sorry," I said.

"That's quite all right," he said with a smile. Putting down his briefcase, he picked up the concert program and flipped through a few pages. "So, I take it you had a good time last night."

"It was the absolute best," I said enthusiastically.

"That's good to hear." He gave me an approving nod as he placed the program back on my desk. "I think you and Pippie are going to make a really nice couple."

"What?" I snapped, then caught myself and changed my tone in a hurry. "Oh, no," I said more sweetly. "I don't know where you heard that from, but we're not a couple." If my plan to seduce Aaron was going to work out, I definitely didn't need anyone thinking that I was dating Pippie.

"Well, yeah, you're not a couple *yet*, but that was only your first date, right?" His comments were meant to be good natured, but I wanted to smack the grin off his Bible-thumping face.

"No, that wasn't our first date. We're not dating at all," I said a little more emphatically. "We went to the concert as friends."

He took a step back from my desk. "No problem," he said. "I didn't mean to offend you."

I realized I must have taken my attitude a little too far. Damn it. I couldn't risk pissing off the bishop and losing this job. Playing this part correctly was proving to be difficult, but the outcome was so important to me that I would do whatever it took.

"Oh, no offense, Bishop. It's just that I'm a single girl and I'm new here, and well, you know how the rumor mill can be in a church. I don't want to gain a reputation," I explained in my best innocent-Southern-girl voice.

He nodded. "Oh, I certainly understand about rumors." There was obviously something behind what he said, and I wondered what rumors had been spread about him in the past. Whatever they were, they made him uncomfortable enough to drop the subject in a hurry.

"Any messages?" he asked, thumbing through the mail he'd picked up from the box where I always left it for him.

I glanced at my message pad. "Yes. You had a call from Ross Parker. He said he needed to talk to you ASAP about a Mr. Jackson Young." I could see the bishop's entire demeanor change when he heard the name Jackson Young.

"Do me a favor, Desiree," he said, sounding very irritated. "Get Ross down here this evening around five. I want to find out what Mr. Young is up to now."

"Right away. Oh, and your wife called for you. She said to tell you she's sorry about last night and that she was still with 'you know who.'" I had no idea who she was referring to, but it sure as hell had me curious.

"I hope you don't mind me asking, Bishop, but is everything all right with you and the first lady? I can't help but notice a little tension between you two." I knew it was way out of bounds for me to be asking such a personal question, but I couldn't help myself. What can I say? I can be very nosy when I smell some juicy drama.

Fortunately, he didn't get mad at me for asking. "It's no big deal, really. She spent the night with a sick friend," he explained. Then he surprised me by adding, "I just wish she hadn't waited until 3 o'clock in the morning to answer her phone and let me know."

I raised my eyebrows, surprised to hear that the first lady hadn't even come home last night, but he quickly cleaned it up by adding, "Don't worry, Desiree. The first lady and I are going to be fine."

"Glad to hear it," I replied, resisting the urge to push for more details.

"So," he said, changing the subject, "have you had a chance to meet our choir director since he's been back?"

"I've seen him in passing, but we haven't officially met. I was thinking about bringing his mail down to him and introducing myself." What I didn't say was that as soon as I heard Aaron was back, I'd headed into the sanctuary and watched the choir rehearsal from the shadows of the balcony, camera phone in hand to capture Aaron in his glory.

"Why don't we take the mail down there together and I'll introduce you," he suggested.

"Well, if it's not too much trouble...I don't want to be a bother, but I would like to meet him."

"No bother at all." Bishop Wilson picked up a box of Aaron's mail. "Come on. Let's make that happen."

When we entered the sanctuary, the choir was singing a song that I'd never heard before. I had to admit that they were blowing the roof off the place.

"They sound amazing!" I whispered to the bishop.

He broke out into a proud grin. "It's Aaron. He's the best thing that ever happened to our music ministry. The choir was always good, but he pulled them together and made them great."

When they finished the song, Aaron spotted the bishop, who waved him over.

"Why don't you all take ten?" Aaron addressed the choir, then he descended the stage and approached us. My heart started racing. This was the moment I'd waited so long for.

"Bishop," Aaron greeted. They shook hands, and I could feel the obvious affection between them.

"This is Desiree Jones," Bishop Wilson said. "She's new to New York, and she just joined our congregation."

"Hello." I extended my hand to Aaron.

"Nice to meet you, Desiree." If he noticed how sweaty my palms were, he was nice enough not to show it.

"I brought you your mail," I told him. "I'm filling in for the church secretary." I smiled innocently, but I knew exactly what I was doing. I wanted to gauge his feelings for the woman who walked out on him. I would have preferred a look of hatred, so I could be sure there was no chance of her coming back in the picture, but the look of distress he gave me would have to do.

"Desiree is from Petersburg, Virginia," Bishop told him.

"Hopewell. Boy, does that town bring back some memories. I'm from Petersburg myself," Aaron shared. Of course, he had no idea just how much I already knew about him. "Bishop won't tell you this, but he has a fondness for those of us from his home state."

"What can I say? People from Virginia always seem to bring me good fortune," Bishop said with a laugh.

Aaron said to me, "There used to be a little bakery in Hopewell, over on Center Street. They made the world's best sock-it-to-me cake. Got my mouth watering just thinking about it. Daggonit, what was that place called?"

"You're too young to be losing your memory," Bishop kidded him.

"The Mocha Expressions Bakery," I offered.

"Yeah. That's it. Mocha Expressions Bakery.

Man, what I'd do for a piece of that cake right now."

"Well, what do you have to offer?" I joked. "I used to work there back in the day. I can make you a sock-it-to-me cake."

Aaron's face broke out in a huge grin. "What do you want?"

I stared at him for a second, trying to keep my true feelings masked. He didn't know it, of course, but this was not the place to be asking me, of all people, what I wanted from him.

An older woman from the choir interrupted. "Excuse me, Bishop. Can I talk to you for a second?"

"Sure, Sister Terrell. If you two will excuse me." He patted Aaron on the back before leading the woman over to the side so they could talk in private.

"So," Aaron said, "who do I have to kill to get you to make me a cake?"

"You don't have to kill anyone," I answered, "but I was hoping to join your choir. I was a member of the choir back home, and there is something about it that heals the soul."

"Amen to that. I just went through some things myself, and this choir has been a huge part of my healing process. Anybody that loves the Lord would be a welcome addition."

"I love singing for the Lord."

"Then we have something in common," Aaron said.

Yeah, I thought, *I can't wait for the day that you find out just how much we have in common.*

Bishop

18

"I thought you might be hungry, Bishop."

Desiree walked into my office carrying a mug of hot chocolate and a small plate of cookies. She was always doing nice things like that. As much as I was worried about Tia and hoping she would be well enough to come back soon, I had to admit I was enjoying Desiree's thoughtfulness.

"Thank you, Desiree," I said. "I don't think there's anything else I need right now."

"I made the cookies myself. They're peanut butter."

"They look tempting, but you know my wife doesn't like me to eat too many sweets," I told her, my mouth already watering from the scent of the fresh baked goods.

"Well, Bishop, seeing as how she's not here, this can be our little secret, okay?" she said with a smile.

I didn't hesitate to pick one up. "I suppose one wouldn't hurt," I said, taking a bite. Once I got a taste, I knew I wouldn't be stopping at just one.

"Is there anything else I can get you before I leave?" she asked.

"Is it quitting time already?" I asked, glancing at my watch. I'd been so busy researching for Sunday's sermon that I lost track of time. "Has Ross Parker called? He should have been here twenty minutes ago for our meeting."

"No, he hasn't—"

Before she could finish her sentence, Ross came into the office, looking a little stressed.

"Sorry I'm late, Bishop," he said as he took a seat by my desk.

"I'll leave you two gentlemen alone then," Desiree said, closing the door behind her as she exited.

"So what's going on, Ross? Your message said you wanted to talk about Jackson Young." Just speaking the man's name made the hair on the back of my neck stand up.

"I wanted to give you a heads-up."

"About what?"

"Well, Aaron and I had a meeting with Jackson Young, and—"

"Wait," I interrupted. "Why was I not informed of this meeting? I expect to be kept in the loop on anything pertaining to my choir."

Ross let my reprimand roll off his back without becoming defensive. "He wanted to talk to Aaron, not the whole choir. I just wanted Aaron to hear the guy out. I thought it would help take his mind off Tia and back onto his career, you know?"

I nodded. "And did it work?"

Ross released a frustrated sigh. "I wish I'd never agreed to meet with the guy."

"I could have told you that," I said. "Nothing good can come out of an association with that snake. So, what happened at the meeting?"

"Aaron actually left after about ten minutes. Said he had a meeting with you."

I leaned back in my chair, recalling the conversation I had with Aaron when we met the other night. We talked almost exclusively about the choir and how he was eager to get back to work. "Well, he didn't even mention Jackson to me, so I guess whatever Mr. Young said to him, it didn't leave much of an impression."

Ross didn't look convinced. "I wish it was that simple," he said. "Jackson planted some ideas in Aaron's head, and I'm worried that in his present state of mind, Aaron might just consider Jackson's offer."

"His offer?" I asked.

"Bottom line is he wants Aaron to be his client, and he's pulling out all the stops to try to get him. He's throwing around a lot of promises—touring, performing at awards shows, and a contract with a major label."

I hated to admit it, but those things sounded great. "You know, Ross, if I didn't have such a personal issue with Jackson Young, I might be asking you to pursue this further. Can you imagine what that kind of exposure could do for the church? Imagine our choir on a national recording label."

Ross frowned. "No, Bishop, you don't understand. He doesn't want the choir. He only wants Aaron. And it gets even worse."

"Worse how?" I asked warily.

"Not only does he want Aaron to leave the choir, but he wants him to stop singing gospel music altogether. He wants Aaron to become an R&B star—the next Trey Songz."

I shook my head. "Aaron wouldn't do that. He's devoted to that choir. That's his ministry."

Ross didn't share my certainty. "I sure hope you're right, Bishop, because this guy's not giving up. After Aaron left, he gave me a list of demands. Said I could either get Aaron to agree to them and stay on as his manager, or he would get Aaron to agree on his own and kick me to the curb."

"That man has some set of b—" This news had me so worked up that I nearly lost my composure in the house of the Lord. "He has some nerve," I said, cleaning up my language. "You don't really think Aaron would go for it, do you?"

"I sure hope not, but like I said, with the way he's

been acting lately, who knows? My problem is that Jackson gave me a deadline to get him to agree, and that deadline is almost up."

"And what is Aaron saying about it?" I asked.

"I haven't talked to him yet. I was kind of hoping you and I could talk to him together. First Jamaica Ministries is like his home, Bishop, and you're like a second father. He trusts you. If anyone can talk some sense into him, it's you."

"Of course I'll speak to him. That snake in the grass is not going to win this one, Ross."

Ross stood up. "Let's go find him now. I don't want Jackson to get to him before we do."

"Unfortunately, the choir is away at an exhibition in Connecticut until late tonight. We can talk to him first thing in the morning," I said.

He started pacing the floor in front of my desk. "Are you sure we shouldn't find him tonight? Maybe drive up to Connecticut?"

I chuckled. "Ross, calm down, son. I have faith that everything will turn out fine. We can wait until morning."

He stopped pacing and looked me dead in the eye. "No, I don't think you understand just how much of a snake this guy is. There's something else about the other day that I haven't told you yet."

"Well, what is it then?"

He sat down again, but he looked very uncomfortable. It took him a long time to start speaking. He finally started with, "Bishop, this isn't easy…" but before he could continue, the door opened and my wife strutted into the room in her usual flamboyant manner.

"And what exactly are you two doing in here behind closed doors?" she purred, a big smile covering her face as she made her way to me. "I hope you weren't talking about me."

A look passed between her and Ross, but he quickly shifted his gaze to a spot on the wall. It was odd; he looked like he was afraid to make eye contact with my wife. She, on the other hand, was her usual confident self.

"I hope I wasn't interrupting anything important," she said. "I just wanted to come by and see my adoring husband." Standing beside my chair, she pressed her body up against me and started rubbing my back affectionately.

"I'm going to leave you two lovebirds alone," Ross said, getting up and heading for the door.

"Hold on," I said. "You were about to tell me something else about Jackson Young. Monique, you don't mind waiting a few minutes for us to finish this conversation, do you?"

She gave me a pout, which always weakened me. "You two can talk about that later. I'm ready to go home."

I knew what that was a signal for, and suddenly I was more than ready to get my wife home too. I felt bad about interrupting my conversation with Ross, but he didn't seem to mind.

"Yeah, we'll continue this later," he said.

Monique waved to Ross as he left, but his good-bye to her was stiff and awkward. The poor guy was so upset by this whole thing with Aaron and Jackson that he wasn't himself at all.

As soon as he was gone, Monique was sitting in my lap.

"I really missed you, honey," she said. "This thing with Tia has me so stressed out. I was hoping you could take me home and help me relieve some tension."

Resting my hands on her generous hips, I said, "You know I'm more than happy to oblige," and planted a kiss on her neck. "But first, fill me in on what's been happening. All I know is you got a phone call from Tia and you had to go rescue her. Where were you? Why didn't you call me right away to go with you?"

She leaned in for another kiss, lingering just long enough to get a rise out of me. "We can talk about that later. Right now I want to go home with my husband so we can get in a nice, warm bubble bath. Can we do that?"

"Whoa! Remember we're in a church." I helped

her up off my lap. The last thing I needed was to get too turned on in my office. It just wasn't right.

"Then take me home, because right now all I want is to make love to my husband—and I don't care if it's in the church or the gutter." She extended her hand to me, and I didn't have to think twice about my response. I may be a man of the cloth, but at this moment I was a man who desperately needed his wife. I took her hand, ready to get the heck out of that church before I lost my religion.

Tia

19

The angry sound of a car horn woke me out of a restless sleep. I was drenched in sweat, my head was hurting, and my heart was pounding, all caused by yet another nightmare. It took me a second to shake the frightening images from my mind and realize that I was safe in Monique's old house. I got up and looked around, realizing that Monique was no longer with me. She'd come back to the house to check on me the day before, and ended up staying through the night because I was too scared to be alone. She must have left when I finally fell asleep.

Through the bedroom window I could see the darkening sky. The clock on the nightstand informed me that it was seven o'clock at night. I'd fallen asleep sometime around noon, which meant I'd slept the entire day away, and now I would probably be up all night. Not that I cared. Sleep wasn't my friend anyway, not with the continued nightmares.

I had believed that confronting one of my rapists,

who I now knew as Vinnie Taylor, would bring me some peace of mind. Instead, I felt more vulnerable than ever. For years, my rapists had been the boogeymen in the next room, kept out by a heavy wall of therapy and service to other rape victims. Now I knew his name, and I could still feel his weight against me as I had when he pinned me to his living room floor. Vinnie and his accomplices were in my thoughts every waking moment, and no amount of positive thinking, praying, or wishing could make them go away.

Another horn blast outside made me jump. I looked out the window to the street and saw a dark-colored sedan near the curb with its lights on. There was a man wearing a baseball cap in the driver's seat, but it was too dark for me to make out his face. I could have sworn I saw a similar car outside yesterday too. Backing away from the window, I sat down on the couch, knowing that if I didn't, my trembling legs wouldn't be able to hold me up and I'd be on the floor.

Take a deep breath, I told myself. *He's probably just picking up someone from a house across the street.*

I sat like that for several minutes, trying to control my breathing and convince myself that it wasn't one of my rapists parked outside Monique's house, waiting for me to come out. I was too terrified to go near the window to see if the car was still there.

Logically I knew there was almost no chance that my rapists knew where I was. After all, Vinnie Taylor hadn't even remembered me, and he definitely hadn't followed me after what I'd done to him. But I was still paralyzed with fear.

My cell phone rang, and I forced myself to get up off the couch to check the caller ID. It was Monique.

"Just wanted to check on you, honey. Are you feeling any better after you got some sleep?" she asked when I answered.

"No," I said, bursting into tears. "I'm so freaked out by the whole thing. My dreams are even more intense and scary than they were before."

"Tia," she said, speaking in a calm, even voice, "just remember they're only dreams. You are safe in my house."

"I can't stop thinking about them. I'm scared that they're coming to get me."

"Oh, sweetie. I'm so sorry you're going through this. Do you want me to come get you?" she asked.

"No," I said. "It doesn't matter where I am. I'll still be scared and I'll still have nightmares. You stay home with the bishop."

She tried for a few minutes to convince me to come to her house, but I wasn't ready to face the bishop yet. I also wasn't a hundred percent sure that Aaron wouldn't be there. She wasn't saying it, but I

knew that Monique and the bishop both hoped that
Aaron and I would work things out at some point.
What if the bishop called Aaron and told him I was
coming to their house? I definitely wasn't ready to
face him in the state I was in.

When she finally realized there was no way she
was changing my mind, Monique sighed and said,
"Okay, but I'm coming to see you first thing tomorrow morning. Maybe it's time we find you a
therapist."

I had no faith that therapy would do any good.
All those years of therapy I'd been through, thinking
it healed me and made me stronger, had proven to
be useless as soon as I spotted Vinnie Taylor working at the bar. One look at his face and I was a
basket case all over again. Why bother to go back to
therapy?

I didn't want to argue the point with Monique,
though, so I just said, "Okay, Monique. I appreciate
everything you've done for me." In the morning I
would tell her my true feelings about therapy, but
for now, I just wanted to get off the phone.

We ended the call shortly after, and I sat on the
bed, wondering how I was ever going to move forward. I'd been in limbo for so long now that I
could barely remember what my life was like before I saw Vinnie Taylor. Longing for some glimpse
of normalcy, I went to the suitcase that Monique

had brought over to the house. Facebook had always been a good way for me to relax and catch up with friends, and I hoped that reading other people's silly status updates might take my mind off the state of my own messed-up life.

Monique had gotten the suitcase from my apartment, where it had been packed and ready for me to grab before Aaron and I headed for our honeymoon after the wedding. That felt like a lifetime ago. Now I had to dig through the bathing suits and cute little dresses I'd purchased for that vacation in order to get my computer. I held back the tears that threatened to escape from my eyes. Grabbing the laptop, I quickly shut the suitcase to get the vacation clothes out of my sight.

I logged on to Facebook and was overwhelmed by the number of messages that had been posted to my wall. After leaving Aaron at the altar, I assumed everyone would hate me—especially the members of First Jamaica Ministries. No matter how much Monique told me they cared about me, I couldn't believe her. Now I sat stunned as I read the messages of concern and love. Instead of hating me, people were praying for me.

Along with the public posts on my wall, I'd received many private messages. Several of them were from women I'd helped through my rape-crisis call center at the church. They wanted to help me now in my time of need. My eyes blurred with tears and my heart swelled with gratitude. This was the kind of healing I needed. Just as I was feeling the most vulnerable and unworthy, these messages lifted me up, evidence of the many people who cared for and loved me. And then I came to the message from the one person who mattered the most.

Aaron had sent me a message not long after I sent him the horrible text message meant to push him away for good. His private message read: Tia, I need you to know that I will respect your wishes, but I will never stop loving you.

I stared at Aaron's words for a long time, knowing that he meant them. A strong urge to reply overcame me. *I could reach out to him and we could start over*, I thought, but then just as quickly dismissed that fantasy. The Tia that he loved, the sweet and trusting woman he knew, was gone. She died the minute I spotted my rapist in the bar.

Just like that, my thoughts were back on Vinnie Taylor, and an overwhelming rage overtook me. Aaron's message reminded me of just how much had been stolen from me, and I could not rest until every one of those motherfuckers paid for what they'd taken. I would handle it differently than I had with Vinnie, not getting close enough to put myself in danger again, but I would find a way to get to each one of them. They couldn't give me back my past, but maybe I could erase them from my thoughts and move forward. I would keep fighting to take back control, and I wouldn't give up until someone put me in a pine box.

I typed Vinnie Taylor's name into the Facebook search and found the same page I'd seen on the computer in his apartment. Seeing his face again made me sick to my stomach, but I ignored the nausea and began to scroll through his friends list, thinking there was a chance the three roommates had stayed in touch. Maybe they even held yearly get-togethers where they laughed and joked about all the women they'd raped.

"Son of a bitch!" I shouted when I came to a friend listing for a man named Clifford White. Sure, he was older, but I would never forget that face. Not only did I have a name now, but once I clicked on his page I knew what college he had attended, along with employment information and a whole lot of personal details. I couldn't believe the line of work he had gone into. The irony was not lost on me. Nor did it surprise me that he'd liked Aaron's page.

Aaron

20

"Man, ain't no food in the world better than Poor Freddie's," Pippie said, finishing the last bite of macaroni and cheese. We'd picked up some takeout from his favorite soul food restaurant on Linden Boulevard and sat in his car while he devoured his meal. I, on the other hand, couldn't stomach it. Ever since the bishop had told me about Tia's reason for leaving me at the altar, I hadn't had much of an appetite. Returning to work had helped distract me, at least during the time I was with the choir, but Tia was always in the back of my mind.

"You okay, man?" Pippie asked, looking down at my uneaten meal.

"Yeah, I'm okay," I said listlessly. I really didn't feel like talking about it, because all the talking in the world wasn't going to change anything. "You want my food?"

Pippie didn't hesitate to grab a piece of corn bread from my takeout container. "You still thinking about what Ross and the bishop told you this morning?" he asked.

He was referring to a conversation we'd all had earlier about Jackson Young. Apparently, after I left the meeting with Jackson the other day, he and Ross had gone at it pretty hard. Ross told me that Jackson wanted me as a solo artist—R&B, no less—and that he would do whatever it took to pull me away from the church choir. Ross and Bishop Wilson came to me all worked up, acting like there was a real danger of me signing on with Jackson. I didn't tell them, but I was actually pretty offended that they doubted my loyalty.

"Nah," I told Pippie. "I'm not thinking about Jackson Young. That guy's out of his mind if he thinks I would ever leave First Jamaica Ministries."

"I know that's right," Pippie agreed. "Speaking of First Jamaica, let's get back there. My lunch break is over."

We pulled away from the curb and headed toward the church. As we arrived in the parking lot, we both spotted Jackson Young at the same time. He was leaning against his Mercedes, texting away on his smartphone.

"What the hell is he doing here?" I muttered. After what Ross told me this morning, I expected Jackson to try to make contact with me, but not to be this bold, coming to the church he wanted to steal me away from.

"Wasting his time," Pippie said as he parked and got out of the car.

I got out too. Unfortunately, Jackson spotted me right away and headed over. Pippie was a few steps ahead of me, and he just kept right on walking, practically bumping into Jackson as he passed him by. I shook my head. I'd have to get on Pippie later for not having my back.

"Aaron," Jackson said, holding out his hand to me as he blocked my path.

I stopped, looked down at his hand, but didn't shake it. He got the hint and dropped his arm to his side. His face still held a fake smile, though.

"You got a minute?" he said. "I spoke to your manager and he told me you were turning down my offer. Mind if I ask why?"

I checked my watch, purposely not answering his question. "I have to get ready for choir rehearsal."

"Mind if I come listen?" he asked. "Maybe I could talk to the choir afterward. You know, fill them in on the details of my offer—see if *they* can change your mind."

This dude must be crazy, I thought. "You mean the offer where you cut the church and the choir out of everything?" I said with disgust. "Don't waste your breath. I'm sure Ross already made it very clear that I'm not interested in anything you're offering."

Jackson looked puzzled. "Cut the church and the choir out? I don't know what you're talking about."

"Ross told me about your little list of demands. You need to understand something about me, though. Gospel music has brought me through some very dark times, and this church is my family. I will not leave them to sing R&B—ever. I don't care how big of a contract you offer me."

He let out an arrogant laugh. "Well, first of all, big doesn't even begin to describe what I'm talking about. I don't think you can even imagine the amount of money we're dealing with here. And as far as leaving the choir, I don't know why you would ever think I wanted you to do that. Gospel music is where it's at, and you and your choir have something special. I'm going to make you the next Kirk Franklin and the Family."

"What about what you said at our meeting? You asked me if I'd ever thought about being a pop star."

He waved his hand as if to dismiss his previous comments. "Oh, I was just testing the waters, you know what I mean? When you left, Ross explained to me how devoted you were to the church, and I knew that solo R&B stuff was a dead end. Besides, gospel is huge these days. I don't want you to leave your choir. I want to make you all stars."

"But Ross said—"

Jackson put a hand on my shoulder to stop me. "Aaron, I don't know what your manager is telling you, but it's false. I am offering you and your choir a chance to put out a recording with Sony."

I was totally confused. Everything he was saying was the complete opposite of what Ross had told me that morning. Ross hadn't even mentioned anything about a recording deal. He had been focused only on telling me what a snake Jackson was and how he wanted to take me away from First Jamaica Ministries.

"But Ross—" I started again, but Jackson cut me off.

"Don't you see what this is about?" he said.

"I have no clue," I said, relieved to see Pippie coming back outside with Bishop Wilson following behind him. Now I knew why Pippie had left me before. He went inside to get backup.

As Pippie and Bishop approached us, Jackson explained, "Your manager is lying to you. He told you I wanted you to leave the church choir behind, which is the furthest thing from the truth."

Bishop Wilson looked at Jackson with pure contempt on his face.

Pippie interjected. "Yo, Aaron, you know Ross has had your back since way back. Ain't no reason for him to be lying to you now."

I nodded in agreement. "Ross is my boy. What reason would he have to lie to me?" I said to Jackson.

Jackson gave me a patronizing smile, like I was a child, too stupid to see the truth. "Mr. Parker is just that—a *boy*. He doesn't want you to move up to the big leagues because he knows he doesn't have the experience to compete. He's afraid that if you sign with Sony, you'll leave him behind."

I shook my head. "You're wrong. Ross is a good manager. Our choir is doing bigger and better things all the time."

"Really?" Jackson said. "When was the last time he got you anything but a small-time gig? Does he have the connections to get you onto BET Gospel?"

Bishop Wilson raised his eyebrows at the mention of the national network. I hated to admit it, but the thought of that kind of exposure excited me too. I also knew that Jackson was correct: Ross really didn't have the power to get us on that network. He had become my manager because he was my best friend, not because of any special skill in the profession. Was it really possible that Ross was that insecure? Would he hold me back for his own selfish reasons?

"Bishop?" I looked to him, hoping he would have some words of wisdom, because I sure as hell didn't know what to do.

The bishop turned to Jackson looking like he wanted to punch him in the mouth. If we hadn't been in front of the church, he just might have. "Mr. Young, I think it's no secret that I have mistrusted you since the moment you set foot in my church. I would like nothing better than to never see you or hear your name again, but somehow you keep popping up, this time with wild claims that completely contradict what Aaron's manager has told us. Can you give me one good reason why we should believe a word that's coming out of your mouth?"

Jackson pulled out his cell phone. "Would you like me to call my lawyers right now? They can explain the contract to you."

"Yo!" Pippie interrupted, sounding pretty pissed off at this point. "If y'all are going to start talking contract negotiations, don't you think you should get Ross down here?"

Jackson shot Pippie a murderous look, but I was glad Pippie was putting the brakes on this whole scene. My head was spinning at this point, full with visions of me and my choir on national television, but also unable to figure out the truth. Add this to the thoughts of Tia that were always in the back of my mind, and I was in no shape to be making any kind of decisions.

"You're right, Pippie," Bishop Wilson said. "We

can't continue this conversation until Mr. Young here provides us with a contract that our lawyers can look over, and of course, until Ross is available to talk this over."

I could see Jackson struggling to maintain his composure. As arrogant as he was, I'm sure he had come to the church expecting to walk away with a new client. This was a man who wasn't used to hearing "no."

"I can assure you," he said, "that once you understand your manager doesn't have your best interests at heart, you'll be signing on the dotted line. I'll be in touch." He headed back to his BMW and drove off, leaving us all in the parking lot wondering who was telling the truth.

Tia

21

I circled the block for the third time then sped down Hillside Avenue, checking my rearview mirror again. The same circular headlights were still about a block behind me, and it was making me nervous. It seemed like the car had been following me ever since I pulled away from Monique's house. Thank God I had Black Beauty in my purse on the seat beside me.

My phone rang, and Monique's name showed up on the caller ID. I was relieved to hear her voice, until I realized she was calling to yell at me.

"Why aren't you at the house?" were the first words out of her mouth. She'd been acting more like my mother every day; at first I appreciated her concern, but now it seemed like she was forgetting that I was a grown woman.

"Wait. How did you know I wasn't at the house? Is that you following me?" I asked, then regretted the slip.

"Following you?" she said, her voice rising an octave. "Are you okay? Where are you?"

I tried to clean it up so she would stop asking questions. "Don't worry. I'm fine. I was mistaken." Surprisingly, another check in my rearview mirror revealed that statement to be true. The headlights were no longer behind me. I breathed a sigh of relief. My paranoia was really getting the best of me these days.

"You didn't answer my question. Why are you out? I told you I'd come by to get you."

"I had some things to do," I answered vaguely, hoping she'd back up and give me some space. When I made my appointment for tonight, I'd forgotten that Monique was planning to come over.

"I knew, should have never given you those car keys back," she said. It took some convincing, because she was worried about me going out alone, but I'd finally worn her down, promising I wouldn't go anywhere without telling her first. Obviously, I'd broken that promise, but I knew she'd forgive me eventually.

"Monique, I'm a big girl. I just needed to get out for a while, go for a little drive, and I didn't feel like waiting for you. Stop worrying about me, okay?"

She let out a big sigh. "I know. I just want to make sure you're all right."

"I'm fine. I promise. I'll call you as soon as I get back to the house, okay?"

"Okay," she said. I could tell by her tone that she didn't like it, but she knew she had no choice in the matter. I had disappeared on my wedding day, and she had to be worried that I could do it again if she pushed too hard.

I ended the call and put the phone down. One more glance in my rearview mirror showed no sign of the car I thought had been following me. Just to be sure, I zigzagged my way around a few more blocks instead of driving straight to my destination.

When I finally arrived at the church, I sat in the car for a minute, making certain I didn't see the car again, and also gathering my nerve. It felt like a lifetime since I'd been in church, and it wasn't the most comfortable feeling to be there now. But this was a conversation that I had to have. As much as I wanted to avoid it, I knew I could never move on if I backed down.

I took a deep breath, staring up at the impressive megachurch where thousands came each week to worship. Unfortunately, that wasn't what had brought me there today. Today was about trying to find closure.

It was late and the church was empty, but he'd told me he would leave the side door open for me and meet me in the sanctuary. As I headed down the corridor, I passed by the choir practice room, and my heart ached. How many times had I watched Aaron rehearsing with his choir, impressed by his talent and proud to be his woman? If only I could turn back the hands of time.

I made my way to our meeting place and slipped into a seat in the last pew. The engraved nameplate on the seat in front of me indicated that the pew had been donated by a Mr. and Mrs. Kimble. I didn't know who they were, but I imagined them to be an older couple, dedicating a pew in gratitude for a long and happy marriage. The image brought tears to my eyes. That type of long-lasting love was something I didn't know if I would ever have, but I really wanted the chance to try. I just needed to be able to breathe again, to be free of the darkness and pain.

I heard the door open behind me and then footsteps moving in my direction. I froze, my body went numb, and a heavy feeling hit me in the pit of my stomach. Despite the fact that I had called ahead to set up this meeting, I was still nervous. This was suddenly harder than I thought it would be, but then again, there was no precedent in how to have a conversation like this.

"I hope you weren't waiting too long." His voice was gentler than I expected.

I didn't want to turn around, but I knew that I had to. I stood up and looked into his face.

"No, I just got here." He didn't look like I'd expected him to. It wasn't just that he'd aged. There was also a calmness and serenity that I didn't remember—and I certainly didn't expect. It may have had something to do with the collar.

"I'm Reverend Clifford White Jr., the youth minister and second assistant pastor here at Mount Olive Church." He held out his hand to shake mine.

I stepped back, refusing to allow him to touch me. "I know who you are," I answered calmly, holding him in my gaze.

He looked uncomfortable for just a second, but covered it up quickly. "I'm very sorry for your ordeal," he said. "Would you like to sit down so we can talk?"

After I found his Facebook page and discovered where he worked, I'd called the church. I got him on the line and told him that I didn't have a church home, but I needed to talk to someone because I'd been sexually assaulted. At first he tried to pass me off to a female church employee, telling me that he was a youth pastor and not necessarily trained in this area. I just carried on, boohooing in his ear so he felt like he couldn't put the phone down. When I'd had him on there long enough, I told him I felt comfortable, and only wanted to meet with him.

We sat down in the pew. I left a good amount of

distance between him and me, and my hand rested on my purse so I could pull out Black Beauty if necessary.

There was an uncomfortable moment of silence between us. I guess he was waiting for me to speak up first. When he realized I wasn't going to, he said, "We have an amazing ministry that helps women who have gone through crisis." He went to place a hand on my arm and I jumped as if I had been burned. "Maybe I should ask one of the women of the congregation to talk to you."

"No. I don't want to talk to anyone but you."

"Okay, I understand. I get it. We have a rapport, and that's a good thing." He used a calming voice, meant to assure me that I didn't have anything to worry about—that he was a safe servant of God who would take care of me. Maybe that worked on his unsuspecting church members now, but I knew the real Clifford White. The only thing I could think about was how he had forced his way on top of me, grunting like a pig.

"So, would you like to talk about the tragic moment?" he said, still trying to fill the awkward silence created by my refusal to speak. As I listened to him pretend to be a kind person, I struggled to keep my anger from boiling over. "Have you visited a hospital, or contacted the police about this incident?"

When the rape occurred, I knew that the logical thing to do would have been to report it to the police, but I'd felt so ashamed and powerless. I hadn't even told my brother for almost a year. This asshole thought he was counseling a stranger to report a rape, when he was the one who had made me feel so worthless I couldn't do that.

I finally spoke up. "Actually, maybe I should have been clearer. I experienced my trauma years ago."

"I see..." he said, and then went silent. If he asked me why I waited so long, I might have pulled out my gun and shot him right then and there. If he was dead, though, I wouldn't have a chance to tell him how he'd destroyed me, and find out who his last accomplice was, which was the main objective of why I'd come there. I swallowed my rage and continued to talk.

"I never went to the police. I tried counseling, support groups, and prayer, and for a while I thought I was doing better."

"Praise be to God," he said. It sounded like blasphemy coming from his mouth.

"Like I said, I *thought* I was doing better, until I spotted one of my attackers recently. Now I feel like I'm back at square one."

"I'm sorry to hear that."

He had no idea how sorry he'd be in a minute.

"So I decided to tackle this thing head on, go

straight to the source. You know, challenge your fear directly."

He gave me one of those practiced looks of compassion, as if he actually wanted to help. At that very moment I felt the heat inside of me rising up and growing into a complete rage. I took a deep breath and attempted to choke it down with a fake calmness.

"That sounds very wise," he said. "I'd like to help in whatever way I can. Would you like me to pray with you?"

That was all I could take. The rage rushed to the surface and I exploded, jumping up from my seat. "No, you can't pray for me, motherfucker! You raped me, you sick bastard!"

He got out of his seat, too, and backed away from me. At first I think it was because he was frightened by my outburst, but then I saw recognition dawn on his face. All of a sudden he realized who I was and why I was there, and he was trying to put some distance between himself and his past.

"Oh my God! You're her?" His hand shot up to his mouth and I could see that he was trembling. Once he looked down and noticed that I was aiming Black Beauty at him, he had to grab the pew to keep from hitting the floor.

Not wanting a repeat of what happened with Vinnie Taylor, I kept a good amount of distance between us. "Yes, you monster, I'm one of the women you raped."

"I'm sorry. I am so sorry," he said as tears ran down his face.

"Are you?" I said as a strange calm washed over me. He was crying; I was the one in control now.

"Please believe me. I have agonized over my wicked past for a long time now," he cried out, as if his pain could even begin to come close to mine. His eyes had doubled in size, and the confident façade had deflated right before my eyes. "Tell me what I can do to make it up to you." His voice cracked under the weight of his guilt, but that only made me feel more powerful.

"You mean make up for destroying my life? For making it impossible for me to marry the man I love? To ensure that I would not be able to allow another person to touch me without flinching and reliving the violence you and your friends put me through? None of you bothered to treat me like a human being, but I'm supposed to absolve you of your guilt now? I don't think so. I won't take away your guilt, just like you can't take away the nightmares that wake me in a cold sweat every night."

"I know. You're right. It is unforgivable. Please, what can I do? I have not been able to get that image of what we did to you out of my mind. Not even after all these years. It has haunted me. You have haunted me," he whined like a little bitch. "That's why I went into the ministry to ask for forgiveness."

"How's that working for you?" I shouted, enjoying his emotional pain. I wanted him to hurt as deeply as I had been hurt. I wasn't about to give him the illusion that we would skip off into the sunset, awash in the glow of forgiveness.

"I've never been able to forgive myself. Ever since that day I have prayed for you. I even tried to find you to make sure that you were okay. When I couldn't, I decided to dedicate my life to helping others in your honor. I joined the Peace Corps and went to Africa to help women and children with AIDS." He almost had me for a minute with that Peace Corps stuff. I almost believed he was repentant, until he said, "I created a ministry to help young boys so that they grow up to respect women and don't make the same stupid mistakes that I did."

"Stupid mistake!" I yelled, waving my gun at him. "Is that what you're calling my rape? Just a stupid mistake?" I smiled as I realized that my outburst scared him so bad he pissed his pants. "Violent, yes. Brutal. Sadistic," I corrected him. "But I'd say 'stupid' is a real understatement."

He looked like he was about to start hyperventilating. "I've given back to the community in every way possible, but I still hate myself every day for what I did to you. I am so sorry."

"I don't care how you feel. You stole my life." I lifted Beauty and aimed at his face.

"I will do whatever it takes to make it up to you. I will go to the police and turn myself in right now," he pleaded with me. I guess a gun to the head will make a man promise to do anything, but I didn't care about telling the police. It was too late for that.

"Shut up and sit down," I commanded. He complied in a hurry.

"I will take full responsibility for my actions. I will do whatever it takes to win your forgiveness."

"Unless you can take back what you did to me, I will never forgive you," I said, still aiming the gun at him. "But you will tell me the names of your accomplices." My voice was so cold and ruthless that I barely recognized it myself. This guy must have had nerves of steel, though, because he refused to give up the others.

He shook his head. "I can't do that. You already have a gun to my head and you're threatening me. If I am going to die, then so be it, but I am not willing to put another man's life at risk."

"Oh, how fuckin' noble of you," I spat. "Your friends deserve everything they have coming to them."

"Please," he begged. "Don't make me tell you. I

don't want to be responsible for another man's suffering."

I laughed at him. "Now you're worried about harming another human being? Afraid it will be a black mark against your soul? Too late for that. You condemned yourself to hell the night you raped me."

He was full-on crying now, tears and snot running down his face.

I pressed on. "Who was the white guy who brought me there?"

"Mark has been through enough," he said, sobbing. "There is no way he can ever be a threat to you again. It's not going to be easy, but one day we're all going to have to put what happened on Washington Street behind us."

"Mark who, goddammit?" I was so close to pulling the trigger and blowing this piece of shit away.

"I can't tell you that."

"Can't or won't?" I asked angrily.

"Both."

"Then you just signed your own death warrant. Any last words, Reverend?"

"Yes, if I'm going to die, I need you to forgive me," he cried out as he dropped to his knees in front of me like the pathetic worm that he was. "Let's pray together. Let's pray to God and ask him to forgive us both." His hands were clasped together as if he truly wanted to pray with me. "Please, Miss, I need you to forgive me so that I can go to heaven."

"Sorry," I snapped, pushing Black Beauty against his temple. "That's never going to happen, because neither one of us is going to heaven."

Ross

22

I checked the clock on my dashboard when I pulled into my parking space at the church. It was already four thirty. Most of the day was gone, but I was happier than I'd been in years. I could barely contain my excitement as I got out of the car and headed for the church. Not only did the bishop and I have a great conversation with Aaron that morning, during which he was totally supportive in not wanting to deal with Jackson, but I'd just taken my pregnant wife, Selena, to the doctor for a sonogram, and we found out that she was having a boy. It felt great being able to put the whole Jackson thing behind me, but nothing made me feel better than the knowledge that I was going to have a son. I couldn't wait to tell Aaron and Pippie the good news. This was definitely a great day, I thought, as I entered the church ready to keep it going.

I spotted Pippie sitting on the edge of Desiree's desk, trying to graduate himself from the friend zone to a contender. Poor guy was too infatuated to realize that a woman that hot was out of his league. The most he could do would be to add her to his fantasy team of women.

"Hey." I nodded to him and waved at Desiree as I approached the desk. "Guess what? Selena and I—"

"Where you been?" Pippie questioned, cutting me off.

Before I could respond, Desiree snapped at me, a little too efficient for my taste.

"Mr. Parker, Bishop Wilson would like to see you in his office right away." She pushed a button on the intercom and said, "Bishop, Ross Parker is here. I'm sending him in." Now, I didn't really know this girl, but she was giving me no warmth. I sure wished Tia was still around, because she always had love for me.

"Send him in," the bishop replied, sounding intense.

I turned to Pippie. "You know what this is all about?"

"Yeah, I think you got set up. But hear them out before you go off, bro." He patted my back as I headed toward the door. I had no idea what he was referring to, but it sure didn't sound good. So much for my great day.

I opened the door to find not just the bishop, but Aaron as well. They were both wearing sour expressions, sitting side by side near the bishop's desk.

"Have a seat, Mr. Parker." The bishop pointed at a chair in front of them. I knew the shit was about to hit the fan when he called me Mr. Parker instead of Ross. My stomach started doing flips, and it wasn't from the spicy lunch I'd eaten earlier.

"What's this all about? Why are you staring at me like that?" I asked as I nervously took a seat.

The bishop said, "Mr. Parker, yesterday you and I had a talk about Mr. Mackie and the choir?"

"Yes, sir, we did," I answered, feeling uncomfortable because Aaron, my best friend, hadn't even glanced in my direction or acknowledged my presence.

Bishop leaned forward in his chair. "You had me approach Aaron about Jackson Young because you claimed Jackson was out to steal Aaron from the church."

"Yeah..." I responded, not liking the bishop's accusatory tone. I didn't know what was going on, but it didn't take a rocket scientist to figure out that Jackson Young had some role in it.

"Look, I've known you for two years. You've never given me reason to doubt you, which is why I'm confused about why you would put me in this position."

"I don't understand," I replied. "What exactly did I do?"

Aaron lost his cool. He jumped up and started

shouting, "You screwed me, Ross! You screwed me and the choir. I thought we were boys. I considered you my best friend, and now you've done this to me."

"Did what?" I asked. "Try to protect you from a guy who really can't be trusted? He doesn't have your best interests at heart. He's not a good guy."

"Oh, and you are?" Aaron said. I was so stunned, I couldn't even speak for a few seconds. Aaron and I had been tight for as long as I could remember. He had never come at me like this.

"Bishop, what is this?" I asked. "Why are we even discussing Jackson Young? I thought we got all this straight this morning."

Aaron continued his rant. "Don't pretend that you don't know what I'm talking about!"

"I *don't* know. I came to you and told you exactly what went down with Jackson. That's what I'm supposed to do as your manager—have your back."

"Man, you're so full of it," Aaron said as he started pacing across the bishop's office. "If Jackson hadn't come to us himself and presented the deal, we would have believed your lies."

"What are you talking about? I told you the deal he was offering. Why would you go behind my back and talk to him when you said you wouldn't?"

"You mean why didn't I let you continue to lie to us? That's what you're really asking me, isn't it?

You wanted to keep me, the choir, and the church small—so that you had complete control."

"That couldn't be further from the truth. Look, I don't know what he told you, but you can't trust that guy."

"See, here's the problem with that," Aaron said. "You *told* me about the deal, but Jackson gave me proof of the truth in writing."

"You met with him?" I asked, feeling completely betrayed and confused. I looked to the bishop for an explanation.

"He came here this morning and told a very different story than yours, Ross."

Aaron grabbed some papers off the bishop's desk and flung them at me. "Choke on this," he said.

Again I looked at the bishop. He explained, "Jackson told us that his deal was for Aaron *and* the choir, not just Aaron alone. And then he backed it up by having a messenger deliver the contract to us."

I picked up the papers Aaron had thrown at me and read a few lines. What the fuck was going on? It was a contract with Sony music, and it was nothing like the deal Jackson had told me about. "What the hell is this?" I asked.

Bishop Wilson looked so disappointed. "I would like to know that myself. Of course I wanted to give you the benefit of the doubt when Jackson spoke to us, but it's all there in black and white. Jackson's offer is nothing like what you claimed he was looking for."

"That contract would have set me up for life, man. It would have set up the church—and even you." Aaron looked like he wanted to cause me serious bodily harm.

I felt my blood start to boil. "I'm being set up, Aaron. This is not what he told me. You have to believe me."

All I saw looking back at me was pure disbelief.

"You're a liar and you've been caught. Man up and just admit you lied," Aaron snapped.

"Yes, Ross, please do what's right," the bishop added.

"But I'm not lying! I swear. Aaron, we've been through too much, especially with what you've just gone through with Tia. Why would I—"

"Don't you dare bring Tia into this."

"But that's what this is about. After the way she dumped you at the altar, you're having a hard time trusting anyone, and Jackson is taking advantage of that. He wants me out of the picture so he can control your career without your best friend looking out for you."

"With friends like you, who the hell needs enemies?" he shouted.

He was still on his feet. I felt the need for us to be

eye to eye, so he could see I was telling the truth. I stood up.

"I am not your enemy! When Tia walked out on you for no reason, wasn't I by your side?" It hurt me to the core that he was accusing me of disloyalty.

"Tia did not walk out on me for no reason. She—" He stopped himself mid-sentence and a look passed between him and the bishop. He knew something he wasn't telling me, although he clearly had shared it with the bishop. I was feeling more shut out by the minute, and it was pissing me off.

"Yes, she did," I shot back. "And she made a fool out of you in the process. Just like Jackson is going to do. Don't you get it?"

"You son of a bitch!" he growled at me. "Don't you ever talk about Tia like that again!"

"Look, Aaron, Tia messed up, but—"

Aaron swung at me. His fist connected with my right eye, knocking me to the floor.

"No, Aaron!" Bishop called out, but it was too late.

"You're fired!" Aaron yelled. "I don't want you near me or my choir." He stormed out of the office.

Bishop Wilson came around his desk and helped me to my feet.

"Jackson? Bishop, you of all people should know you can't trust him." I pleaded with him to understand.

"Me of all people? What is that supposed to mean?"

My eye was throbbing from Aaron's punch, but the bishop was having trouble seeing things for what they were. After the way Jackson had disrespected him at that first meeting, I wouldn't expect the bishop to believe a word the guy had to say. Yet here he was, buying Jackson's bullshit, apparently blinded by the promise of big money and fame. I had to make him understand the truth.

"He took your wife out to an expensive meal, champagne and all. It was obvious to me that he was trying to get with her."

"What?" He stepped back, his brow furrowed in confusion.

"Yeah, I saw them together," I said, grateful for the chance to reveal what I should have told him the day Monique interrupted us. I needed him to understand that Jackson was nothing but poison—not just to me, but to all of us.

"You saw my wife out with Jackson Young and you didn't respect me enough to tell me man to man? Aaron's right, what kind of damn friend are you?" Bishop reared back and punched me in the other eye, laying me out.

Bishop

23

I walked out of my office into the common area of the church flexing the fingers on my sore right hand. I hadn't broken anything punching Ross, but I was already feeling the repercussions of my actions. Poor Desiree was sitting at her desk looking at me like I'd lost my mind. I'm sure with all the fussing and fighting in my office, she must have heard everything that was said. I was sorry for that, but unfortunately, I didn't have time to explain myself or worry about what she thought. My main objective was to find my wife and get to the bottom of Ross's allegations.

"Where'd Aaron go?" I asked Desiree.

"He went toward the front door. I think he left."

"That's probably for the best." I'd talk to Aaron about all this later.

"Bishop, are you okay?" Desiree was staring at my hand. In that short period of time, it had already begun swelling. What the hell had I been thinking about, hitting that boy? Desiree had an expression on her face that made me wonder if she'd run screaming back to the South, telling everyone about the crazy bishop who punches his employees. I'd always prided myself on my ability to stay calm under pressure and somehow stay above the church drama, but at this moment Bishop Wilson was off duty and I was an angry husband.

"I'm fine," I said. "But I need to find my wife. Have you seen her?"

"Uh, she hasn't been in the office today," Desiree said, quickly looking down at the stack of mail on her desk as if she were eager to get back to work—a little too eager, as far as I was concerned. Was she in cahoots with my wife, keeping her secrets?

I retrieved my phone from my pocket and dialed my wife's number. It went straight to voice mail, which made me even more concerned. That meant she had turned her phone off completely or was in a dead zone, which was pretty unlikely in a borough as populated as Queens.

"Use your phone to dial my wife," I ordered Desiree, my tone clipped with impatience and frustration.

She didn't hesitate to comply. She picked up the phone and called Monique, staring up at me with a panicked expression on her face as she handed over the phone. Again it went straight to voice mail. When I gave the phone back to Desiree, her eyes told me there was something else she wasn't telling me. My years as the head of a congregation had taught me to read subtle signals.

"What is it, Desiree?" I asked.

"Nothing, sir. Just..." She stopped herself.

"Just what?" I barked. Her silence was making me even more suspicious that she might be involved in some sort of cover-up for my wife, and I was beginning to direct my anger toward her.

"Bishop, I don't want to get into the middle of this. This is between you and your wife."

"No, this is between me and whoever is standing in the way of me getting to my wife. In case you forgot, I'm the one who gave you this job and a place to live. You owe me some loyalty, Desiree," I reminded her, knowing full well how far outside of my bishop's role I was stepping. I was setting a very poor example for a man of the cloth, but I couldn't help myself. Ross's statements about my wife were making me crazy.

"I understand that, but I don't feel comfortable sticking my nose in your personal business," she protested.

"I'm going to give you a piece of advice: Don't ever get in between a man and his wife." I guess my tone was serious enough to change her mind about not talking.

"I'm so sorry," she said. "That's not what I

thought I was doing. I did see your wife earlier. She was talking to a man in the parking lot, but then she never came inside. That's all I know."

"Was it Jackson Young?" I asked and then started praying to God it was just one of the other deacons or a member of our church community.

"I've heard the name, but I'm not sure who Jackson Young is."

"But you saw him?"

She nodded.

"About forty, brown skin, a little over six feet, clean cut, with pretty-boy looks. Probably wearing an expensive tailored suit?"

"Yes, that was him," she confirmed.

"Son of a bitch!" The words flew out of my mouth.

"Bishop!" she gasped.

"Now, usually I hold my tongue, but—"

"No, it's not that." Desiree flew from her desk and hurried past me.

I turned to see a battered Ross stumbling out of my office looking like he'd just lost a prizefight. I felt bad about letting my anger get the best of me, but there was nothing I could do to take it back now, so I stayed focused on my main objective—finding my wife.

"Thank you," Ross mumbled as Desiree reached him, placing his arm around her shoulder to help him maintain balance. I had to admit he looked a lot worse than I'd expected. I guess I didn't know my own strength, especially since I wasn't in the habit of behaving like a caveman and resorting to physical violence. I certainly hoped that I wouldn't have to harm another man before the day was done.

I hurried out of the church and got into my car, my mind racing all over the place with X-rated images of Monique and Jackson playing on a loop in my head. Within seconds I had clicked on the button that would help me answer all of my questions and hopefully restore my peace of mind.

"OnStar, may I help you?" a friendly professional voice spoke through my car's sound system. I was so busy having an internal argument with Monique in my head that I didn't answer him the first time. He repeated himself. "OnStar, may I help you?"

"Oh, yes, this is Bishop TK Wilson. I need to locate my other car. My wife can't remember where she parked it."

"No problem, sir. Can you give me the account number and password for the vehicle?" he requested.

"Sure. Just a moment." I reached into my wallet and pulled out the card that held all the important numbers I needed. I gave the man the information *he* needed, and he put me on hold while he checked the account. Yeah, it was great being alive in the post-technology age—at least for me. If my wife was doing something she wasn't supposed to, then this was not a good day for her.

As I waited for the OnStar representative to come back on the line, I tried to come up with another explanation for my wife's disappearance. Monique did a fair amount of outreach with women of the church, including wives, widows, and the elderly. Maybe she was just off somewhere, helping a parishioner through a crisis. That would be the best possible outcome: I would find her visiting someone at a hospital, and then I could laugh at myself for letting my jealousy get out of hand over nothing.

The representative came back on the line. "Mr. Wilson, your vehicle has been located in Forest Hills, Queens." He gave me the address. There was no hospital or nursing home anywhere close to that location. "Can I help you with anything else?"

"No, you've been very helpful," I said as I disconnected the call and then swung my car out of the parking lot, headed to Forest Hills and God knows what else.

Monique
24

"No! No! No!" Jackson was obviously frustrated with me. "How many times do I have to tell you? You have to put more passion into it. If I can't feel your commitment to the piece, how the hell do you expect the audience to?"

"I'm trying, Jackson. I'm really trying." The last thing I wanted was to mess up my big chance; however, it looked like my words were falling on deaf ears.

"Well, you're not trying hard enough." He picked up his suit jacket from the chair beside the couch where we were sitting. "Time is money, and you're starting to waste my time."

"One more time, please, Jackson. I'll do better. I promise." I grabbed his arm, my eyes pleading with him for another chance.

"You don't understand. You're getting ready to audition in front of one of the biggest and most important casting directors in the industry. I pulled a lot of strings to get you this audition. I won't risk my reputation by sending you in there like this, all uptight and stiff. You'll never get another shot, and my reputation is too—"

My phone rang in the middle of his tirade. Jackson shook his head and tossed his hands into the air. "Unbelievable," he said.

"It's TK," I said. This was the tenth time he'd called. "He never blows me up like this."

His body language screamed, *I don't give a damn*!

"You here to work or to talk to your husband on the phone?" he barked. "This is taking up my valuable time, so if you're not really interested in this opportunity, then I need to know now."

Taking a deep breath that didn't help relieve my anxiety, I shut off the phone and placed it in my purse. I knew it would cause problems with TK later, but this opportunity was too important. I'd have to call my husband as soon as I was done, but right now I couldn't risk Jackson thinking that I wasn't taking this seriously.

"I'm ready," I told him.

Jackson sat back down on the couch facing me. "Listen to me. This is very important. You just have to engross yourself in the character. You're not Monique Wilson right now; you're Lana Washington, a middle-aged sex kitten who knows what she wants and isn't willing to take no for an answer. She's the hunter, not the prey. You got it."

You can do this, Monique. You can be a star, my internal voice coached.

"Oh, I can be the hunter when I want to," I said in my best sex-kitten voice.

"The question is: Can you be one for the camera?" he asked. "Can you make the audience believe it?"

I nodded, and he said, "Action!"

I cleared my thoughts and got into character, staring at Jackson hungrily.

"Why are you running away from me?" I began.

"Because you're a married woman and your husband's my best friend."

"My husband's asleep, but you have awakened something in me I've never felt before. Can't you feel it?" I picked up Jackson's hand and placed it over my heart.

"Yes, but we can't act on it," he said, looking not into my eyes, but down at the place where his hand rested. I wondered if he could feel my heart pounding as I prepared for the part of the scene that was hardest for me.

"Why not?" I leaned in close, committed to giving it my all. Pulling him to me, I pressed my lips against his. Jackson got into the part, too, wrapping his arms tightly around my waist and resting his hands on the small of my back. I knew I'd finally convinced him that I was good enough to go to the audition.

I was feeling so good about my performance that I abandoned any inhibition and slipped my tongue into his mouth, pushing him backward on the sofa. Suddenly I was really getting into the part, becoming my character—and I have to admit that he made things much easier because he was one hell of a kisser. By this point, we were so engrossed in the scene that neither of us heard the door to his office open.

"Monique!" The booming voice startled me. I jumped back to find my husband standing in the doorway with a look of distress on his face. That was quickly replaced by a dark cloud of rage.

"You son of a bitch! I'll kill you!" TK stormed over to Jackson, a harried assistant on his heels. Next thing I knew, my husband's hands were clenched around Jackson's neck like a vise grip, shaking him as he gasped for breath. Jackson was struggling to break free. My husband had become a madman.

The assistant was trying to pull TK off, and I jumped in to help. TK had him in such a death grip that I knew if we didn't stop him soon, he would kill Jackson. "Please, TK! Please stop!"

"I don't know who the hell you think you are, but that's not some cheap whore you're trying to bed. That's my fucking wife!" I'd never seen or heard TK act like this. It scared the hell out of me—but it also turned me on.

Finally, we managed to pry TK's hands from around Jackson's neck. Jackson took a few deep breaths as he staggered away, but he didn't get far enough. TK lunged at him again. This time, without thinking, I reared back and slapped him as hard as I could.

"Stop it!" I yelled. TK froze, glaring at me, and a wave of fear rushed through me. I wrapped my arms around his, hoping to restrain another attack.

Jackson managed to recover enough to scurry away to the other side of the sofa. "That bastard is crazy!" he said, rubbing his neck.

"You haven't seen crazy yet," TK spit. I held on to my husband as he seethed, his body heaving as he tried to regain his breath.

"I'm sorry, Mr. Young. He just forced his way in," his assistant apologized. She was standing between Jackson and TK like a sentry. "Would you like me to call the police?"

Jackson smoothly shook off the attack, straightening his tie and regaining his composure as if nothing had happened. "I don't know. Maybe we should let the first lady decide."

"No, we'll leave," I said.

"Stay the hell away from my wife. This isn't over!" TK raged. He broke away from me, trying to take a step toward Jackson. The assistant's question stopped him momentarily.

"Should I call the cops, Mr. Young?" the assistant asked again, but Jackson stood there smirking, completely calm now. Watching his amused expression, I understood that this was a man who thoroughly enjoyed the circus.

"No worries, Lynn. Bishop Wilson won't be a problem anymore." Jackson waved her away. "Not unless he wants his mug shot on the front page of the *Post*."

"No, he doesn't," I answered for my husband.

"Good." Jackson turned to his assistant. "Can you give us a moment?"

She shot him a look of protest.

"Don't worry. I got this," he said.

She shrugged then got the hell out of there, closing the door behind her. She was smart to avoid the drama fest. Believe me, I wished I could have gone with her.

"TK, it's not what it looks like," I started, wanting desperately for him to believe me. Catching me making out with anyone was bad, of course, but I knew the fact that it was Jackson made it so much worse in TK's eyes. TK had felt disrespected by Jackson at their first meeting, and nothing I had said since then could change his mind about the man. That's why I had chosen not to tell TK about my meeting with Jackson as I prepared for my first audition. I'd always believed that it was better to ask for forgiveness than permission, but I was rethinking that philosophy now that my husband had tried to kill a man.

"It's not what it looks like? Really? Because to me it looks like I should kill this motherfucker." He clenched his fist, shaking it at Jackson.

"TK, your hand!" I shouted. It was grossly swollen. He didn't bother to even acknowledge me. I cringed when I noticed the veins in his neck were bulging. I'd only witnessed it once before in our relationship, and I swore I never wanted to see it again. His anger was about to blow out of control.

"No, you have to believe me," I said, feeling close to panic. I reached out and touched his arm, hoping the physical contact might bring him down from the edge. "It's not what it looks like."

He shoved my hand away. "What it looks like is that my wife is lying to me."

"I'm not lying!"

It was obvious nothing I said was making a difference. Jackson tried to come to my defense. "You have a very honorable wife."

"Don't you dare try and talk to me about my wife! I know exactly why you brought her up here, and it wasn't to talk about her imaginary acting career."

"Honey, it's not imaginary. We were practicing

for an audition. Reading our lines." I grabbed the pages off the table and tried to show him. "Look, this is the scene."

He pushed the pages away. "Auditioning for what? Some porno? Because his tongue down your throat was not PG-rated!"

As much as I wanted to, I couldn't protest—first because I had been the one to initiate that tongue-kiss, and second because Jackson really had gotten into it. I guess he was doing what they call "method acting." Either way, I knew it looked bad to my husband.

I tried a different approach: Steer the topic away from the kiss. "Jackson got me an audition. It's a really big movie. It's starring Angela Bassett."

TK's look told me he didn't give a shit.

"You have to believe me," I begged. "Have some faith in me and in our marriage. I'm not about to risk everything."

"You already have!"

"Honey, please just listen to—"

"Get in your car. We'll talk about it at home," he said.

I couldn't believe that he was treating me like a child in front of the man I was trying to build a working relationship with.

"Why are you not supporting her?" Jackson took a protective step closer to me, and for a second I felt a sense of satisfaction. *How dare TK order me around like that?*

Then I caught a look of sheer rage on TK's face, and I took a step away from Jackson. If he had actually put a hand on me at that moment, anything could have happened, and none of it would have been good. I tried one more time to calm him down.

"Honey, we were just practicing a scene so I can go to this audition. I have to be able to play a romantic lead in the movie."

He remained unmoved. "You are not an actress, and you need to get that through your head. You are my wife, and you have a full-time position, which you neglected today to come here and do God knows what behind my back with this guy."

He sneered at Jackson, who didn't look like he was bothered at all by the drama in front of him. Working in show business, he was probably used to clients acting a fool all the time.

"Jackson, will you please tell him that's all we were doing?"

"Man, she's got real potential. Women like your wife don't come along every day. Believe me when I say that Aaron's not the only star at First Jamaica Ministries." I was pleased by his praise, but he hadn't directly said that the kiss meant nothing. TK was unmoved.

"This whole thing is over," he said to Jackson. "You need to get yourself another actress. My wife is no longer available for this mess."

"Don't you think your wife can make her own decisions?"

"I don't need you filling my wife's head with this nonsense," TK shot back. They were like two vicious pit bulls fighting over a bone.

"Oh, so since you don't approve, it has to be nonsense? You don't have to be threatened by her dreams." Jackson looked at me as if he pitied me.

TK looked at me as if he wanted to punish me. "I am not having this conversation in front of this goddamn liar. Now, get in your car and we will discuss this at home."

"Hey, man," Jackson said, actually sounding amused by his power struggle with TK. "I'm just here to support her dreams. That's my job. I'm a dream maker. But if you really want to hold her back..."

I felt my dream slipping away from me. My husband was going to ruin my career before it even got started.

"You stay the hell away from my wife, or I *will* be on the front page of the *Post*—and you'll be six feet under." His words were not hollow. He meant them. He grabbed ahold of me and shoved me toward the door. "Monique, you are finished here."

Tia

25

After my incident with Clifford White, I decided it was for the best that I let go of everybody connected with First Jamaica Ministries, including Monique. Being around her made me think of the church, and more specifically of Aaron, and that's not what I needed right now. So, I packed up all my stuff and moved out of Monique's house.

With all of my things crammed into my trunk, I got onto the expressway and headed east to a university on Long Island. I'd never been to the campus before, so I had to ask a student for directions to the library, where I hoped to find the information necessary to continue my mission. The library was packed with students—some studying, some simply hanging out, and others sleeping at their workstations—and the atmosphere brought me back to my own college days, before my life went horribly wrong. Anger rose inside of me as I faced the image of yet one more part of my youth that my rapists had poisoned.

My life, and all of my memories, would be forever distorted through the lens of "before the rape" or "after the rape."

Glancing around, I noticed a black woman pushing a cart full of books to be put back on the shelves. She looked young enough to be a student, probably working in the library to help pay tuition. I approached her.

"Excuse me?"

"Yes?" She smiled at me, extra bubbly. Her nametag told me that her name was Niecy.

"Does your library have a collection of past yearbooks? I'm looking for a former student."

Her face didn't register any suspicion, but I still felt the need to explain why I would be seeking a former student.

"Well, actually," I said, putting on my best impression of embarrassment, "I'm looking for this guy I had a one-night stand with in college. He was really, really hot."

"Hot? Damn, girl. Why didn't you tell me?" Niecy gushed, losing the bookish persona and letting her sista-girl surface. "I am so sick of looking for textbooks on the theory of this and research articles on the theory of that and blah, blah, blah. A hot guy with a good dick sounds like the kinda research I can get behind."

"Did I say he had a good dick?" I felt like vomiting. If this girl only knew that he had the kind of dick that deserved to be chopped off.

"Honey, if you came all the way to this library to find him, trust he had a good dick," she said with a laugh.

"Yeah, you got me," I said weakly.

"These days I have to get mine vicariously. I'm heading into finals, so there's no time to play, if you know what I mean."

I nodded silently, hoping this girl would get the hint and drop the subject when I didn't play along with her sexual banter.

"Follow me," she said as she headed toward a row of computers in the back.

As we passed by a row of windows overlooking a parking lot, I noticed a burgundy-colored sedan parked near the curb. It hadn't been there when I arrived.

"Shit!" The word escaped my lips before I could stop it.

Niecy whirled around and stopped in her tracks. "Is everything okay?"

My eyes were still on the suspect ride outside. "You ever get the feeling that you're being followed?"

"Yeah, every day. These forty-four triple Ds are like a homing device," she said, looking down at her oversize breasts. "Somebody is always trying to follow me home." Something about how comfortable she was with herself put me at ease. In another time, I was certain that we would have been friends.

"Maybe I'm just imagining it," I said, trying to shake off my worry. "I could swear I've seen that same car for the last couple of days. Everywhere I go, it shows up."

She turned around and kept walking, chattering the whole time. "Isn't it like when you get a new car and suddenly all you see is that car? I got a Prius, and now I can't go anywhere without seeing a million. And don't let me in a parking lot. I'll spend hours looking for my car. All I was trying to do was save gas, and now I can barely find my car."

"Yeah, you're probably right. Thanks," I agreed, feeling relieved.

We arrived at a table with a row of desktop computers. "These computers house the college archives," she said. "A lot of the old yearbooks have been scanned. If you tell me what year you're looking for, I can see if it's in the system."

I took a seat in front of one of the computers and leaned to the side so she could type her password in to access the archives. "I'm thinking he was probably a senior sometime between 2006 and 2009," I said.

She entered the dates, and a few files popped up on the screen. "Here you go. I'll check back on you in a while to see if you need anything else. Happy searching," she said, then went back to her cart full of books.

My search would certainly not be happy, but I sure hoped it would be fruitful. From their Facebook profiles, I had learned that Vinnie and Clifford both attended this college. The dates were a guess, based on the fact that I was twenty-one at the time of my rape, and Michael and his roommates looked like they were around that age too. Since they were all roommates, I was making the assumption that they had met at college. It was a shot in the dark, but I was determined to do whatever it took to track down the men who had ruined my life, and this was the best lead I had right now.

I opened the first file and started scrolling through pages until I came to the head shots of that year's senior class. That's when I realized what a big job I had in front of me. There were pages and pages of faces to look at, and after a while, my eyes were so tired that everyone started looking the same. I pushed on, determined to find the person I'd come looking for. I would not rest until each one of them had paid for their crime against me.

Deep into the second book, I stopped scrolling for a moment when I found Vinnie Taylor's photo. He was all smiles in his cap and gown. The photo looked, for lack of a better word, typical. In it, he seemed like every other proud college grad on those pages. Except I knew what evil lurked behind his eyes.

But it wasn't Vinnie I was looking for. Now I was certain I'd found the right year, and I would look at every single photo, hopefully to find the last monster I was seeking. I scrolled more slowly, scrutinizing the features of every male student's face. My heart was pounding with anxiety. I didn't want to see this man's face ever again, but I also longed desperately to find him so I could get closure.

Somewhere near the end of the set of senior portraits, I was beginning to think Vinnie was the only one of my rapists who had graduated in that year. Then I came across Clifford White's picture. The sight of him made me sick, but I did get some small satisfaction from a memory of the fear I witnessed as he was crying and begging for my forgiveness the other day. It was a far cry from the prideful smile he displayed for the camera in his senior portrait.

"May you rot in hell, you bastard," I whispered.

"Did you find what you were looking for?"

I nearly jumped out of my skin when Niecy approached me from behind. Scrolling down the page to get Clifford's face off the screen, I turned around and tried to keep a neutral expression on my face.

"Uh, no, not yet. I found a few of his friends

that I recognized from the club, but not the guy I'm looking for."

She glanced down at the screen and suggested, "Maybe he wasn't a senior like his friends. Why don't you try a year later?" Then she turned around and wheeled her cart down another aisle to put more books back on the shelves.

Taking her advice, I moved on to the next year's set of seniors with a renewed sense of determination. It turned out Niecy's suggestion was the right one. It didn't take me long to find his picture among the crop of smiling seniors from that year. Looking beneath the photo, I saw a different name than the one he'd given me at the club, but I was positive it was him, the man who had introduced himself as Michael.

"Got you, Mark King, you pig," I whispered to the photo staring back at me.

I closed the file and got up from the computer. My smile had brightened considerably as I sailed past Niecy.

"Girl, you look like you found what you were looking for," she said with a conspiratorial wink. "I bet he's going to be happy to hear from you."

"We'll see about that." I waved good-bye and continued on my way to wreck someone's day.

Bishop
26

As a man of God, I know that life can be full of hardships, but I certainly had never expected the one I was dealing with now. As I stormed out of Jackson's office, desperate to put some distance between him and me, I could not shake the image of my wife with her tongue down his throat. Everything I thought I knew about Monique and our marriage had just been blown to bits.

"TK, slow down," she shouted at me from behind, her ridiculously high heels clicking against the pavement as she tried in vain to catch up to me. But I kept stepping. The last thing I wanted to hear were more excuses and lies.

By the time she caught up to me, I was in my car with the key in the ignition. She tapped on the window.

"TK! TK, talk to me," she pleaded through the glass.

I rolled the window down just enough to shout, "Get in your damn car! We'll talk at home," then rolled it up again. I wasn't sure how a conversation would happen anyway, since I could barely stand the sight of her face.

I stayed in place long enough to make sure she'd gotten into her car before I raced away from the curb, nearly sideswiping another car. The driver blasted his horn at me, and rather than apologizing, I put up my middle finger, surprising even myself. Thank God I wasn't wearing my collar. The behavior was so unlike me, but my wife had taken me to a dark place I'd never been.

"Lord, how could she do this?" I screamed in anger, but really I was fighting back the urge to cry. I'd never felt so low in my entire life. There was a time when I would have turned to James Black, my good friend and confidant, for advice, but he'd died a few years back. He was the one person, other than my wives, who I'd trusted with my secrets, my sadness, my truths. Now with him gone and Monique's betrayal, I felt utterly alone.

I pulled into my driveway and rested my head on the steering wheel, trying to regain some composure before going inside to deal with my wife. There are certain things that no person should have to put up with, and a lying, cheating spouse is one of them. I doubted I would ever be able to get past this, so there was really only one course of action.

By the time Monique made it to the front door,

I was in our bedroom. I'd pulled out her suitcases from the closet and flung them onto the bed.

"What are you doing?" Monique shouted when she entered the bedroom. "You can't leave, TK."

"I'm not. You are!" My booming voice shook the floorboards. I ignored the shocked expression on her face, refusing to be affected. "You need to pack your shit and leave!"

"I'm not leaving, and neither are you. We need to talk, and I'm not going anywhere until we resolve this." She sat down on the edge of the bed and crossed her legs all ladylike. Ha! I'd just seen her in action, and she might be a lot of things, but a lady wasn't one of them.

"I don't see the point in talking. I've already made up my mind."

"Well, unmake it," she said. "Our marriage is the most important thing in my life. I'm not going to let you throw it away because of a misunderstanding. Now, I'm sorry about how things turned out, but you need to get over it." She folded her arms defiantly.

"Get over it? You want me to get over catching my wife straddling some man with her tongue down his throat?" I grabbed one of the suitcases and threw it against the wall.

"Jesus, TK, you're scaring me!"

Hell, let her be scared, I thought. Maybe it would

light a fire under her ass and help her get to stepping.

"I want you out of here!" I screamed.

"I love you!" she proclaimed, trying to look
wounded, like she was the one who caught me
cheating and not the other way around.

"Don't even try using those words to manipulate
me. You don't love me. You don't have the slightest
idea what those words mean."

"Of course I do!" she shouted, but I didn't
care—or at least I didn't want to. I felt sick to my
stomach because part of me still wanted to believe
her. Part of me wanted to rewind to the beginning
of the day and have it go differently.

I flung open the door to one of her closets and
started tossing piles of clothes into the suitcases.
This woman broke our wedding vows and made an
absolute fool of me. This could not be what God intended for me. I didn't care how much I loved her,
she had to go.

Monique jumped in front of me, snatching the
clothes out of my hands and trying to stop me from
taking more out. As soon as she touched me, an
electric current shot up my arms. I snatched away
from her as if I'd been burned. That's when the tears
came down my face.

"TK, I'm sorry. I told you that we were practicing
a scene for my audition," she said, still holding on

to that lame excuse. This was not the woman I had married. Not at all.

"I can't do this anymore. I'm done." I tried to free my arms and walk around her, but she refused to budge.

"No, dammit! I'm not losing my marriage over some stupid audition!" She was frantic. "If you'd just listen to me, you'd see that you're overreacting. It was just a scene for a freaking movie audition. I wasn't cheating on you, so we're not done."

"Yeah, we're done. Finished. You got a house; go live in it."

My phone started to ring, a welcome distraction.

"Don't answer that. We're talking." She said it like she thought her wishes would still have some influence over me.

Calmly, I answered my phone, not really giving a crap about our so-called conversation. "Bishop Wilson."

"Hello, Bishop. This is Deacon Samuels from Mount Olive Church in Brooklyn." Mount Olive was our sister church. "I have some sad news to tell you. Reverend Cliff White was found murdered in the church this morning."

"Clifford was murdered?" I reached for the bureau to steady myself as I digested the devastating news. Pastor Clifford White was one of my closest friends among the local clergy.

"No, not Pastor White. His son, Clifford Junior."

"Little Cliff?"

"Yes."

"Dear God." I sighed heavily, thinking about how devastating it would be if my son, Dante, was found dead. There is a natural order to things, and when it comes to death, the parents should always die first. "Let the pastor know I'm on my way."

"I'll do that, Bishop. I'm sure he can use your support."

I hung up and looked at Monique, unable to muster half of the anger I'd felt before. Despite everything that had happened today, it didn't remotely compare to what the White family was going through.

"What?" Monique said, sensing the bad news.

"Clifford White's son was found dead in the church. I have to go to Brooklyn."

"Oh, no." Her hand flew to her mouth and her eyes filled with tears. "Let me change my clothes. I'm coming with you."

"Oh, so all of sudden you're the first lady again?" I snapped.

"TK, what you fail to realize is that I never stopped being the first lady. Now, Cliff was a good boy, and his mother and father must be devastated. It's our job to minister to them. So for now, let's just go play our roles and be done with this discussion."

Desiree

27

"Mmmm. This is so good," I said to Pippie before taking another bite of a Jamaican beef patty. The spicy beef in a crisp pastry shell made my mouth sing. "I've never had anything like this before."

"Glad you like it," Pippie replied after he finished a mouthful of coco bread.

We had been on our way home from the church when Pippie asked if I would mind making a pit stop for something to eat. Now we were sitting on a bench outside a Jamaican restaurant on Guy Brewer Boulevard.

"Sorry to hear about your car," he said.

"It's okay. Hopefully I'll get it out of the shop in the next couple of days. I just appreciate the ride."

In truth, there was nothing wrong with my car. I'd told everyone at work that it was in the shop, because I was hoping Aaron would offer me a ride home after choir practice. That was before I found out that choir practice was canceled. Apparently, with World War III raging between Bishop Wilson,

Ross, and him, Aaron was in no mood to direct the singers. So I was stranded until Pippie, being the gentleman that he was, offered me a ride home.

"So what did you think about all that drama at work today?" I knew the basic details, but I was hoping he'd have some more to share. "I mean, you can't make this stuff up. I was there and I still can't believe it."

"What can I say? Things are getting a little out of hand." That vague answer was not nearly enough to satisfy me, so I tried again to get him talking.

"A little out of hand! That's an understatement, don't you think? The bishop knocked the hell out of Ross and gave him a black eye."

"What? No!" He shook his head. "Bishop didn't hit Ross. Aaron did that."

"No, Bishop Wilson hit Ross. You shoulda seen his hand. It was swelled up like a grapefruit."

Pippie looked confused. "But when Aaron and I went outside, he told me that he punched Ross in the eye."

"Well, maybe they did a tag team or something, because I'm positive the bishop hit him too."

"I can't believe it. I mean, I'm not surprised about Aaron hitting him, 'cause that boy has a temper, but the bishop? Day-um!"

"So, Aaron has a temper, huh?" I asked.

"Yeah," he answered without elaborating. Pippie

might have been a good source of information—if only I could get him to open up. Finally I asked the right question that got him talking.

"How'd you meet him, anyway?"

"We met back in the day. Elementary school. We really didn't like each other. He was one of those pretty boys who was always the teacher's pet. Not like he didn't do no dirt, but he was slick. Never got caught. He wasn't obvious about his stuff like me. Man I hated him," he said with a laugh.

"Really? I couldn't even imagine you two not getting along. Actually, I couldn't imagine you not getting along with anyone," I said. In the short time I'd known him, Pippie had definitely made an impression on me as a real "people person," always with a kind word or an offer to help out.

"I was a different person back then," he said. "My life at home was terrible. My dad skipped out and just went MIA. Moms was bitter, overworked, with five kids she couldn't afford. She had a revolving door of dudes coming through. Home just sucked, and I kind of took it out on other kids at school. It's hard to admit, but I was a straight-up bully. Hated kids from happy homes."

"Yeah, I know what you mean." It slipped out before I could take it back.

Pippie looked over at me, surprised. "Really?"

"Yeah, but we'll talk about me later," I said, definitely not ready to go there with him. "I want to know about you."

He hesitated for a second, like he wasn't going to let me off the hook that easy. I raised my eyebrows and kept my lips tightly pursed to let him know I wasn't saying another word. He took the hint and continued his own story.

"Eventually, the school gave up, Mom gave up, and I started running with the wrong crowd. Break-ins, armed robbery, drugs... Hell, you name it; I did it. I messed up every opportunity I had to choose a different path. Did my share of time for it too."

"Wow, I just can't even envision you in jail. You're such a sweet guy. I can't imagine you being a hard-ass."

"Well, imagine it, because I was as hard as they come. I got the prison tattoos to prove it." He pulled up his sleeve to show me. "I was just one more messed-up kid, angry at the world. My last prison stint I had twenty years over my head, and it taught me that I wasn't nearly as tough as I thought."

I couldn't help but ask, "They didn't rape you, did they?"

"No, I had too many friends for that. But they did break me."

I stared at him. He didn't look like a broken man. "Really? How?"

"All that time over my head was more than I could stand. It's one thing when they give you a year or two—hell, even five—but twenty years puts you in a different class. A different mentality. Twenty years is just a different word for life." There was tension in his voice, like just talking about the sentence was stressful. I could only imagine how much worse it had been to be locked up for that kind of time.

"If you had twenty years, why are you out now?" I asked.

His face softened into a grin. "That's where Aaron comes in."

"Yeah, I think I heard that Aaron went to jail," I said vaguely, careful not to mention how I knew this information or how much else I knew. "Did you do time with him?"

"Yeah, he was locked up with me. In fact, that's how we bonded. Wasn't a lot of people from Hopewell in the joint, so when he got there, I kind of looked out for him as my homeboy. I knew he wasn't the kind of person who belonged in there. He kept his head down and did his time. Didn't get mixed up in prison politics. He was basically a good guy who made one stupid mistake. And me, I made so many that I lost count."

"So you felt sorry for him? What? Did you become like his protector?"

"Oh, I whispered in a couple of people's ears, but

actually it was the other way around. He helped me survive a hell of a lot more than I helped him."

"I'm confused."

"Aaron taught me through example. Unlike me, who was angry and blamed everybody for my situation, Aaron took full responsibility for his actions. He owned his mess and taught me how to do the same."

"Interesting," was my only comment. Given what I knew of Aaron and of Pippie, this story was not what I would have expected.

"His faith was always so strong," Pippie continued. "One day we got to talking, and eventually we got to praying. If you told me that I would ever be one of those people who believed in God, I would have laughed in your face, but he introduced me to God in a way that I could understand. In a way that made me feel like I was no longer fighting an uphill battle alone."

"So wait, what are you trying to say? Aaron is the reason you believe in God?" I would have assumed it was the other way around.

"Not the reason, per se, but God used him as a vessel. He's the one who showed me the way. Without him, I wouldn't be here."

I gave him a skeptical look. I mean, I knew Aaron was popular at the church, but Pippie seemed to be lifting him up to some kind of mythical status. He was a singer, not a miracle worker. "So you're saying that Aaron got you out of jail?"

"I never thought of it that way, but yeah, kinda. I do know I would have never gotten paroled if I hadn't gone down the path he led me on. And then when I got outta jail, Aaron convinced me that I needed to get a fresh start. He got the bishop to talk to the church to give me a job. Plus he gave me a place to stay, and here I am. And I'll tell you this: I am never looking back. Onward and upward."

"Well, however it happened, I'm glad you're out, and I'm glad you're here," I said with a genuine smile. I really liked Pippie. He was truly a nice guy—even if I believed he was giving Aaron too much credit.

We sat quietly for a while, Pippie finishing his coco bread while I sat and digested everything he'd just told me. I really couldn't get over his dedication to Aaron.

"You know, I really have to say I've been surprised by many things since coming up here from Virginia," I said.

"How so?"

"I swear this is not like any church I've ever been to."

This comment got a swift reaction from Pippie. "Well, I sure hope it doesn't run you outta here," he said, looking a little worried. It was sweet that he cared. Pippie really was a good guy. I liked the way he made me feel. If things had been different...

"Please!" I said, waving away his concern. "I just want to be able to do my job." *At least until I accomplish what I came here for,* I thought.

"That's good to hear," he said. "I like having you around."

"Thanks."

"Wanna go inside and get another one of those patties?" Pippie asked as he stood up.

"You tryin' to get me fat?" I joked, getting up too. "You can't keep taking me to these places with all this good food. You're going to make me big as a house."

"I'm just trying to show you a good time, Desiree, especially after everybody else almost ran you back to the South with their drama." His voice suddenly had a sweetness to it that touched me in a way I didn't want to acknowledge. "You have no idea the places I wanna take you...if you let me."

He took a step closer to me, invading my personal space for the first time. Up until this moment he'd been a perfect gentleman anytime we were together. Now he was so close I could feel the heat coming off his body. I wasn't quite sure what he was about to do, and even more, I wasn't quite sure how I would react if he did make a move. I couldn't risk doing the wrong thing, so I took a step back.

I glanced at my watch and announced, "Oops. I gotta get home."

He looked disappointed, but he didn't press the issue. "Yeah, I guess you're right."

"So, what's your favorite kind of food?" I asked, making small talk to ease the tension as we got back in his car. I knew he felt let down, but I wanted to make sure he was willing to continue with the status quo. Plenty of guys will never talk to you again once you put them in the friend zone. Fortunately, Pippie wasn't one of them.

"It changes week to week. Today it might be this"—he held up the last bite of his second patty and popped it into his mouth—"but you never know in New York, because there's so much to choose from. You can get a lot of good eats in Virginia, but nothing like here in the city. I wanna introduce you to all of them—Cuban, Dominican, Russian, Korean, Caribbean, Ethiopian—"

"You still haven't told me your favorite," I interrupted, because he sounded like he was still trying to steer the conversation toward a date.

He took the hint and slowed his roll a little. "When I was locked up, the one thing I craved was some barbecue. Man, I dreamed about ribs. Even woke up drooling a few times," he said with a laugh.

"If you love BBQ so much, why'd you leave the

South? Everyone knows the best ribs are down South."

He laughed. "There's some truth to that, but you've never been to Poor Freddie's rib shack. Our next little field trip is going to be there."

"You don't have to ask me twice!" I said, not worrying about his intentions for the moment. If there was one thing I loved, it was some good barbecue.

"Bring your appetite and some napkins," he said as we turned the corner onto my block.

"Well, thanks for the ride," I said. "It's good to know I can rely on someone." As much as I was worried about how it would complicate things, I really was glad to have gotten to know Pippie. I'd never really had a male friend. Without thinking about it, I leaned over and gave him a kiss on the cheek.

As I turned to open the door, I spotted Lynn sitting on the front steps. She'd obviously seen me kiss him, because her face was contorted into a nasty scowl.

"Oh shit," I mumbled under my breath.

"You all right?" Pippie asked. He followed my gaze and noticed Lynn. "Not sure who that is, but she sure looks pissed."

"I forgot that I was supposed to meet a friend after work." He had no idea the nightmare I was walking into.

"It's my fault. You want me to go over to her and apologize? She doesn't look too happy."

"No, it's not a big deal." Pippie talking to Lynn would make it worse. He couldn't hide his crush on me, and that would only piss her off more. "I owe her some money and was supposed to meet her for dinner to pay it back. I'll handle her."

"Okay, then. I'm gonna go on and get back to the church. See you tomorrow."

"Sure thing. I'll see you tomorrow, Pippie." I got out of the car and prepared myself to face Lynn's wrath.

Monique

28

TK barely acknowledged me during the ride over to Mount Olive Church, but after the blowup at Jackson's office earlier, I was surprised he'd even agreed to wait for me. It gave me a glimmer of hope—our marriage was rocky, but not dead. I guess the news of Clifford Jr.'s death had shocked him out of his rage. Death had a way of putting everything into perspective.

I couldn't fathom why anybody would want to kill Cliff. I'd met him when TK and I attended an event held by his youth group, and he seemed perfectly nice. His father told TK he was grooming him to one day take over their church. This was a young man who had his whole life ahead of him, and I couldn't begin to imagine the pain his parents were experiencing. Times like this made it hard to have faith in the human race.

When we arrived at the church, the parking lot was full. Inside the church, the entrance to the sanctuary had been taped off. I saw a group of police officers in there, probably working to gather evidence. I shivered at the thought that the body must have been discovered in there, in a place reserved for holy things, not murder.

An officer guided us into the rec room, where clusters of people were standing around in shock, crying, talking, and just being there to support Pastor White and his wife, First Lady Vanessa. TK headed right over to Pastor White, and I went to see the first lady.

"Monique." Vanessa greeted me with a warm, tearful hug as soon as I approached. Out of all the first ladies I'd had to deal with in New York, she had been the first one to accept and embrace me. We'd actually become friends, having lunch together once in a while.

"I am so sorry for your loss. Clifford was such a nice young man. This was just…" I stopped, at a loss for the words to verbalize a tragedy so horrendous that no parent should ever have to experience it.

"Thank you for coming." She gave me a half smile then pulled back, attempting to maintain her control. We were both wiping away tears.

"Vanessa, you don't have to be strong for any of us. Right now it's our job to be here for you in whatever capacity you need. Let us be your rock the way you've been for so many." The women around me started chiming in with "Amen" and "Yes, Lord."

We were all in agreement on this. Being the first lady of a megachurch, I knew from experience that Vanessa's life was spent in service to those in her congregation.

"Thank you." She pulled me close again, and this time she really allowed me to hug her tight.

By the time I headed over to TK and Reverend White, the group of women had swelled around Vanessa, offering her comfort. I could see that TK and Reverend White were in a serious discussion. I almost stopped, but then my husband caught my eye and motioned for me to join them.

"Pastor, I am so sorry for your loss." I hugged Pastor White. Unlike his wife, Clifford didn't show his emotions on his face. If you didn't know he was the grieving father, you might think he was just another one of the supportive clergy that seemed to be hanging around.

"Do they have any idea who might have done this?" I asked.

Reverend White shook his head. "Far as I know, Cliff didn't have any enemies. People liked him. I mean, everywhere he went he made friends. I just don't understand this."

"We are going to find out who did this. That's a promise," TK said.

We looked up just as two plainclothes cops were heading in our direction.

"Pastor White, I'm Detective Turner, and this is my partner, Detective Dugan." The man who spoke could have been straight out of central casting under "big-city detective, medium build, dark hair, and a thick Brooklyn accent." His partner looked like he'd be more comfortable behind the desk in a law firm. "Our captain asked us to bring you up to speed. Is there somewhere we can talk alone?"

"Bishop Wilson and his wife are like family. You can speak freely in front of them," Clifford replied. "Have you gentlemen arrested anyone?"

"No, sir, our investigation is still in its preliminary stages, but we will do everything we can to solve this crime," Detective Dugan answered.

"Well, do you have any leads?" TK questioned. My husband was not letting them leave without getting some answers for his friend.

"Well, possibly. We're just not quite sure how it fits in."

"What lead?" Clifford asked. The detective hesitated for a moment. I got the sense that this was more information than they would usually share about a case. TK and Clifford were men who commanded a certain amount of respect, however, and the detective soon gave in and discussed what little the police knew so far.

"There was a murder in Queens a couple of days

ago with a very similar MO. A young Jamaican-American male about the same age was found dead of a single gunshot wound. Same caliber gun, and like your son's murder, there was nothing of note taken."

"Do you think the same person who killed him also shot my son?" Pastor White asked.

"It's possible. Did you or your son know a man by the name of Vincent Taylor? He was a bartender in Queens."

"Vinnie Taylor. Big, burly guy?" Clifford blurted out in recognition. He wasn't the only one who recognized the name.

"Yes. Do you know him?"

Clifford's face revealed his emotion for the first time. "Yes, Vinnie and Cliff played football together. Do you think their deaths are connected?"

I couldn't concentrate on the detective's reply. In my mind, I was back in my house with Tia, the night that Jackson and I found her racing out of her rapist's apartment. She was an emotional wreck that night, and half of what she said sounded like the ravings of a madwoman, but I clearly heard her say the name Vinnie Taylor more than once. Given the fact that Tia had first spotted her rapist working at a bar during her bachelorette party, I felt certain that this dead bartender from Queens was the same guy.

I forced myself to tune back in to what the detectives were saying.

"We're waiting to get the ballistics report to see if the same gun was used in both crimes."

"This just doesn't make sense," Pastor White said sadly.

"Were your son and Mr. Taylor close? Did they keep in touch?" Detective Turner asked. Pastor White shook his head.

"Cliff tried to bring Vinnie into the church, but he had other interests. They hadn't seen each other in person in years because Vinnie had taken a pretty dark path into drugs and alcohol."

"All right. We'll let you know something as soon as we get the report," Dugan said.

"They seem to be on it," TK said after the two detectives were gone.

Pastor White didn't answer. The news that his son's murder might be related to another killing had pushed him over the edge. He looked like he was on the verge of breaking down. TK recognized this, and offered to take Clifford into his office so he could grieve in private for a while.

"Thank you, TK," Clifford said. "I think I will take a few minutes away from my congregation, but there's no need for you to escort me. I appreciate your coming."

"Absolutely," TK said, pulling Clifford in for a

hug. "I'm here whenever you need me. You or Vanessa."

After Clifford left, TK turned to me and said, "Let's go." His tone still held a little of the chill from our earlier fight, but I had faith that we would be okay.

As we exited the church, TK spotted Jeff Watson, a police officer who also happened to be a member at our church and the coach of our youth basketball team. "Hold on," he said to me.

I followed him over to the police car, where Jeff was standing with a fellow officer.

"Jeff, can I have a word with you?"

Jeff excused himself from the other officer and stepped aside with us.

"Bishop Wilson, good to see you, sir." He offered his hand.

"You too," TK said, then wasted no time with small talk. "The black clergy community is extremely tight knit. We're like family, so I need you to tell me whatever you can about Cliff's murder. I hear it's possibly related to another recent murder."

Unlike the other detectives, Jeff didn't hesitate to share what he knew. "Look, this isn't for public consumption, but both this man and the murder victim in Queens were found with the letter *R* written in blood on their foreheads. We don't know what the significance of the letter is yet. That's all we have so far, Bishop, but I will make sure to keep you in the loop."

"That's all I ask," TK replied.

"You know, while I have you here, Bishop, do you have a minute to discuss some issues with the basketball team? A few of the boys have been getting to practice late, and I'm worried about what they might be getting into."

Of course, TK obliged him. My husband was dedicated to all the members of our congregation, but he felt an extra responsibility for the young men who could so easily fall prey to the many temptations out there on the streets.

"TK, I'm going to head back to the car while you two talk," I said, relieved for the chance to separate from him for a minute. Jeff's information about the murders had my heart slamming against my chest, and I had to make a phone call that I did not want TK to hear.

Jeff might not have known what the *R* stood for, but I feared that I did. It stood for "rapist"!

In the car, I struggled to pull myself together and make sense of what I'd just heard. When did Vinnie Taylor's murder happen—and even more terrifying, was there some connection to the night Tia was there? I was ashamed to admit to myself that I'd never even asked Jackson about that night in front of Vinnie Taylor's. What happened after Tia and

I left him there? I'd been so busy caring for Tia that I'd kind of buried my head in the sand, preferring not to give any thought to a rapist. Jackson, too, seemed to have no interest in discussing that night. When we'd met to go over lines, he had been all about getting down to business. Neither one of us mentioned that night. With the news we'd just heard from Jeff, I needed some answers now. When I'd finally calmed down a little, I picked up my phone to call Jackson.

"Hello. You've reached Jackson Young, talent agent at Johnson Morris Agency. I'm away from my phone right now, so please leave a message."

"Jackson, it's Monique. I need to talk to you about something very important. Call me back as soon—"

TK's hand on the door caused me to jump. I quickly ended the call and dropped the phone onto my lap.

"Who are you talking to?" TK snapped. The guilty expression on my face must have been a dead giveaway.

"Um, nobody," was all I could muster.

He snatched the phone out of my hand. At this point, I was too emotionally spent to even protest. TK opened up the Recent Calls list and dialed the last number. He put the phone to his ear, and I knew the second Jackson's voice mail recording started playing. The look of rage that came across TK's face scared the crap out of me.

"After everything that happened today, you're calling him?" he said. "You are not the woman I married."

Aaron

29

Walking into the church for the first time since my altercation with Ross, I felt more uneasy than I'd ever felt in that building. The way people were quietly eyeing me as I made my way down the corridor, I was sure the gossip mill had been in full effect the past couple of days. Let them talk, I thought. It wasn't like Ross deserved any less than my fist in his eye after the way he'd tried to sabotage me. I had nothing to be ashamed of, I decided, as I straightened my shoulders and marched down the hall toward the bishop's office to share the good news about our choir's future.

"He in?" I asked as I stopped at Desiree's desk. She seemed like a nice enough girl, but I still had trouble even making eye contact with her, no matter how many times she'd tried to chat with me. To me that would always be Tia's desk she was sitting at.

"Yes. Just knock on the door."

"Thanks." I moved past her and rapped on the door.

"Come in," the bishop called out.

I entered his office to find him standing behind his desk, dressed in a wifebeater and dress pants. There was a large suitcase open on his desk, and he was sorting through a mountain of clothes. I won't sugarcoat it; he didn't look happy at all, and the whole thing just seemed strange for a man of his stature.

"You moving in?" I joked.

"Feels like it," he said under his breath.

"What's going on, Bishop?" I asked, taking a seat.

"I don't want to talk about it." He spoke in that authoritative tone that usually made people defer to him, but not this time.

"Wow, I remember saying the same thing to you. Remember?" He didn't answer, but glanced up from his search long enough for me to see the pain in his eyes.

"I don't know what's going on, but I'm your friend. I think I've proven that to you over the years."

"I know you are, Aaron." He sank down in his chair, took a deep breath, and let out a sigh. Suddenly he looked much older and wearier. Whatever the hell was going on, it was obviously taking a toll on him. "To make a long story short, Monique and I are having a lot of problems as of late. I'm thinking about filing for divorce."

His words came as a complete shock. I knew there

had been some tension between him and the first lady recently, but I had no idea it was that serious. "Nah, you don't mean that," I said, wishing for it to be true. If the bishop and Monique couldn't make it, what the hell chance did the rest of us have?

"Yes, son, I did. I meant every word," he said sadly.

"You wanna talk about it?"

"Thank you for your support, but I can't talk about it right now," he said, standing up again to return to his search through the suitcase. "Not sure if you heard, but Pastor White of Mount Olive, his son was murdered. I'm going to the wake, and I need to show up clearheaded and able to be of service to my friend. I can't do that if I delve into my personal problems right now."

I understood all too well how difficult it was to put on that professional face when you're suffering on the inside. I had struggled with it myself the first time I faced my choir after Tia left me at the altar. It was best to let Bishop Wilson set aside thoughts of Monique for the moment.

"So, I do have some good news," I said in an effort to change the subject.

"What's that?" he asked as he put on a white dress shirt that frankly could have used a good pressing.

"I had dinner with Jackson Young last night, and—"

"Don't mention that man's name to me," he said with a scowl.

"But—"

He cut me off again. "I'm starting to believe that Ross may have been right. I don't think we should work with that guy."

Now I was thoroughly confused. "What do you mean? We discussed this, and I thought you were on board with me signing the contract. I gave it to him last night."

He hung his head and took a few deep breaths to calm down before he spoke. It was a good thing, too, because for a second he looked mad enough to rip my head off.

"Fine," he said with a sigh. "So we have to work with this guy, but I can't. You're going to have to be the point person on this and deal with him personally. I don't want any interaction with him unless it's through you—or our lawyers."

"I understand," I lied, not grasping the reason for his sudden flip-flop on Jackson. Yeah, I knew the two of them didn't have a love connection, but this deal was too advantageous for all parties involved to let personal jealousy block the flow. Whatever was going on between him and his wife must have been pretty serious, because he was acting like he'd lost his mind.

A knock on the door prevented us from discussing it any further, although I doubted the bishop was going to give me details anyway.

"Hey, I need to talk to both of you," Pippie said when he came in with an uncharacteristically morose look on his face. He was the most upbeat person I knew, but he was looking like somebody stole his new puppy.

He flopped into a chair and explained the reason for his expression. "Ross is in jail. He got arrested last night on an aggravated DUI. He needs us to help bail him out."

"He's got a wife. Let Serena deal with it," I snapped.

"She's pregnant, man." Not long ago, I would have been just as protective of Ross and his family, but right now I couldn't manage any sympathy for him.

"That's not my problem. There is no freaking way I'm coming to his rescue."

"You can't be serious." Pippie gave me a look of disappointment that normally would have gotten a reaction from me and made me change my tune, but not today. Nah, the Ross thing was a wrap. I didn't feel no way about it.

"He got himself into this, so as far as I'm concerned, he can get himself out of it."

"That's cold, man." Pippie shook his head. "The guy is hurting. He's been drinking like a fish ever since your fight."

Bishop Wilson was a better man than me, because he stepped in to offer his help. "Pippie, let me get my things. We can get to the bank before I go to this wake."

"Great. You two can handle it," I said, standing up to leave the office before Pippie tried again to guilt me into forgiving Ross.

I breezed by Desiree's desk without saying good-bye, but stopped in my tracks when she called my name.

"Oh, sorry. I didn't mean to be rude. See you later, Desiree. You have a nice day now," I said.

"Oh, thank you. You too. But that's not why I stopped you."

"What is it?" I asked, hoping she wasn't going to offer up her advice about my feud with Ross—which she'd practically witnessed firsthand from her seat right outside the bishop's office.

"You think you can give me a ride home after choir practice? My car is in the shop." Then she added this to increase her chances of a yes: "I made some sock-it-to-me cake."

"Well, all right then. You definitely have a ride."

Desiree

30

I got out of Aaron's car, waving good-bye to him as I walked toward my apartment building. As soon as he disappeared out of sight, the smile dropped from my face and I stomped my foot on the sidewalk in a hissy fit. I couldn't believe I had come that close to having him upstairs in my apartment only to be thwarted by some supposed "personal emergency" he had to take care of. I had plans for Aaron that went far beyond sock-it-to-me cake. He had no idea what surprise I had in store for him upstairs, but now it would have to wait.

I struggled with my key in the lock, frustrated by the unhappy turn my night had taken. One minute I was about to have Aaron Mackie served up for dinner, and the next I'm stomping up the stairs to my apartment. I entered in a huff and threw my things down on the counter. The First Jamaica Ministries Choir songbook landed with a thud on the floor. I'd study those songs another time, I fumed. There was no way in hell I was in any mood to sing church songs.

"Hey," a voice called out from the living room.

I turned to find Lynn stretched out provocatively on the sofa. She was wearing a body-hugging teddy with garters and fuck-me-now pumps, her long curly wig falling past her shoulders. Girl had a figure that made men want to pounce: big luscious breasts, tiny waist, and ass ripe enough to make you want to take a bite. She pierced me with her hazel cat eyes narrowed into a frown.

"What happened? Where is he?" she pouted.

"I don't want to fucking talk about it." I kicked off my heels and started pacing the length of the room like a caged zoo animal.

"I thought you were bringing him home."

"I was this close to having him come up, and poof! It all went away with one mention of Tia," I fumed. "He's got that wench on the brain."

"Get the fuck out of here," Lynn snapped. Even she couldn't believe that a man could resist my game. She shifted her tone when she saw how upset I was getting. "Hey, sooner or later he'll come around. Your time will come. It always does," she added knowingly.

I stopped pacing and stood near the couch, my whole body tight with tension. "If we want this to happen, then we need to get rid of Tia. That bitch is in the way."

Still lying on the couch, Lynn looked me up and down, taking in every single curve. "Fuck Tia. I'll take care of her ass personally." She reached out and placed a hand gently on my leg. "We're gonna make this happen."

"But I wanted it to be today!" I whined. It hurt to get so close to something you've been longing for, only to have it snatched away.

"Hey, aren't you the one who taught me about patience?" she teased me, trying to lighten my mood. "All those months you made me wait to be with you, to taste how sweet you really are."

"Yeah, but you were a lady-killer. You had a rep-utation of being over the ex one and on to the next one, what, every two months?"

"I bore easily," she said casually. "But then again, there is no one like you. Desiree, you've waited this long to get what you want. Relax. You'll get it, and Aaron will get the surprise of his life." Lynn's hands worked their way down my body. "Hmmm. Well, enough about Aaron Mackie. You take your pills?" It was her way of letting me know that she cared about me no matter what.

"Yes, I took the last one yesterday."

"Good, 'cause this is nothing to play with. It's your life."

"Look, stop babying me. I took the medication just like the doctor ordered." She was starting to get on my nerves and she knew it.

"You know what I'd like to do?" She was all smiles as she reached out to touch my inner thigh.

"I'm too wound up." I clenched my legs together, feeling as stiff as a board.

"Let me see if I can make you feel better." She gripped my hips between her hands. Next thing I knew, her head was up under my skirt. I felt her teeth snatch the rim of my thong and pull it down. She buried her head into my crotch and began licking and pulling at my pubic hair. My knees felt ready to give out.

"I gotta lay down," I murmured. Lynn released me and I lowered myself onto the couch. She snatched my legs apart and dove down in between them as if this was the last meal of a dying man. She kept teasing me, licking and blowing on me, bringing me to the edge. As soon as I raised my hips up off the couch in anticipation of an orgasm, she would stop.

Lynn slid up my body and unbuttoned my blouse. She helped me out of it, and then she reached around to the back of my bra and unsnapped my ladies like a real professional. She lowered her mouth onto my nipple, gripping it between her teeth as she tugged it, suckling and licking me into submission.

Damn, I needed this, I thought. Even when you think you're not in the mood, the right touch turns it all around.

"You wanna come?" Lynn taunted me once she returned to my clit, licking and flicking it with her tongue.

"Yes! Please!" I begged.

"How badly do you want to come?"

"So bad, baby."

"Do you like this better than being with a man?" Her voice was hoarse.

"Fuck! Yes!" I shouted as she brought me closer to orgasm. I would have said anything to make her continue. I grabbed the back of her head, her curly hair twirling between my fingers. She pursed her lips and sucked down on my clit, sending me into spasms of ecstasy. "Yes, yes, yes!" I cried out as my back arched and then relaxed, moving in rhythm like a wave.

Once I caught my breath, I grabbed Lynn and flipped her down on the couch doggy style, so that her tight, round ass was sticking in the air. I snatched her teddy up over her cheeks and began to lick her from one end of her ass to the other.

"Oooh," Lynn cried out. I reached my fingers under her and started to massage the area around the

opening of her vagina. I loved that she went Brazil-
ian to make my job easier. There was nothing to get
in the way of her smooth pussy.

And of course she was so predictable. If I ever
went near her, she immediately got moist in anticipation. My fingers slid inside of her easily, getting
drenched in her juices. I wriggled my fingers until
she crashed against them, rubbing her walls against
my hand. I expertly brought her to orgasm after orgasm.

She leaned up and grabbed me, wrapping her legs
around my waist. "I love you."

"I love you too," I responded, feeling all open and
safe. She was the first person since my dad died who
had allowed me to be myself, with all my issues and
fears and anger, so when I said those words to her, I
really meant it.

After my father died, my mother sank into a
deep, dark hole of grief that she never fully emerged
from. I hadn't just lost one parent; I lost them both.
This was what made my rage over the situation so
deep and endless. Even after my mother got a job
and became able to function again, I had already
learned to be independent—and lost my ability to
trust.

"We're gonna make all your dreams come true."
Lynn shook me out of my sad stroll down Memory
Lane. She knew me well enough to know what was

on my mind. I knew she had my back no matter what.

"Even if they are other people's nightmares." She laughed and kissed me on the lips, letting me know this was only the beginning of our evening.

"Hungry?" I asked between kisses. After this first round of lovemaking, my stomach growled, reminding me that I hadn't really eaten since breakfast.

"Hell yeah. That stupid-ass cake you made looks terrible."

"Yeah, well, that cake is gonna get me exactly where I want to be," I reminded her. "You do understand this whole plan is about one thing?"

"Yeah," she said, giving me that devilish smile I loved. "Aaron Mackie."

Ross
31

Staring out through the metal bars that confined me in the Queens Central Booking holding cell, one thing had become painfully clear: I'd fucked up royally. Most of my life I'd done all the right things. I'd gone to college, married the woman I loved before getting her knocked up, and I regularly tithed ten percent to the church. And yet, here I was, sitting on a bench next to some big stank brotha with a tattoo that said *Bubba* on his arm, like he was too damn stupid to remember his own name. I felt foolish and ashamed. I was in a complete free fall, and it was all because I underestimated that son of a bitch Jackson Young. Not only did he take my best friend and client and turn him against me, but now he was the cause of a serious rift between me and my pastor. The bruises left behind when both Aaron and the bishop decided to land their fists against my eyes as part of my severance package were a physical reminder of how much I hated Jackson Young.

What was I thinking in the first place? Driving

drunk like some irresponsible teenager instead of a grown man with a pregnant wife and a mortgage to pay? I swore that when I got out of here I was recommitting my life to God and getting back on the straight and narrow. Somewhere along the way I'd gotten lost, and this was my wake-up call. This was as bad as things ever needed to get.

"Anybody got a smoke?" a wiry kid who looked like he wasn't old enough to shave asked no one in particular. Instead of receiving an answer, he got a hostile look that cut him down quick.

"Nah, I don't have any," I responded, feeling bad for the kid—almost as bad as I felt for myself. Jackson had set a trap, and my dumb ass had stepped right into it, hollering and acting like a fool, letting him make me look crazy and possessive. I was determined to fix that as soon as I got out of this place.

"Ross Parker!" An official-sounding voice barked out my name. As I approached, an officer holding a clipboard met me at the door. "You made bail."

A couple of the brothas in the cell started hating on me, but I was so relieved to have my freedom back that I barely paid them any attention. I followed him through a series of doors until we were back in the waiting area where I had turned over my personal belongings. Pippie stood there looking as tired as I felt.

"You all right?" he asked as I signed for my things.

"Yeah. Is Selena here?" I looked around, eager to see my wife.

"Nah, I never reached her. The bishop put up the money to bail you out."

"He did?" I was surprised. I didn't expect any help from him or Aaron anytime soon. Except for the moment he lost his temper and hit me, I guess he really did practice what he preached.

"Yeah, but he didn't stick around. He had a funeral to go to."

"Guess he's really done with me, huh?"

"He's not happy with you," Pippie confirmed, "but he didn't want to see you in jail. He told me to tell you to stop by the church tomorrow."

I was relieved that Bishop Wilson seemed willing to forgive and forget, but his wasn't the only friendship that Jackson had stolen from me.

"What about Aaron? I gotta talk to him about Jackson. I was thinking about it while I was in here, and this just ain't adding up. That is one bad dude."

Pippie gave me a look that said he thought I was wasting his time by stating the obvious.

"No, man, I mean it's more than just the contract thing. Not only did the guy set me up, but I really think he's got something else going on. Something's not right. I'm telling you, I got a bad feeling here. Aaron—"

Pippie cut me off. "Ross, Aaron's got nothing for you right now. It might be best if you went home to your wife and let things continue to cool off between you and him. Go home and get a good night's sleep."

There was no denying that he was dead right about that. I really needed to see my woman. Selena instinctively knew how to make me feel better. She could always see the bright side when I couldn't. Boy, did I need her warm arms and soft lips right now.

"Yeah, you're right," I said as I got in my car. This time I was leaving the driving up to Pippie. I passed out in the passenger seat not long after we started moving.

"You're home, man," Pippie announced when we pulled into my driveway sometime near midnight.

"Yeah, and it's a good thing, 'cause I'm beat." I gave Pippie a high five. "Hey, thanks for everything."

"That's what friends are for."

I got out of the car, watched Pippie pull off, and then walked to the front door. I'd been away from home for almost two days, so I fully expected to get an earful from my wife. Funny thing was, I was okay with it. I'd messed up and I knew it. As long as she let me in the front door, I was okay with whatever cussing out she wanted to give me. I knew that once she got it out of her system, we could make up and make love.

Before I could put my key in the lock, the door-knob turned.

"Here it comes," I thought.

The door swung open and I saw that it wasn't my wife standing in the doorway, but her brother. We called him Tank, because he was built like one. He was carrying a suitcase that I recognized as one of Selena's. First thing that came to my mind was that she had gone into labor.

"Hey, man, is Selena all right?" I wanted to push by him, but his girth took up almost the entire door-way.

"What the fuck did you do to my sister?" He gave me a look that I don't think I will ever forget. Tank and I had always been cool—hell, we were like brothers—so his choice of words had me confused and concerned.

"What do you mean, what did I do to her? I didn't do anything. I was in jail."

"Is that where your face got jacked up?" he said.

I'd forgotten how bad I looked. "I got in a fight."

"Looks like you lost. Same thing's gonna happen to you again if you touch my sister. She's already in there crying her eyes out." With that, he pushed past me and stepped outside, pulling out his phone.

I hurried inside and stopped dead in my tracks at what I saw—or rather, what I didn't see.

"Selena!" I called out from the living room, and my voice reverberated back at me like I was in an echo chamber. I stumbled through the dining room, which was also empty, still calling out for my wife. I wasn't even sure I was at the right address anymore.

She didn't answer, which worried me even more. Then I heard a light tapping sound, like something hitting against the hardwood floors. I followed the noise through the house and into the bedroom, only to find my wife sitting in the center of the empty room in a lone rocking chair.

"Selena, what's going on? Where is all of our furniture?"

"It's in storage," she responded, wiping tears off her face.

"Storage? What the hell? What happened?" My mind went immediately to Jackson. He'd already ruined my friendship with Aaron. Was he out to destroy my marriage now too?

"The doctor's office called," she said.

"Is the baby okay?" I took a step toward her, but she put out a hand, warning me to keep my distance.

"He better be," she said in a tone full of hate.

"The doctor gave me a prescription for antibiotics. He also gave me a prescription for you." She tossed a piece of paper at me.

"Selena? What the hell is going on? Why do we need prescriptions?" I couldn't fathom what Jackson had done to trick her. I was utterly confused.

She pierced me with a hard look. "You know, before today you couldn't have paid me to think that my husband would ever cheat on me. Now look at me. Don't I look like a damn fool?"

"Honey, what are you talking about? I never cheated on you," I swore. I tried to take another step toward her, but the look of sheer hatred stopped me in my tracks.

"Selena! I didn't. I swear."

"You never cheated? Never?" she raged at me.

"No, never!" I insisted.

"Really." She sighed. "Then how come I have syphilis?" I was stunned silent. "Go ahead. Make up some shit that makes sense, please, because the blood test doesn't lie."

"Oh my God! That stripper at the bachelor party!" The cold expression on her face made me realize that I'd said the words out loud.

Selena jumped up. "Are you fucking kidding me?" Her face was crimson. "You risked both our lives and our baby's life to fuck a nasty-ass stripper at a bachelor party?" She looked ready to collapse. I reached out to her, wanting to take away the pain and hurt. I tried to pull her into my arms, but she fought me like a wildcat.

"Please, baby, I love you. I fucked up, but I'm so sorry. Please." I reached out and placed my hands on her face, tears rolling down her cheeks. "I really fucked up, but, baby, I love you. I love our family."

"Get your motherfuckin' paws off of me. You disgust me!" She pulled away.

"Selena, please. I can't lose you!" I fell to my knees and held on to her legs, desperate to save my family.

"Get off of me!" she screamed. "I hate you! I fuckin' hate you!" she raged at me, but at least she had stopped moving toward the door.

"I can't lose you. You are my life."

"Get off of me, Ross!"

"I won't let you go!" I gripped her even tighter.

"Get off of her!" Tank, whose six-foot-three, 260-pound frame seemed to grow right before my eyes, grabbed the back of my neck with his massive hand.

"Man, stay out of this. This is between me and my wife."

"Ross, if you don't get your hands off my sister, I'm gonna break your fucking neck." He tightened his grip to let me know he was capable of doing just as he'd threatened. I released Selena and fell back onto the floor. Tank took Selena's arm and led her out of our house. As I watched her leave, it felt like the end of my life.

Desiree

32

I'd been sitting at my desk all morning waiting for Aaron to stroll by. Instead of my normal low-key secretary outfit, I'd worn something a little more eye-catching: a mint-colored scoop-neck dress that showed off the tops of my breasts without being too hoochie-mama desperate. It would definitely get a man's attention. Now, if I could only make sure it was the right man, I would be set.

"Hey, Des." Pippie strolled into the reception area. He got a good look at what I was wearing and momentarily stopped in his tracks. To his credit, though, he resisted the urge to whistle at me, instead giving me a small nod. "You look nice today." I have to give credit where credit was due. Pippie had made it very clear that he was interested in dating me, but he'd never once stepped out of line when I told him I just wanted to be friends. Despite his criminal past, he was a true Southern gentleman.

"Hey, Pippie, I haven't seen you since yesterday," I said, smiling. I'd gotten so used to him being my welcoming committee every morning that his absence had been noticed.

"Yeah, I had some errands to handle for Bishop and then..." He grimaced.

"What?" I said, expecting something terrible.

"A friend of mine got a DUI, so I had to help get him out of jail."

"Oh. Yeah, I heard about Ross's arrest." I was expecting something terrible, not news I'd already heard from the church rumor mill.

"That's First Jamaica Ministries," he said, shaking his head. "That's why it's better to be on the straight and narrow, 'cause folks around here will know your business—sometimes before you do."

"I know that's right," I said with a laugh. I was truly enjoying Pippie's company, and as usual, he didn't bother to hide the fact that he enjoyed mine too. Most guys would play it cool, but not him. With Pippie, what you saw was what you got. I found it really refreshing. If I didn't have things I'd already set out to accomplish, I could have definitely fallen for a guy who treated me like that.

"You eat lunch yet?" I asked, acting on impulse and deviating from my morning's plan.

"Nah. Why? You wanna go grab some lunch together?" He looked hopeful.

"No, I actually brought my lunch from home, but I have something for you." I reached behind me into my lunch sack and pulled out a Tupperware container. I handed it over to him.

"What's this?" He seemed genuinely pleased by my gesture.

"Sock-it-to-me cake. I thought you could have it for dessert."

"You made this?" He looked surprised. I nodded. "*And* you can cook. You gonna make some man really lucky one day."

"Thank you," I said, blushing. "I really like cooking for people. I guess that's my Southern roots, you know?"

"Amazing. Most women today ain't thinking about cooking for a man. They want to be taken out and wined and dined."

"No, I like all of that," I said, "but there is something about being able to satisfy a lot of different needs."

"Amen to that, my sister," Pippie joked. I knew his mind was in the gutter.

"Let me know if you like it. I still have half a cake at home."

"Thanks, Des. I'm gonna tear this cake up. I'm already putting in my order for another piece."

"You got it," I said, genuinely pleased by how much he appreciated my small gesture.

"Well, I better get back to work."

"See you later, Pippie."

"Yeah, you can be sure of that," he said then left happily with his slice of sock-it-to-me cake.

His little visit left me in a good mood, but the next person to approach me was a whole different story. He ducked out of one of the rooms nearby. It was pretty obvious he'd been listening to my conversation, waiting for Pippie to leave.

He straightened out the lapels on his suit then checked out his cuff links before arrogantly striding over to my desk. He was good looking for a man of his age, there was no doubt about that, but he took conceited to a whole other level.

"Have you lost your mind?" I snapped. "Bishop Wilson could walk in here at any moment."

"So?" Jackson Young said arrogantly. "The hell with Bishop Wilson. I wish he would come out here."

"You didn't say that when he had his hands around your throat," I reminded him. As far as I could tell, he must have been conked on the head and lost his natural-born mind showing his face here.

"Hey, I told you that in confidence, not for you to ever bring it up again." He pierced me with a stare that told me to back the hell up. I did, but it still wasn't going to do either one of us any good if Bishop walked in here right now.

"You shouldn't be here. It's not smart." I knew

that Jackson was going to do whatever he wanted, but he wouldn't be able to say that I didn't warn him. After what happened with Ross, I now knew that the mild-mannered man of God was only one side of Bishop TK Wilson. "Worst-case scenario, you could cause me to lose this job. Then where would we be?"

"Relax. You're not going to lose this job. I heard you tell the little church thug that the bishop isn't here." Jackson smiled, revealing a mouthful of perfect teeth. "I didn't come to see him anyway. I came to see you."

I leaned in and hissed at him, "Are you not hearing me?"

"Loud and clear. But I need an update," he said, lowering himself to a comfortable seated position on the edge of my desk.

"I'm doing my part. Things are going according to plan." He raised his eyebrows, obviously not satisfied with my answer. "Look," I said, "you got to get out of here before anybody comes by and recognizes you." We were lucky no one had come by already. This church was a hotbed of activity with folks coming and going all day.

"Did you get the check?" he pressed.

"Yeah, I got it," I said, hoping that would satisfy him enough to leave before this all blew up in my face.

"Good, now there's nothing standing in our way." A sadistic grin began to form on his face.

"Jackson?" We both turned as First Lady Monique entered the reception area. I shot him a smug look as if to say, "I told you so."

The first lady looked about as happy to see Jackson as I was. In fact, she looked downright uncomfortable. He, on the other hand, seemed to be enjoying himself. First Lady Monique quickly looked past me toward her husband's office.

"He's not here yet," I said, and her relief was palpable.

She took Jackson by the arm and led him to a corner. I pretended to be busy sorting through the papers on my desk, but I would have had to be blind and deaf to miss the exchange between her and Jackson.

"What are you doing here?" I heard her voice catch. She was obviously trying to play it cool, but there was no disguising her worry.

"I came to see you." Jackson, ever the smooth player, acted as if being there after the conflict with Bishop Wilson was the most natural thing in the world. "You really left me no choice. You haven't answered my calls, and something's come up. We need to talk," he said, his voice dripping with concern. Hell, this was better than any reality show or daytime soap opera I'd ever seen.

"You're right, we do need to talk but we can't talk here." Monique lowered her voice to a whisper. She took out a piece of paper and handed it to Jackson. He read it, nodded, and was out the door, followed by the bishop's wife. I didn't know what was going on, but things had certainly gotten interesting.

Monique

33

Jackson stood up as I approached his table at Junior's, the famous cheesecake restaurant in downtown Brooklyn. Even though we had left the church at the same time, I'd taken longer to arrive because I parked my car ten blocks away, in case TK decided to use that OnStar tracking device again. He wouldn't think to look for me here, because it wasn't the kind of place I'd dine at in the middle of the day. It was one of those places I usually only went to for graduations or birthday celebrations.

Jackson opened his arms for a hug, and I fell into it without hesitation. I should have felt self-conscious in a room full of people, but the truth was, I really needed some support, and after my fight with TK, I knew I couldn't get it from him. As first lady of the church, I had to be very careful about who I talked to and what I shared; the slightest rumor could put my husband's reputation at risk, so very often I kept things to myself. Given what I'd learned about the recent murders, though, I needed to talk to someone. Jackson was the logical choice.

"Thanks for meeting here," I said as I sat down. "I wanted to make sure that we weren't in Queens. Things are not good with me and TK, and seeing us together would only make it worse."

"Of course," he said. I appreciated the way he let the mention of TK's name pass without making a big deal of it. After all, TK had tried to strangle him, so the fact that Jackson was even still speaking to me said a lot about his character. "I took the liberty of ordering your lunch. You don't look like you've been eating," he said.

"I haven't had much of an appetite," I admitted.

"What's going on? I've been worried about you ever since...that day."

"I've been relegated to the guest room." I hated to admit out loud how bad things had gotten between us. Jackson was the first person I'd said anything to.

"The guest room? Are you serious?" He seemed shocked, but then again, most people would be. TK was a great preacher, and that was usually the only side they saw, but he was also a man with a lot of stubborn pride. Couple that with the fact that he no longer trusted me and the situation was much worse than even I could have predicted.

"Yeah, he tried to kick me out at first. I had to

fight like hell to even get a spot in the guest room."
I could feel tears forming in my eyes.

"But we were only practicing."

"I know that, you know that, but my husband
disagrees." I wiped my eyes with a napkin, refusing
to break down. I had bigger things to discuss with
Jackson, and I needed my wits about me. "But that's
not why I wanted to talk to you today," I told him.

He leaned back in his chair. "So what are we doing here, Monique?" he asked with a confident look
on his face. I didn't think he'd have that look on his
face for long once I told him what had happened.

"Vinnie Taylor is dead," I said.

He took a sip of his water. "Who?"

Was he serious? "Vinnie Taylor, the guy you said
you were going to talk to."

Still no reaction from him.

I leaned closer and spoke quietly. "Tia's rapist."

"Oh, him," he said casually.

"Yes, him, Jackson. Tia told us she hit him on the
head with the lamp, but now I find out he's dead.
Shot, and Tia has a gun."

"Guess he got what he deserved," Jackson said,
still unfazed by the news. His behavior was starting
to make me nervous.

"Jackson, I need to know what happened when
you went in to see him that night. Was he still alive
after Tia hit him?"

We paused our conversation for a minute while the waitress set our plates on the table. I couldn't even think about touching the sandwich Jackson had ordered me, but he dug in, enjoying a few bites before he answered my question.

"I never went inside," he said.

"What? But when I left with Tia you said—"

"I was going to, but when I got inside the building, I didn't know which apartment it was."

"So you just left?" I asked, totally confused. That night, he had been so adamant about going to confront the guy. Now he was admitting that he made barely the minimum effort. Not that I necessarily expected him to be a hero or something, but his lack of effort, added to his lack of concern about the guy's murder, didn't fit with my initial impression of his character.

"Yes. I never went in. So, why exactly does that bother you so much? The guy was a rapist and who knows what else. He probably had lots of enemies who could have done this to him. I say good riddance to bad trash."

"There's more," I told him.

"Like what?"

"There's another dead guy in Brooklyn."

He gave me a patronizing smile. "Monique, this is New York. There are dead guys in all five boroughs every single day."

"The guy in Brooklyn knew Vinnie Taylor. Both of them were killed with the same type of gun," I said, my breath catching in my throat as I revealed the most frightening piece of evidence: "And they both had the letter *R* on their foreheads."

"The letter *R*?" he asked.

"*R* for 'rapist,'" I whispered.

He let out a low whistle. For the first time, he showed some concern. "Whoa, that doesn't sound good. Have you asked Tia about this?"

"No. I haven't even called her. I think I'm afraid of what she might say," I said, my body trembling as I admitted that awful truth.

He thought about it for a second and then said, "Look, you have no way of knowing if she has anything to do with this. It could be one hell of a coincidence...Maybe there were other victims and someone else delivered their justice."

I looked up at him with tears in my eyes, wanting so badly for his version to be correct. I did not want to believe Tia was capable of murder.

"Look, regardless of who pulled the trigger, here's the bottom line," he continued. "Those guys committed a heinous crime. Could you really blame a victim if she did go rogue?"

I shook my head adamantly. "God should be the one to take care of those men, not her."

He looked doubtful. "Is that what you would do

if you were in her position? Sit idly by and do nothing except hope they get their punishment in the next life?"

As a preacher's wife, I would have liked to think I could "turn the other cheek," but when I imagined myself in Tia's position, I had to admit something to myself: I would never be able to live up to that standard.

"There wouldn't be a rock big enough for them to hide under if they did to me what they did to her."

Jackson was staring at me with a look of pure admiration.

"And if you were my woman, I would be right there with you, squeezing the trigger. I would not wait for the cops to exact justice for you."

"What am I going to do?" I asked.

"Well, just have faith that the same God that looks after you will also be there for Tia."

"That sounds like something TK would say...if he was talking to me."

"Monique," he said, reaching out to hold my hand, "he doesn't deserve you."

Tia

34

Ever since I found his name in the college yearbook, I'd become obsessed with finding Mark King. Nothing and no one else mattered to me, and it would be that way until I could confront the guy who lured me into the trap that wrecked my life.

I'd been staying at my brother's house and parking my car a few blocks away so no one would know I was there. My brother was at work most of the time, so we rarely saw each other, which was just fine with me. I really didn't want to talk to anyone these days. Monique was the only one still calling on a consistent basis, but every once in a while someone else from the church would ring my cell phone and leave a message to tell me they were still thinking about me. I knew they meant well, but the last thing I needed was some nosy biddy from the church taking it upon herself to find me and try to "save me." I could just picture one of them getting it in her mind that she would be the one to get me and Aaron back together.

I had been thinking about Aaron a lot lately. My heart ached when I admitted to myself just how much I missed him, but I knew that us getting back together was not possible, at least not until I had a face-to-face with Mark King. If I was ever going to speak to Aaron again, I needed to be able to approach him as a grown woman, not a wounded girl.

I let out a frustrated scream, grateful nobody could hear me as I drove through the nighttime streets of Queens. Maybe I was being delusional. I'd already done so many things that I couldn't take back, and there was no way that I could expect Aaron to forgive me. But I wanted to believe it could happen. Hell, I needed to believe that. Holding on to that dream kept me going.

As I turned onto a side street, I glanced in the rearview mirror and noticed the car that had been behind me for a few blocks also turned. It wasn't the same one I'd seen the other day, but the way it stayed on my ass when I turned and then switched lanes made me suspicious. Maybe I'd watched too many cop shows on television, I thought, because my active imagination had me worrying that someone had actually been following me for days, and had changed cars to throw me off.

"Shit!" I cursed, worried that I might be in some real danger out here alone. Once all the possible theories started playing around in my head, they seemed plausible to me. What if there was more than one person following me? What if Mark King had found out that I was searching for him and now he was hunting me?

I looked in the mirror again, and the car looked like it was straight-up on my tail now. I made a quick turn into the parking lot of a small shopping center. If the car didn't follow me, then I would know I was just being paranoid.

"Damn!" The car stayed right on my behind. "Think, Tia. Think!" The lights were off in the dollar store, the wig shop, RadioShack, and an over-charging check-cashing place. A handful of cars were left in the lot, probably folks parking for free on their way someplace else. I had to get out of there.

I sped up and shot down an alley that I thought would lead me back to an always-busy Jamaica Avenue. Halfway down the alley, I realized my mistake. An oversize Dumpster was in the middle of the alley behind the dollar store, blocking my exit. Even worse, behind the Dumpster they had erected a chain-link fence. I put the car in reverse and turned my head to back up, but the other car was creeping down the alley behind me. Out of options, I grabbed my purse and retrieved my gun with trembling hands.

The car pulled up right behind mine, but the

bright headlights shining into my car made it impossible for me to see who was getting out of the driver's side. I watched, terrified, as the silhouette of a man approached my car. In no time, he was walking around the side to my door. I shut my eyes tight, waiting for the worst.

"Tia? What are you doing, girl?"

I nearly jumped out of my skin when he spoke my name. Whipping my head to the side, I saw Pippie standing there, looking down at me with a puzzled expression. He reached down and opened up my door. Adrenaline still coursed through my body; to my terror-stricken brain, everyone was an enemy right now, even Pippie. Acting on pure animal instinct, I jumped out of the car, pointed my gun at Pippie, and ran to the other side of the car to put some distance between us.

His hands shot up defensively. "Whoa!" he yelled. "Tia, it's me, Pippie. What are you doing? Put down that gun."

"Why were you following me?" I shouted at him, taking another step back and keeping my gun raised.

"I was coming from that Chinese spot on the Avenue when I saw you drive by me, so hell yeah, I followed you," he said, his voice a combination of nervousness and anger. "No one's seen you since you left my boy at the altar. You think I was going to see you and not try to talk to you?"

"How do I know that you haven't been following me for days?" I yelled.

"'Cause if I had found you before tonight, believe me, we would have had a conversation. Like, where the hell you been? Are you all right? How could you do this to Aaron? Are you coming back?"

He kept his hands up but took one cautious step toward me.

"Stop right there!" I ordered. "And stop asking me so many questions."

"Tia, I'm not the enemy here." He did not stop his slow advance toward me until he realized I was not putting the gun down. He now stood just a few feet away from me. "I only want to help you."

"Mind your business and leave me alone, Pippie." I couldn't control the shakiness in my voice, and I was sure he noticed it too.

"This is my business! You're my little sister, re-member?"

At one time, Pippie and I had been extremely close. When he got released from prison, he'd lived with Aaron while he was getting on his feet. Over that time, he'd become like a big brother to me. But just like everything else from before the night I spotted my rapist, that relationship was dead to me now. Pippie couldn't help me. The only thing that would make me whole was confronting every one of my rapists, and I did not need Pippie hindering that plan by telling anyone he'd seen me.

"Pippie, walk away. Just pretend that you didn't see me," I begged. "It would only hurt Aaron. It's better if he just forgets about me."

He shook his head. "No, that's not right. Aaron loves you. If you're in some kind of trouble, he would want to help you. You two were meant for each other. Let me help you fix things."

A single tear escaped and rolled down my face, but I refused to give in to my feelings for Aaron.

"Nobody can fix this," I said. "Not you, not Aaron, not even the bishop can help me."

Pippie kept trying. "Love can fix almost everything. Trust me on that. Aaron loves you, Tia. He's not going to stop loving you."

"You spent too much time in prison," I spat. I was becoming angry at the way he kept trying to tug at my heartstrings. I was in control of my own destiny now, and no man was ever going to be allowed to change my course. I pushed away any lingering tenderness from my mind. "You think because you got out of jail, now life is gonna turn out like one of your fantasies. That everything and everybody can have a second chance. Guess what? Not everybody gets a second chance. And that other fantasy? Please. Love can't fix shit. Not my life or yours, so don't talk to me about love."

"Look," he said, reaching into his pocket. "Let me just call Aaron and get him down here. I have faith that you two can work this out if you just talk to him." He pulled out his phone.

"Don't you call him!" I screamed out, waving my gun in the air.

He lowered his phone, staring at me wide-eyed. "What is going on here? You are not the Tia I knew."

"Yeah, well, you don't really know me then. But if you know what's good for you, then you will back the fuck up and let me out of here!"

Aaron

35

I walked into the church, pulled out the chair next to Desiree's desk, and stared her down. I'd just come from a conversation with some very influential church members and the main topic of the conversation was Tia. I wasn't surprised to learn that many of them felt the same way about her that I did.

"Why are you staring at me?" she asked, sounding nervous. "Do I have something in my teeth?" She covered her mouth, rolling her tongue around to check.

I answered her question with a question of my own that had nothing to do with her dental hygiene. "Who are you, and why are you really here?"

"What do you mean, who am I? You know who I am. I'm Desiree Jones, the church's secretary. I work here. You're sitting on my desk," she answered with a little humor in her tone.

"You can cut the BS, okay. It's just you and me. We both know you're not who you say you are, and you darn sure ain't no church secretary."

Her facial expression went blank. Now she was staring at me. "My name is Desiree Jones. You wanna see my ID?" She reached for her wallet and pulled out her ID.

"Okay, so your name really is Desiree. That still doesn't explain things." I chuckled, but she did not look the least bit amused. In fact, she was getting downright defensive.

She leaned forward. "What exactly do you need explained, Aaron?"

"Well, for starters, explain that story you concocted about just moving to the neighborhood from Virginia, like it was some coincidence that you ended up here. 'Cause me and a few of the choir members were just talking, and—"

Her eyes opened wide, and she looked truly scared. "What? Y'all were talking about me?"

I realized I better let her in on the joke before she fell apart. "Yeah, we don't believe you moving here was a coincidence. We believe it was divine intervention."

"Huh?" The fear was gone, replaced by confusion.

"Nobody comes all the way from Virginia to New York without prompting and no family to lean on, unless God's behind them—or possibly the devil. And, well, we all know you have the voice of an angel," I said with a smile.

"So, I'm not fired?" Her face softened.

"No, you're not fired. Truth is, I'd like to offer you the chance to do a solo with the choir."

"A solo?" she shrieked, loud enough to make me worry about my eardrums.

"Oh, I'm so sorry about your ears. I'm so sorry. You really think I'm ready for a solo?" she asked excitedly. I nodded. She seemed genuinely surprised, which I expected. Most of the solos in our choir had gone to the same four women for quite some time now. It had become pretty much a foregone conclusion when I assigned parts that the solos would go to one of those four. But I felt like we needed to shake things up. I'd been noticing recently that Desiree had a mean set of pipes on her. When I heard some of the choir members agreeing with my assessment of her voice, I knew it was the right time to make the change. If the other choir members recognized and respected her talent, it might be enough to keep any jealous grumbling to a minimum.

"Absolutely. You have an amazing voice. If I didn't know better, I'd think you were a professional."

"No, nothing like that," she said with a modest smile. "I just sing for pleasure."

"What? Are you gonna tell me that you weren't a lead in your last choir?"

"Yes, but it wasn't First Jamaica Ministries. I

mean, we hadn't won any awards or recorded albums or toured. We were small time." She laughed, and I noticed for the first time how pretty she was. Sure, I'd checked out her figure before, but I'm a guy and that's second nature, like holding the door open for an elderly person or putting ketchup on fries. But I'd never taken the time to really look at her—or any other woman, for that matter—ever since Tia left me. Not that I was ready to make a move, but it felt good knowing I could still find a woman attractive. Yeah, it felt real good. Normal.

"You are going to love the song I have picked out for you. I knew you were perfect for the solo once I heard that high note you hit the other day. This song really fits your voice."

"No, no, no! That's not going to happen! I don't want you in my house!" The sound came booming through the closed door to Bishop Wilson's office, and both Desiree and I fell silent.

"TK! Please, just listen to me!" Monique yelled back just as loud.

We both tried to act natural, like we hadn't heard a thing, when the door to the bishop's office flew open. We weren't the only ones trying to put on an act. Immediately, both Bishop Wilson and First Lady put on their game faces and acted like everything was all right.

"Aaron," Bishop greeted me, although he

couldn't maintain eye contact for more than a second. The first lady pretended to be busy searching for something in her oversize purse.

"How's it going, you two?" I asked.

"We're fine." First Lady gave me a curt smile.

The awkward silence lasted for only a few seconds, interrupted by two white men dressed in inexpensive blue suits who strode into the office.

"Can I help you?" Desiree addressed them.

The taller of the two flashed his badge. "My name is Detective Dillon, and this is my partner, Detective Barron. Do you have a John Nixon who works here?"

Desiree started to answer, "No, no one by that name—"

Bishop Wilson stepped in to address the officers. "John Nixon does work here. People here call him Pippie. How can I help you gentlemen?"

They shared a knowing glance that made me nervous. Pippie was on his last year of a five-year parole, and doing a great job of staying out of trouble—or so I thought. Unfortunately, it would only take one small slipup for him to violate and be sent back to prison to complete his original sentence, probably with extra time thrown in.

"Is he in some kind of trouble?" Bishop asked.

"Bishop Wilson, there's no easy way to say this. John Nixon is dead." The detective's words caused a collective gasp in the room. "Uniforms found his body in an alley off of Jamaica Avenue around six this morning."

I felt my knees go weak. I would have fallen to the ground if the bishop hadn't caught my arm to hold me up. God, it felt like my life was totally falling apart. First Tia left me at the altar, then Ross betrayed me, and now Pippie was dead. What had I done to deserve this?

Ross

36

As Bishop delivered Pippie's eulogy, his words were punctuated by the sounds of sobbing throughout the packed church. I was only hearing half of what the bishop said, because I had my own internal dialogue going on. I'd been plagued with these thoughts, running like a loop through my head, ever since Selena left me, and they weren't cutting me any slack even at my best friend's funeral service. All the things I'd done wrong in the past month had fucked up my life royally, and Pippie was the one person I could lean on. Just the fact that he believed in me bolstered my faith, made me think that I might be okay again someday. And now he was gone. Murdered.

I tuned back in to the bishop's words. "Pippie wasn't a saint, but when you were around him, he made you believe in God!" He preached the absolute truth. "He had a way of making you believe in miracles, setting a quiet example through his own life story of triumph over adversity."

I glanced around at the folks in the audience. Pippie had impacted so many of their lives in some way. He always had a kind word and a willingness to help people, and as a friend, you just couldn't do better. Lately, I'd been calling him up at three a.m., and not only would he talk me down off the ledge, but he'd show up and do it in person. What kind of person gets up from a dead sleep in the middle of the night just so you didn't have to be alone with your demons? And I'd had plenty of those days recently. I didn't have any idea how I was going to do this without him, because without him, I was now completely alone.

"He had a way of letting you know that you mattered," Bishop said, and I felt a pang of guilt. I wasn't so sure that I'd let Pippie know how much *he* mattered to *me*, how much I appreciated his love and friendship.

A small smile crossed my face as I realized that Pippie would have been the first one telling me not to beat myself up over something like that. Even after I told him about Selena getting sick, he didn't lecture me. His response was, "Even good people do bad shit sometimes."

Bishop Wilson wrapped up his eulogy and returned to his seat. First Lady was in the seat next to his, but there was a coldness that was apparent between them. They weren't holding hands the way they usually would during services, and neither one stole so much as a glance in the other's direction.

The church filled with the sound of "Precious Lord, Take My Hand" sung by the choir. Before they'd finished the first verse, tears were streaming down my face. Aaron directed the choir, and after their final chord, he approached the podium, his face wet with tears too. The thought crossed my mind that if it had been me in that casket, he might not have shed one tear, and that hurt me deeply. Aaron and I were so tight; we should have been there for each other, grieving this loss, but Jackson Young had destroyed any chance of that.

"Good afternoon." Aaron addressed the congregation, and I could see how hard he was struggling to hold himself together. I had the urge to go up there and put a hand on his shoulder, offer him support, but of course, those days were over between us. Out of respect to Pippie, I stayed in my seat, no matter how painful it was.

"Brothers and sisters, I really have no idea what I'm doing up here. What can I say to make any of this better for anyone, including myself? Tragedy seems to be hanging over me like a black cloud lately." I heard some people in the church murmuring in agreement. Everybody there had witnessed their beloved choir director being left at the altar, and most of them probably knew about our fight.

"It's all around me to the point where I can't get away from it. And this, the reason we're here today, is the worst of it. This is permanent. Unfixable. John Nixon, the man we knew as Pippie, was an amazing human being. He was, and will always be, my best friend. He was a good man.

"Like a lot of us, he made some big mistakes in life, but his love and commitment to his friends remained consistent. He was there for me when I made some pretty stupid mistakes too. He had my back through it all, the good and the bad. He was the most loyal person I knew. Once he had your back, he had it for life."

"Amen!" somebody shouted out from the audience. I was squirming in my seat. Was Aaron taking a jab at me, talking about loyalty? Would he really take his grudge that far, to carry it right into the middle of Pippie's funeral? I turned my head, trying to look everywhere except at Aaron up at that altar, insulting me like that.

"Well, that makes me think of someone else. It makes me think about my other best friend—my brother, my heart, and the one who originally coined us 'the Chocolate Musketeers' way back when." I sat up in my seat, unable to believe what I was hearing.

I turned to face Aaron, and our eyes locked. The look he gave me was everything.

"Pippie made a point to remind me that 'you can't make new old friends,' and boy, was he right," Aaron said with a sad laugh. He moved away from the podium and spoke directly to me.

"Ross, I know we ain't been right lately, but we both know that if Pippie were here, he would tell us to get our acts together. That with him gone, we need to lean on each other, and we can't let nothing get in the way of our friendship. We owe him that. We're family, man, and I need you." Aaron motioned toward me, a waterfall of tears streaming down his face.

"Yeah, me too," I shouted out, overwhelmed by the love he'd just given me. Damn if Pippie wasn't right.

"Then what you doing? Get up here, man," Aaron ordered as people jumped up and started shouting, clapping, and stomping their feet in support. I raced up the stairs and joined him, hugging and blubbering and throwing "I love you"s back and forth.

"We been through it, and now I know we have to stick together. I'm sorry. I love you, man," I told him. I swear it felt like Pippie was watching over us, pushing us back together. This was exactly what he would have wanted.

Aaron returned to the podium, bringing me with him. He waited for the crowd to settle back into their seats before he spoke.

"After this service, we're going to go into the meeting hall for some food, but it won't be just about eating. No. There is going to be some celebrating. Pippie liked to have a good time, and it's up to us to have a good time for him."

"Amen!" people shouted from the audience. The mood in the place had lightened considerably, until Aaron brought it crashing back down.

"Holy shit!" he said, still holding the microphone so that everyone heard him.

I hit him with my elbow, whispering, "Man, what's wrong with you? You know we're in church." He ignored me, his gaze fixed on something in the back of the church. I looked back there, and then I understood what had him so worked up.

"Oh, shit. Tia." The words left my mouth this time.

The entire congregation swelled in unison and turned to face the back of the church. There was Aaron's ex-fiancée, standing in the entrance of the church.

Desiree

37

Tears were forming in the corners of my eyes as I listened to the bishop eulogize Pippie. There were a lot of people who deserved to die, more than a few I knew personally, but Pippie wasn't one of them. Pippie was the one person who had consistently shown me genuine kindness and tried to make sure I felt at home in New York. He was one of the good guys, and his death had really affected me. It reminded me how completely random and unfair life could be. But it wasn't the first time I'd experienced an unexpected loss. Maybe that's why this was hitting me so hard.

I hurried out of my seat, down the aisle to the back of the church, and out the double doors as a waterfall of tears poured down my face. It took a few minutes, but I finally pulled myself together. I wanted to be back in there to pay my respects to Pippie. As I turned to head back in, I heard footsteps rushing toward me.

"What is wrong with you? I know you are not

crying over this dude," Lynn seethed when she got close enough to see my face.

I dropped my hand from the door to the church and pulled her away from the entrance where we wouldn't be heard. "He was my friend," I said, trying to wipe away the evidence of my connection to Pippie before it caused any further drama.

"That dude was not your friend." She spat out the words, her tone tinged with a blind jealousy. Lynn was not the kind of person to share me, at least not emotionally, and to see me broken up over him sent her on the warpath. She grabbed me by the shoulders and stared into my eyes intensely. "All he was doing was being nice so he could screw you. And getting in the way of your goal. Remember that? The reason you came here?"

I refused to let her talk that way about Pippie without defending him. "He was my friend, and he was a really decent guy," I responded, staring her down in the hope that she would back the fuck up.

She let go of my shoulders but stayed up in my face. "Yeah, well, you done met a whole lot of decent fucking guys over the years. In the end they all wanted one thing, and once they got it they were gone. Only difference is this one's not gonna have that chance," she said with not the slightest bit of sympathy for the fact that the man was murdered.

I did love this woman, but she didn't understand that I could have feelings for men that didn't travel in a sexual or romantic direction. Unlike her experience of being lesbian from birth, I considered myself bisexual and had thoroughly enjoyed sexual relationships with men in the past. Lynn was my first full-on relationship with a woman. Consequently, she was always insecure, afraid that deep down, I still craved the D.

"He was my *friend*!" I hissed at her. I just wanted to be left alone to grieve without having to justify my feelings to anyone.

"So, what? You were into him?" She kept at it, unable to process the idea that a man and a woman could be just friends.

Instead of letting things escalate further, I took things in a different direction and tried to reason with her. "He looked out for me. He even went to the pharmacy and picked up my medication."

She sucked her teeth, unimpressed. "Yeah, well, I should be the only one who looks out for you, and don't you forget it." She grabbed me and pulled me close. I pushed her away, my anger growing.

"I can't have friends now?" I challenged. I'd been forced to become independent at an early age, so there was no way I would stand for another person trying to control me now. Not even a lover—a really good lover. I'd rather walk away and be by my damn self than be a slave to anybody.

"You better remember we are here to do a job. You need to get your shit together," she shot back. Changing the subject was her subtle way of backing down, so I relaxed.

"I know that," I agreed, my tears stopping as quickly as they had begun.

"Then you know that you need to go in there and use that emotion to get Aaron into our bedroom."

That certainly wasn't my purpose for going to the funeral, but maybe she was right and there was a way to turn my grieving into an advantage with Aaron. After all, we both had a connection to him. People fell into bed at funerals and weddings for a whole lot of reasons, including shared grief. I stopped brushing away the wet spots on my cheeks and decided to let them glisten for everyone to see. I would have to thank Lynn for her smart idea later, in private.

"Let's go back in," I said. We headed back toward the entrance, where I caught sight of someone else stepping inside. My mouth dropped open. I stopped dead in my tracks, causing Lynn to bump into my leaden form.

"What the hell, Desiree?" Lynn said, nudging me to move forward, but I couldn't take my eyes off the woman as I watched the door to the church closing behind her.

I turned around to Lynn. "You are not going to believe this."

"What?"

"That was Tia. She's here!"

Tia

38

I took a moment to pause and gather my nerves before walking up the steps to First Jamaica Ministries. At one time, this place felt like coming home; the people here were my family. I had so many good memories of this church, but now everything was tainted by the pain and anger that had become my constant companions ever since I spotted Vinnie Taylor at the bar. If only I could turn back the hands of time...

But I wasn't there to relive the good old days. I was there to pay my respects to Pippie. As hard as it would be to set foot in this place, to face the inevitable stares and whispers, I owed it to him to be there. I needed to make amends in some way, even if that meant showing up to a place I'd run from the past few weeks.

If only Pippie had listened to me that night. His life might not have ended so tragically. I would live with the guilt for the rest of my life. I know some people say everything happens for a reason, but why did Pippie have to spot me driving by him that night? If only I had driven a different route, we wouldn't have ended up in the alley, and none of this would have happened.

But it was happening, and as I set foot in the sanctuary, I realized I had underestimated the reaction my presence would bring. I had foolishly imagined that I could slip into the last pew, unnoticed, and say a few prayers for his soul. Instead, Aaron spotted me from the altar, where he was standing with Ross, and soon every head swiveled in my direction, their stares piercing me.

Standing before the mass of people, my body rooted itself to the spot. Even if I wanted to run, I couldn't. When Aaron stepped down from the podium and headed toward me, I willed my feet to move, to no avail. My heart was pounding as I watched the man I loved coming down the aisle.

"Where have you been?" His voice was tinged with anger, but in his eyes I could see relief. It was the first time we'd laid eyes on each other since our wedding day. Oh, how I longed to feel his arms around me.

I stood there mute. How could I even begin to answer his question, to share with him my horrible secrets?

"Tia, answer me."

"This was a really bad idea," I said, taking a step

back, ready to bolt for the closest door. "I can't be here."

I turned to flee, too ashamed to face him any longer, but I felt a large hand on my shoulder, preventing me from going anywhere.

"You okay?" Bishop Wilson said in a voice that instantly soothed me. I began to cry quietly.

Monique came toward me and put an arm on my shoulder, whispering kind words in my ear. "You're okay, Tia. You're safe here with us."

"Tia, I need to know why you left," Aaron said, still sounding agitated. As desperate as I was to escape, he was just as desperate to get some answers. I had caused that poor man so much pain. Just one more thing I would forever feel guilty about.

"Give her a minute, Aaron," Bishop said. "I think she needs a little time to calm down, and then maybe we can all talk."

I was trembling as he took my hand. "Come on, Tia. Let's go in the back together," he said to me. "Monique, get one of the assistant pastors to continue the service, please, and Aaron, get back up there. Your choir needs you."

"But—" His face was full of resistance.

"Come on, son. Pippie deserves no less," he said. "I'll come get you later when Tia feels ready to talk."

Without protest, I allowed him to lead me down the aisle toward the front. I kept my eyes straight ahead, avoiding eye contact with anyone in the pews. Unfortunately, that meant the only place I could look was straight ahead, where Pippie's body lay in a casket.

I paused my steps, staring at Pippie's lifeless body.

"Would you like to pay your last respects to your friend?" Bishop asked.

My eyes flooded with tears as I approached the casket. "Oh, Pippie, I'm so sorry. I'm so sorry," I whispered, then turned away, wiping my tears.

When he thought I was ready, the bishop took me by the arm and led me out of the sanctuary toward his office. It felt so strange to be back there, passing by the desk where I had worked happily, never suspecting the way my life would soon be turned inside out. There were unfamiliar objects on the desk; it was obvious someone else was working there now. That caused me a pang of jealousy, though I fully understood why they had hired someone new. As dark as my soul had become, I no longer felt worthy of that position anyway.

"Have a seat." Bishop directed me to the chair in front of his desk.

I sat down, still shaking with emotion that threatened to overwhelm me. Coming back to this church, and especially seeing Aaron, had proven to be much harder than I imagined it would be. Now, sitting before a man I respected like a father, I felt small and pitiful. What would Bishop Wilson think of me if he knew how far from grace I'd fallen?

He sat down behind his desk and leaned forward, hands folded, waiting for me to look up and meet his eyes. When I finally did, he said, "I think it's time you told your pastor just what is going on with you." It was a command, not a question.

I took a deep breath. "Bishop, if I did, I'm not sure you would believe it."

Monique

39

Amazingly, Deacon Washington was able to get everyone to settle back in their seats after the drama of Tia's appearance. "People, out of respect for the departed, we are going to continue this funeral service. I would ask that you all remember we are in the house of God right now." His announcement was enough to get everyone back in their seats, where the chatter died down to a minimum. The people would hold their gossip—at least until they were outside the sanctuary.

The rest of Pippie's funeral service was a blur to me. I couldn't concentrate on a word anyone was saying as people made their way to the podium to speak about how Pippie had touched them. When the choir began to sing, some people jumped to their feet, raising their arms high in passionate worship. I couldn't join them, though. I was too distraught, and had been since early that morning, when TK received some horrifying information from Jeff Watson. Jeff had promised to keep TK in the loop if anything new came up pertaining to the murder of Clifford White.

We were in TK's office preparing for Pippie's funeral service when Jeff came in. TK and I were still not on good terms, but just like when Clifford Jr. was killed, we came together as a couple to fulfill our responsibilities in the face of death. Little did we know that the two deaths had more in common than just bringing the two of us together.

"Bishop, I have some news I thought you should hear," Jeff said.

"Can it wait until after the service?"

Jeff shook his head. "The department is working around the clock to solve these murders, so I can't stay around until after the service."

"I understand," TK said. "Well, I need to eulogize Pippie Nixon today, so any information you have on Clifford White's murder can wait. Just come back whenever you have a chance." TK still had every intention of helping his friend find his son's murderer, but at the moment he was focused on one of our own flock who'd just lost his life.

"That's just it," Jeff said. "This *is* about Pippie Nixon. And about the other two murders."

TK sat down at his desk. Jeff had his full attention now. "What are you saying?"

I felt dread growing in the pit of my stomach.

"Just like the other two victims, Pippie Nixon was

found with a red *R* on his forehead. The murders are somehow related."

I stifled the scream that welled in my chest. How the hell had Pippie become involved in all of this? If the letter *R* did in fact stand for "rapist," then did that mean Pippie was a rapist too? And then my mind went to an unthinkable place: Did that mean Tia killed Pippie?

Now, as I sat through Pippie's funeral service, I tried to consider every possible angle in my mind; tried to find another explanation for the coincidence, but I kept coming back to the same conclusion. Tia was a murderer. I was left to struggle with my own conscience. When I thought she had killed her rapists, a part of me wanted to protect her, to keep her secret. Now I wasn't so sure. I needed more details. I needed to hear it from her mouth why she would have killed Pippie. She was in the back office with TK, while I remained at the funeral, squirming in my seat. I wanted to know what she was saying to my husband. Was she confessing everything to him? And if she was, how would he handle it—especially if he found out I had been with her outside Vince Taylor's apartment?

When the service was over and everyone had cleared out of the sanctuary, I raced toward TK's office. Aaron was right behind me. He had his own obvious reasons for wanting to talk to Tia.

TK was just coming out of his office, closing the door behind him, when we arrived back there.

"Where is she?" Aaron asked. "I need to talk to her."

"She's gone," TK said calmly. "I let her go out the back door." His expression revealed no emotion. I wondered whether he was struggling to conceal his true feelings, maybe of shock or disgust? Or maybe she hadn't told him anything.

"What do you mean she's gone?"

"I let her go out the back door," he said. "She said she wasn't ready to talk to you yet."

"Bishop, I can't believe you did that. I need to talk to her!" Aaron yelled.

"Not yet, Aaron. You have to trust me. She's not ready."

Aaron started pacing back and forth in the small area. "Well, what did she say to you then? I need to know something. Anything."

TK put his hands on Aaron's shoulders to stop him. Looking into his eyes, he said, "Son, you know I can't tell you what she said. That's between Tia, God, and me, her pastor."

Desiree

40

I had felt like I was on the verge of a nervous breakdown ever since Lynn dragged me away from the church when Tia showed up. We'd worked so hard to put our plan into place, and in one day, it looked like it could all be falling apart. It was bad enough that Pippie's death was affecting me the way it was; Lynn was totally pissed off about that, warning me that I'd be off my game if I let my emotions get in the way. Then Tia had the nerve to stroll into the church like the Queen of England or something. That bitch was supposed to be so far out of the picture by now that no one would even remember her name. Instead, she'd shown up and thrown a monkey wrench in my plans.

Jackson's efforts to drive a wedge between Aaron and Ross had been just about as unsuccessful. Everyone was talking the next day at church about how Pippie's death had brought the two of them back together. They claimed it was God's divine plan to make something good out of something so sad, but I sure didn't see it that way. Nothing we had planned was working. At this point, I wasn't even sure if destroying Aaron's support mechanism was realistic anymore.

That's why I'd driven over to Jackson's office. I was so frustrated by our lack of progress that I was ready to give up. If anyone could reassure me, it was him.

When I entered the office, nobody was there. I didn't even bother to turn on the lights as I sat down to wait for him. The darkness seemed appropriate for my mood. I had phoned him and asked to meet at his office, so I hoped he wouldn't keep me waiting too long.

Twenty minutes later, I heard the doorknob turn, and he entered the room and turned on the light.

"What are you doing in my chair?" he snapped.

"Nice to see you too," I shot back. "You're late."

He gave me a smirk that let me know he had kept me waiting on purpose. It was typical for his arrogant ass to do something like that. Coming around the desk, he stood so close I could feel his breath on me when he spoke. "Can you get out of my chair?"

"Technically, it's my chair, since I paid for it." I sat back, rocking a few times for effect. He might have come up with most of the plan, but clearly I had to remind him who the boss was in this little arrangement of ours.

"In principle, you're right," he said, "but technically, for it to be your chair, I'm gonna need you to give me that next payment you promised."

"At least you're consistent." I chuckled, though I was not feeling the least bit amused. "All you care about is money, money, money." I stood up and moved out of his precious seat.

"I wouldn't say it's the only thing I care about, but it's up there on my list of priorities." He sat down in front of his desk then leaned back and put his hands behind his head. "So you wanted to talk, let's talk. What's on your mind?"

"Ross Parker's on my mind."

"Ross Parker's a nonissue. I got rid of him like the amateur he is," he said confidently. "I drove a wedge between him and Aaron that brought them to blows. You told me that yourself. I am now not only the agent for Aaron Mackie and the First Jamaica Ministries choir, but I manage them too."

"Well, Mr. Manager, I guess you don't keep up with current events."

I have to admit, I liked his look of confusion. "What are you talking about?"

"Aaron and Ross made up last night at Pippie's funeral. They are the best of friends again. That can't be good for our plan," I explained.

He looked a little rattled by the turn of events,

but covered it up quickly. He was too arrogant to admit failure. "A minor setback. Don't worry. I'll take care of Ross. I deal with chumps like him on a regular basis."

"Please do. And what the hell are you doing with the first lady?" I asked. He would never admit it, but I was starting to think he was smitten by her. Maybe my feelings for Pippie as a friend were troublesome, but his desire for Monique was ten times worse. I was worried he wouldn't be able to complete his mission if he was developing feelings for her.

"When I'm ready to seal the deal with Monique, it will be done," he said. Just as I expected, there was no way he would admit that he liked her. He was really starting to piss me off.

"What the fuck's that supposed to mean? I'm not paying you to work on it. You're so busy trying to romance and impress the woman that now the whole plan is falling apart. Why don't you just bed her so we can send the pictures to her husband? He's already on the ropes." I stared him down until the smug smile dropped from his face. "You're sitting there acting all nice and shit. That's not helping me. I want all the people in Aaron Mackie's inner circle destroyed so that he doesn't have any of them. And I want it done soon."

"Fine. I'll deal with it. But I find it interesting

that you're getting on me about handling my business, and you haven't come close to handling yours." He sat back in his chair and smirked because now it was my time to squirm. "Why haven't you slept with Aaron yet? It's the reason you came up here to New York to begin with, isn't it?"

"I'm pretty close to getting what I want from Aaron." I lied, and I was pretty sure he knew it.

"No, you're not. You should have screwed that guy a long time ago," he snapped. "If you want to make sure Tia doesn't come back in the picture, then you better hurry up and get some video of him in bed with the new church secretary." Suddenly the tables were turned; he was in charge, and I looked like an incompetent fool, despite the fact I was the one paying the bills.

"It isn't that easy," I pushed back at him. He knew that Aaron was a devoted fiancé who'd been faithful to his future bride. "He's not like most guys. He's more stuck on her than I thought."

"Well, then find some other way to get her out of the picture," he said. "Hell, for the right price, I'll get her out of it."

"No, I think it's best if Lynn takes care of Tia. She already has a lead on where Tia might be staying."

"Okay, but do me a favor and try not to let her

handle Tia the way she handled Pippie. I've got a feeling Pippie's death is the reason Aaron and Ross are back being buddies."

"What? What are you talking about?" I demanded.

A look passed over his face that I couldn't interpret, but it was quickly replaced by his usual arrogant smirk. "I guess you and Lynn don't talk as much as I thought you did. Oh, well. Every relationship has its secrets," he said, and I was left wondering what he was trying to say. Was he saying Lynn had something to do with Pippie's death? Or maybe he was just trying to stir shit up between me and Lynn. For some reason, he got a kick out of seeing us fight.

"What the fuck are you talking about?" I asked a second time.

"Why don't you talk to Lynn about that? Right now we got more important business to deal with." He shut me down quickly. It would be useless to keep pressing him. If there was one thing I knew about him, it was that he did things only when he damn-well pleased.

"More important things like what?" I asked.

"My money!" He held out his greedy hand. "There's a small balance in the amount of twenty-five grand you owe me."

"Haven't I paid you on time so far?"

"As long as you owe me money, then we have a problem. Now, did you bring the check?"

"And what if I didn't have your money? What would you do then?"

"Remember, I know every single detail of the plan, so if I were you, I wouldn't forget who you're talking to and what I can do to you."

"Uncle Willie, I know exactly who you are." I smiled as I lifted my purse and took out my wallet, writing him a check for the payment I owed him. Thankfully, there was only one more payment due when this whole thing was over. I'd be thrilled to write that last check, and I'd be happy to put some distance between me and my uncle. Family or not, he was one giant pain in the ass—an expensive one, at that.

He snatched the payment out of my hand. "Nice doing business with you. You know you're my absolute favorite niece." He grinned as he raised the check to his mouth to kiss it. "And anytime my niece wants to sit in my chair, it's fine with me."

Tia

41

It's not going to be easy, but one day we're all going to have to put what happened on Washington Street behind us.

Clifford White's words had been echoing in my head ever since the night I confronted him, but even more so now, as I came to one dead end after another in my search for Mark King. Other than his picture in the old yearbook, I had no information on him. No Facebook profile, no number listed in the phone book. All I had to go on now was one small clue: Washington Street. When I left the club that night, Mark King had taken me to a house that he said was his. If he was telling the truth and he did in fact own it, then maybe he was still living there now. Based on what Clifford said, it was safe to assume that house was on Washington Street. The problem was that I had no idea what town it was in. Back then, when I was innocent and trusting, I hadn't even paid attention to where he was driving when I went home with him. The only thing I knew was that we were somewhere on Long Island.

A quick Internet search told me that just about every town on Long Island had a Washington Street. I was pretty sure the drive to his house had only been about half an hour, but it wasn't like I'd been timing it. To be safe, I decided to check every Washington Street in every town within an hour's drive from Queens.

I started my search in Huntington, on the western edge of Suffolk County. I would drive down every Washington Street until I found the two-story colonial that at first had impressed me and then had become the setting for every nightmare I'd had since then.

I drove all day long, stopping only long enough to put more gas in the car and get another cup of coffee. Eight hours later, I was exhausted and frustrated as I drove into Elmont, one of the last towns before Nassau County becomes Queens. This Washington Street was a tree-lined street filled with modest single-family homes that all looked alike. To be honest, it looked like most of the other Washington Streets I'd driven on—until I spotted the house.

"Holy shit," I muttered, my heart pounding. "That's the house."

I stopped in the middle of the street, stunned that I'd actually found it, and that it looked exactly the way it did in my nightmares. The thing that made me scream, though, was the car in the driveway. It was definitely his. The car was the one detail I'd paid attention to that night—his expensive foreign car that impressed me so much it blinded me to the foolishness of my actions.

I felt a shock wave of emotions. Like an avalanche, where one loose rock gives way, and then everything comes rushing at once. And I lost it. My body released years of pain and sorrow and regret. Apparently there is no end to grief; it lies dormant under the surface, until the day it reappears, reminding you that you will never be truly free from it.

I imagined Mark inside the house, lounging on his couch, watching a game and drinking a beer without a care in the world. He didn't think about me. I was nothing to him. Less than nothing.

I must have circled the block fifty times before I finally stopped about five blocks away after the sun went down. I watched that house for the next hour, standing across the street in the shadows, wondering about how I would get myself in there. There was no way I could walk up to the front door and announce my presence. I'd done that with the first one and it hadn't ended too well. I'd barely gotten out alive.

"Tia, you can do this," I said, gathering the nerve to move closer to the house. I pulled the gun out of my purse and headed across the street.

As I stepped near, I saw that the same beige drapes with blue stripes were hanging in the front window. Sneaking around the side of the house, I peered inside a window and saw that the kitchen was just as outdated. A movement inside the house startled me, and I ducked down, but it was too late. Someone had seen me.

I heard a woman's voice, calling out, "Who's there?"

Crouching beneath the kitchen window, I was trying to figure out my best route for escape when a light came on, illuminating the entire backyard. I had lost the cover of darkness. There would be no escaping without being seen.

The back door opened and she came outside. "You there. Stand up, young lady," she said. She had his face. This had to be his mother. Her tattered robe and headscarf had seen better days.

For a moment we just stared at each other.

"I knew eventually one of you would come." She didn't seem the least bit surprised to see me, a stranger, standing in her backyard.

"One of us?" I said.

She pointed to the gun clutched in my hand. "You're here to kill him, right?"

"How…how do you know that?" I asked, confused and scared.

"I've seen the tapes," she said. "I couldn't believe my eyes. That my own son would do the things he did to you girls…No mother wants to believe that her only child could be a monster, but he is who he is." There was no emotion behind her words. This was a woman who had resigned herself to the awful truth a long time ago.

"You know what he did?" I asked, horrified.

"Yes," she answered. The weight of it must have been so heavy, because she dropped down to the ground and sat leaning against the house. Staring straight ahead, she began her explanation. "I had moved away to take a job in Tennessee, thought about staying and eventually retiring one day. He stayed here, rented out the rooms to his college friends, and paid the mortgage. One year after they all graduated, I thought about selling the house, so I came back to clean it out. Started going through closets, cleaning things out, and I found a box of videotapes. They were all neatly labeled and numbered in his handwriting.

"It seemed so unlike him to take that much care with anything, and so I got curious. I started to watch the first one and I got so sick that I almost gave up; but then I realized I needed to watch them all. I needed to see exactly who my son was, so that I couldn't make any excuses for him."

I was crying now, and although her expression remained blank, she had tears running down her face too. "Oh my God. It wasn't just me?"

"No, it wasn't. And I don't blame you for wanting to kill him. I'm going to take you to him." She got up and went over toward the stairs. I thought she was going to climb them, but instead she went to another door that opened into a small room, separated from the rest of the house.

He was in there, watching television like I'd imagined, but he looked nothing like the man who had seduced me and then raped me. His body was slumped over in a wheelchair, his head tilted to one side. Drool traveled down his face and onto his shirt.

"Oh." I didn't know what else to say.

"God does not like ugly. He did all those things to you women, so it had to come back to him. He has Lou Gehrig's disease. He can die in a couple of years, or live like this for the next ten." She walked over and turned off the television. "Go ahead, tell him how you feel. His body may not work, but he understands everything you're saying."

I stood there staring at this semi-vegetable. The man who had brutally torn my soul apart couldn't go to the bathroom by himself.

"Go on," his mother prodded me. "You've come this far."

So I went over to him.

"Daaah," he murmured, nodding his head in jerky little movements as if he was already protesting whatever I was about to say. His blue eyes, strangely alert, watched my every movement.

"You took something from me that I will never, ever get back. My innocence. I used to believe that people were basically good, and you changed that for me," I said in a shaky voice. "What gave you the right to touch me without my permission? To violently abuse me. To rape me!"

"Daah! Daah!" He tried to scream, but his body failed him. He might as well have been neutered, and I was glad.

"You could have walked away when I told you that it was my birthday. When I explained that I had never done anything like this, going home with a stranger. But you still did it. And I hated you. Every moment of every day, I have hated you." I raised the gun and pointed it at him.

"I don't care if you're in a wheelchair. I want you dead. You deserve nothing. Not even the air you're breathing."

His breath became more labored as he twitched his hands, trying in vain to move his wheelchair. He was powerless. He had no choice but to listen to what I came to say to him.

I pressed the gun to the side of his head. This useless motherfucker had hurt too many women. I needed to do this not just for me, but for all the other women he had raped.

His mother caught my eye, and for a full minute we stared at each other.

"Just know that taking a human life isn't something you can change," she said. "I agree that he deserves to die, and he will, but are you willing to destroy your life to do it?"

"So, are you gonna tell on me? After what he did?"

"No, I'm not your maker. That's who you're gonna have to answer to."

As I considered her words, I turned back to look at this drooling, helpless man in the wheelchair. Regardless of what he was now, this was the man who had raped me. My life was already destroyed. I had already traveled too far down this dark road to change things.

"Good-bye, you bastard."

Bishop

42

I was just finishing up my evening prayers when Desiree entered my office carrying the mail and a cup of hot tea for me. I really appreciated her kindness; it was magnified by me receiving the opposite from my own wife. I was still living out of my office, although that little arrangement was about to change.

"Thank you, Desiree," I said as she handed me the tea.

"Bishop, is there anything I can do? Maybe take your suits and shirts to the dry cleaner to have them cleaned and pressed on my way in this morning?" She glanced over at the abundance of clothes I'd shoved into my suitcase in haste. I hated that anyone knew about the problems between me and my wife, but seeing how I'd been living in my office, there was no way to avoid Desiree knowing.

"Sure. That would be really nice." I got up to sort through my suitcase, but she beat me to it.

"Don't worry. I'll do it," she said. I was glad I kept my undergarments in a separate laundry bag.

"Thank you, Desiree. You're a godsend."

"Bishop, I know that I'm not an equal or any-thing, but you do know you can talk to me if you want. It's not like I know anybody here, so you don't have to worry about me gossiping. Pippie was my only friend here." She glanced over at me with a forlorn look on her face. It hadn't even occurred to me how much Pippie's death affected her.

"I'm sorry, Desiree. How are you holding up? I know you and Pippie were close. I'm sorry that I've been so distracted that I hadn't thought to check on you."

"I'm okay. You don't need to worry about me. You knew him so much longer."

"A friend is a friend. Doesn't matter how long you know them, it still hurts the same."

"Thank you. I'm only sorry you're going through so much, Bishop. You remind me of my dad."

"Thank you. That's a great compliment." I sensed that she wanted to talk about her father, but that conversation was not to be, because Monique barged into the room.

"Hello," she called out as she flew in the door, looking way too sexy for church. She wasn't slick at all. She was wearing my favorite red dress with a plunging neckline, the same one she'd worn the night I decided to propose to her. Lord help me, but I was a breast man, and normally that vision would have been enough to sway. Except this wasn't close to normal. She took one look at Desiree with that armload of my shirts, and her mood visibly darkened.

"Sweetie, can you give us a moment?" Desiree, who was smart enough to sense the tension, smiled and left, closing the door.

"TK, when are you going to quit this foolishness and come home?" She leaned in toward me so that I could get a closer view of her mounds of pleasure, but I wasn't about to be manipulated or seduced. I backed away as if I'd been burned—and technically, I had been. It felt important to cut this short.

"Were you with Jackson the other day?" I asked her, wondering if she'd tell me the truth or if it would be one more in a series of lies and omissions. Monique's eyes met mine, accusing.

"What? Were you following me?"

"No, but I had someone following you," I admitted, seeing that my words dropped like a bomb on her because her eyes grew to twice their normal size.

"What?" She actually had the nerve to look offended, as if she hadn't given me reasons, plural, to check and see what the hell was going on between her and Jackson.

Now that I was feeling more in control of my emotions, I walked around to the front of my desk. Leaning against it, I looked her right in the eye.

"You have broken every rule to a marriage," I started with a heavy heart. This would be a very difficult conversation to have.

"You don't understand why I was with him," she said, pleading. "It had everything to do with Tia."

"Tia, huh? Tia doesn't even know Jackson. He didn't show up until after the wedding."

"That's true, but—"

I cut her off, sick of this foolishness. I couldn't bear to hear one more lie. "You know what? I don't have anything more to say. I'll be filing for divorce by the end of the week."

"TK!" she cried out, her voice breaking from the shock. "You can't do that!"

I steeled myself, took a deep breath, and continued because at this point, I didn't really have anything to lose by being honest. "Monique, I've been living in my office, functioning out of a suitcase, and instead of working to get me back, I find out you're out meeting with Jackson. I can't live like that anymore, not knowing if I can trust you. I love you with all my heart, but I almost killed a man over you. Me, a person who has dedicated my life to God. It's better to put an end to this now, before things get even more out of hand."

"Are you serious?" Tears began rolling down her cheeks. I knew that she was broken up, but I couldn't make myself reach out and comfort her. I knew it was not the way a man of God should be acting, and I would certainly pray on it, but at the moment, I felt no sympathy for her. I believed in the sanctity of marriage, and she didn't. It was simple as that; and as much as I hated to see a woman cry, her tears were no longer my business.

"My mind is made up. You broke my trust and my heart, and there is no way in the world to unbreak it."

She wiped her tears and straightened her shoulders, a determined look on her face. "We can get separated, but we're not getting divorced."

"Yes, we're getting divorced." I held my ground, reiterating my decision to move on without her.

"No! Separated, and that's that!" she announced, then got up and strode out of the room.

As I watched her walk away in that red dress, I felt genuine physical pain at the loss of our relationship. I had loved Monique fiercely and completely, even when members of my congregation were trying to convince me she wasn't worthy of the position of first lady. Her recent behavior had shown me that they were more right than I could have imagined. I would have to search my soul deeply before I could understand the lesson God meant for me to learn from this chapter of my life.

Tia

43

It took me a minute or two to get myself together once I reached my car, but I finally drove away with a sense of accomplishment. I had confronted my last demon and defeated my fears. The cloud was lifted. I felt like I was alive again. After all the fear, self-doubt, and sleeplessness, it was surreal to discover that the big, bad rapist in my nightmares had been reduced to a wheelchair-bound invalid, shitting in a bag and drinking through a tube. Never again would I be held hostage to my terror; I would never again worry that they were coming after me.

The freedom was exhilarating, but I was also physically exhausted. Truthfully, it had taken all of my energy to even walk into Mark's home, let alone to do what I had done, but it was well worth it. Now that I had finished what I started, I would be able to release the past.

And now I wanted to put as much distance as possible between me and this place.

From the safety of my car, I took one last look at

the house of horrors, marveling at the woman I had met inside. If you had asked me before that day about the bond between a mother and her child, I would have sworn it was impenetrable. A mother's love means throwing herself on top of a grenade if it means saving her child. The woman in that house, though, didn't conform to any standard definition of the mother-child bond. If someone had come to harm us, my mother would have taken the bullet, no matter what we had done to deserve it. Mark's mother, on the other hand, basically told me her son was a monster and gave me permission to end his life. That was some cold-ass shit right there.

Ready to rid my mind of the dark thoughts that had consumed me for so long, I turned on the radio for the first time in weeks.

"Reunited, and it feels so good..." The old-school Peaches & Herb song was playing, like some sick cosmic joke. The reunion I'd just experienced felt anything but good. I quickly changed the station.

"Don't forget about us..." Mariah Carey's chart-topping vocals reached out to me like a message from the man upstairs. That tune was so spot-on that I couldn't help but giggle at the irony. Boy, did it feel strange to have a lighthearted moment, even by myself in my car. There really was no getting around the fact that Aaron still had my heart, and I deeply believed that one perpetrator at a time, I had finally placed myself in the position to win back my life. A slow smile spread across my lips at the thought of reuniting with Aaron. Would this mean that I could finally move on with my life? That I could allow the man I loved to make love to me?

I picked up my gun off of the front seat, feeling the cold steel in my palm. "Black Beauty, you're going into retirement," I said gratefully.

As badly as I wanted to sleep, I knew that there was one more thing I had to do that night. I picked up my phone and dialed a familiar number.

"Hey, it's Tia. I know it's kind of late, but is it okay if I swing by so we can talk a bit?"

"Come on home, baby girl," Bishop answered, and I felt one step closer to true freedom. I hung up the phone feeling ready to go forward and, most importantly, to tell the truth. It was time to go see my pastor, to cleanse my soul and to let go.

On my way to the church, I made a quick stop at my brother's house to change out of my soiled clothes and wash off the mascara that had run down my face. I wanted to start my life over, and the first step would be to wash away the vestiges of my last dramatic encounter.

By the time I jumped back into the car and pulled

away from the curb, my heart was soaring. I exited the highway near the church, feeling lighter and freer than I had in weeks. I was so tired of running, and returning to First Jamaica Ministries felt like coming home.

I parked close to the entrance, since it was after hours and the lot was nearly empty. If this were Sunday, I'd be lucky to nab a space at the overflow lot a block away.

Shutting off the engine, I pulled down the visor for a final check in the mirror—just in case Aaron happened to be in the building. I almost jumped out of my skin when I saw the reflection of a woman rising up in the seat behind me. Before I could react, she slipped a belt around my neck, pulling it just taut enough to pin me to the headrest.

"You are one dumb bitch," she hissed in my ear. "Don't you know you should never leave your car doors unlocked in the city? I knew you'd return to your brother's house sooner or later, but I had no idea you'd make it so damn easy for me to get at you."

"Who are you?" I croaked through my constricted windpipe.

"Bitch, you're about to die."

My survival instinct kicked in, and I began flailing my arms in an attempt to loosen the noose around my neck. I reached up my hand, trying to snatch it away, but the next thing I knew I was fighting for my life. The more I moved, the tighter she pulled the strap.

My mind went to the gun in my purse, but there was no way I could reach it. The situation was hopeless. I was about to die. After everything I had been through, all the demons I had confronted, why would God bring me this far only to let me die right in front of the church?

He wouldn't, I decided. I was not supposed to go out like this. I had to see Aaron again, to apologize and tell him how much I loved him. With my last bit of strength, I pressed on the horn and held it down, letting out a sustained blast. It startled her for a second, and she loosened her grip on the noose as she tried to pull my arm off the horn. It was just enough of a release to allow me to scream.

We struggled some more as she tried to maintain her grip on the belt and I squirmed in my seat, trying to break free. I reached for the horn again, and that's when I heard the rear door being snatched open. Just like that, the pressure on my neck was released, and my assailant flew out the opposite door.

I stumbled out of the car, coughing and gasping for air.

"Tia! Are you okay?" Bishop grabbed me and held me up.

"Who the hell was that?" I muttered in shock as

we watched the woman booking her ass down the block.

"I don't know who she is, but I've definitely seen her before." We stared at each other, the shock of what just happened striking us mute.

"Did you call the police?" I asked.

"Don't worry about it," he said, with a deadly calm in his voice. "I'm going to take care of it myself."

Desiree

44

I walked up to my apartment and almost pissed my-self when I saw Uncle Willie sitting in his car in front of my stoop. I searched the street to see if any-one I knew was around then quickly opened the door and slid into the passenger seat. That fool had the nerve to smirk as he pulled off.

"What the fuck are you doing here?" I yelled.

"I needed to talk to you." He grinned, amused by my discomfort, like the asshole he was. Every time I saw him, he made me regret even more my choice to involve him in this whole thing.

"You ever heard of a phone? There are church members that live in my building. You could have blown everything."

He shrugged, totally unconcerned with anything but his own agenda. "Your cell phone went straight to voice mail. We need to talk, so here I am."

"My phone's dead. I left my charger at home." I made a mental note to never do that again. The less I had to see of my uncle, the better. I sighed, buckling my seat belt. "So what do we need to talk about anyway? Please don't tell me this is about money again, because I don't wanna hear it until our plan is completed."

"Well, to get right to the point, it is about money. A lot more moneeeeeyyyyy." He dragged out the word like he was rapping. I sucked my teeth, wanting to punch his stupid ass.

"More money for what?" I snapped. "I've paid you everything I owe you so far. It's what we agreed on—and it was more than generous."

He shook his head slowly, ignoring my rising anger. "Well, the situation has changed. The first lady called to tell me that the bishop asked for a divorce. It's only a matter of time until shit comes together." He pulled into a grocery-store parking lot, looking self-satisfied. "So, I think I need a bonus."

"Well, I think you're crazy."

"It doesn't really matter what you think. I need more money. I've developed real feelings for the first lady, and I can't support her without money." He popped the collar of the Hugo Boss blazer that I had purchased, along with numerous other designer pieces. Once I hired him, his broke ass insisted on a $20,000 wardrobe allowance. He told me if he was going to play the part of a successful agent, then he couldn't be dressed in Walmart T-shirts. I fell for it, blinded by my desire to succeed. If I had known it would cause his greed to balloon out of control like this, I never would have bought the stuff. I couldn't give in to his demands now, or he'd keep coming back until he took every last dime I had.

"I don't give a damn if you developed feelings for the Virgin Mary. We had a deal and you agreed, so we're done. I don't even know why we're talking about this anymore. Take me home," I snapped.

"Well, I don't agree anymore."

"A deal is a deal." I said it slowly, as if he had a mental condition that kept him from grasping reality.

"Well, then let me put it in a context that you'll understand," he said coldly. "Let's just imagine I went to the congregation and told them every-thing—I mean *everything*—about you and Lynn and our master plan. Those folks would run your ass out of town so fast . . ."

The last part sent a chill through me. I couldn't bear the thought of being chased out of the church before I had a chance to fulfill my goal.

"How much money would it be worth for you to stop me from having my little crisis of conscience?" he asked.

Part of me was so scared of failing that I wanted to write him a check immediately, but looking at his smug grin, I couldn't let him think he'd defeated me so easily. "Don't get it twisted," I said, forcing myself to stay calm. "I'm not giving you a dime more than we agreed to. And if you do tell anyone about this, I'm not even gonna give you that. You need to just do what you're supposed to and stop this nonsense so you can get paid."

He was unimpressed by my speech and pushed back even harder. "Sure you won't reconsider? Because I'd hate to have to visit you in jail." He pierced me with a look that was meant to scare me.

I rolled my eyes. Now he was trying a little too hard, I thought, making up baseless threats. "Oh, please. I haven't done anything that's going to get me arrested. And even if I had, you're just as guilty as I am."

"Not for the murder of Pippie Nixon I'm not. I had nothing to do with that, but you and your girl Lynn? How much time do you think you're gonna spend behind bars for that murder?"

"Oh, come on, Uncle Willie. Now you're just making shit up to try to scare me. I didn't murder Pippie, and neither did Lynn." Just the thought that he would accuse me of doing something to Pippie had me pissed off. He was really barking up the wrong tree with that accusation.

"Oh my God," he said. "Either you're just plain stupid or more naive than I ever imagined. Maybe you didn't have anything to do with it, but Lynn killed that boy."

"Shut up, Willie! Shut the fuck up!" I jumped right up in his face, grabbing his lapels, ready to beat the black off of him. I didn't care that he weighed twice as much as I did, or that he could crush me. He was stepping way out of line by suggesting that Lynn would do something like that, knowing how I felt about Pippie. "She did not kill Pippie!"

"Yes, she did," he said matter-of-factly. "According to Monique, the cops said Pippie had a bloody *R* on his forehead, just like the others. Do you think that was just coincidence? I sure as hell don't."

The truth was, neither did I. Monique had told him a while back about the bloody *R* found on two other recent murder victims. Supposedly both guys were tied to Tia somehow, and the first lady actually thought Tia had committed the crimes. When Willie told me and Lynn about it, we actually had a good laugh. Lynn even said something like, "That's good to know. If I ever have someone to kill, I'll just put a letter of the alphabet on their head, and the cops will tie it back to Tia."

"She didn't do it," I whispered, not sure if I even believed my own words. I let go of his lapels, frozen in place, as the gravity of his words sank in. At first all I wanted to do was find Lynn and rip her head off, but then I wanted to know, "Why? Why would she do something like that? Pippie wasn't a threat. He was my friend."

"That's why she did it," he replied. "Because he was your friend."

"What are you saying?" I asked, not wanting to believe what he was suggesting—that somehow I was responsible for Pippie's death.

"I'm saying she's in love with you. People do strange things when they're in love. You of all people should know that. Wouldn't you kill someone for somebody you love?"

He already knew the answer to that.

"What am I supposed to do now that I know this?" I asked sadly. When I left Virginia to execute my plan, I had no idea that it would lead to something like this.

"You stick to the plan, that's what you do. You can't bring that boy back, and Lynn is your biggest asset next to me."

As far as I was now concerned, neither one of them was an asset.

"In another two weeks she'll be in Afghanistan, ducking bullets from the Taliban. If God is just, she'll catch one and your misery will be over."

"What?" I shouted. "I'm mad at her, but I don't want her dead." There'd already been too much loss in my lifetime.

"Then act like it. Get over this guy Pippie and move on with our plan...Speaking of which, there's still the issue of my money," he said, bringing the conversation right back to his original purpose. "I need insurance just in case this blows up in our faces."

"I'm not giving you more money."

He sighed, tired of my defiance. "Maybe you're not exactly understanding grown folks' talk. Either you give me the money first thing tomorrow morning, or your shit is on full disclosure, and I will make sure you don't have a chance to get Aaron Mackie. Is that clear enough for you?"

I felt every bone in my body shaking with rage. The fact that this motherfucker was my only living family made his blackmail ten times worse.

"Fine. I will be at your office tomorrow to give you exactly what you deserve."

"I knew you'd see this my way. Don't make no sense that you get to keep all that money to yourself. It's much better to share the wealth." He had the audacity to try to give me a hug. I shoved him away.

"Don't touch me!"

"It's like that?" He laughed, pulling out of the parking lot to head back toward my house.

When Uncle Willie dropped me off, there was a light on in my apartment, which meant that Lynn was there. I bolted from the car, wanting to get away from my uncle and get inside to confront my so-called lover.

Lynn was sitting on the sofa with a freaked-out look on her face, as if she already knew I was on the warpath. I assumed Uncle Willie had called her, giving her a heads-up as soon as I got out of the car. It turned out I was wrong.

"We got a problem," she said the second I walked through the door.

"Damn right we got a problem!" I marched right up to her and slapped her as hard as I could.

"What the—" Surprisingly, she didn't even flinch, just placed a hand on her cheek and looked up at me like she was perplexed as to why I would do that to her.

"Did you kill Pippie?" I shouted. "Did you kill him?"

She stared at me with no response.

"Goddammit, Lynn. Did you kill Pippie?" Inside, I was begging her to say no, though a part of me already knew she wouldn't say that.

Finally, she admitted in a blasé tone, "Yes, I killed Pippie."

I'd never been in a fistfight, but suddenly I knew what it felt like to be punched in the stomach. Things were not supposed to turn out like this. "Why?" I croaked.

"Because I love you. That's why."

"You don't love me. You killed my friend!" I leaped at her, swinging my fists like a maniac. She grabbed my wrists and we wrestled for a minute until she pinned me to the floor.

"Get out! Get the fuck out my house, you dike bitch!" I yelled as I struggled to free myself. It was useless. Lynn was a trained soldier, and I was no match for her strength. Before long I gave up and stopped fighting, lying limp on the floor.

She attempted to explain. "You asked me to come to New York to help you, Desiree. I did what I did because that man was the enemy and you couldn't even see it. He was Aaron's best friend, and nothing good could come out of your friendship with him. He was standing in the way of you achieving your goal. Don't you see? I was helping you."

"I didn't ask you to kill him," I sobbed.

She released my arms and moved away so I could sit up. Then she held my hands and looked into my eyes. "You're right. I fucked up. I was jealous of him, and maybe I overreacted. But I did it for you. I love you, Desiree. All I want is for you to get what you want."

"But I didn't want him to die."

"Of course you didn't," she said. "Because you're a good person. But if you set aside your emotions and are honest with yourself, you know he would have gotten in the way. Ask yourself one question: In the end, what's most important to you, Pippie or Aaron Mackie?"

We both knew the answer to that one. Aaron was the whole reason I'd left Virginia and come to New York in the first place.

"Pippie was just collateral damage," she said, wiping away my tears. "His death wasn't your fault."

I collapsed against her and she held me tight, stroking my hair to soothe me. "I will always protect you, Desiree. I will always do what's best for you."

I turned my face toward hers. "I love you," I said, sealing the proclamation with a deep kiss. Lynn may have done the wrong thing when it came to Pippie, but she would always do the right thing by me. I trusted her. I had to. She was all I had.

"I don't ever want to lose you," she said, stroking my face gently.

We held each other quietly for a while, too emotionally spent for anything else.

"Hey, Des, can I ask you a question?" she said after a few minutes.

"Sure."

"How did you know it was me?"

I swallowed any lingering anger at her and said, "Well, I wasn't a hundred percent sure it was you until you admitted it, but when Uncle Willie told me about the red *R* on Pippie's forehead, I thought—"

"Fuckin' Willie," she spat. "Why couldn't he have just kept his mouth shut?"

I agreed with her on that one. He already knew I was sad about Pippie's death, and then he had to make it worse by revealing that the woman I loved was responsible. If I didn't know better, I'd think he had his own little plan in the works—to destroy me.

"Yeah, fuckin' Willie," I said. "You know he just came to me saying he needs more money? He says he'll reveal our whole plan to the church if I don't give him more."

"What!" She jumped up and started pacing. "Des, that motherfucker won't be happy until he's spent every last dime of your insurance money."

"I know. But if I don't give him the money and he tells it all, I'll never get Aaron."

She stopped pacing and looked down at me with a determined expression. "I will *not* let that happen. All I ever wanted was to make you happy, baby, and I will do whatever it takes." She resumed her pacing. Under her breath, I heard her mumble something along the lines of "That's what I was trying to do tonight."

The tension in her body gave me an uneasy feeling. "Lynn, what are you talking about?" I asked warily.

"The bishop saw me tonight."

"So? He doesn't know who you are."

She corrected me. "He does know me. Remember when he came to your uncle's office to fight over

Monique? I was the one who tried to stop him. He knows me as Jackson Young's secretary."

"Well, did he say anything to you tonight? I mean, it's 'Jackson Young' he has a problem with, not his secretary." I still wasn't understanding why she thought this problem was so serious—but that was only because she hadn't shared the worst details yet.

"He saw me at the church while I was trying to take care of your Tia problem," she admitted.

"My Tia problem?" I repeated, and then it dawned on me what she was implying. "Oh, Lord. Please tell me you weren't doing what I think you were."

She gave me a look that confirmed my fear. "I almost had her, Des. I had the belt around her neck. She would be gone right now if the fuckin' bishop hadn't rolled up on me."

"Shit! Shit, shit, shit! What the fuck were you thinking?" I yelled.

"Desiree, I'm sorry, but you did say to take care of her."

"Yeah, but I didn't say kill her, dammit!" Now I was the one pacing back and forth frantically. "Did he see your face?"

Her shoulders slumped. "Yeah. He looked right in my eyes," she said in total defeat. She had fucked up beyond belief.

"We've gotta go," I said.

"Where?"

"To see my uncle. He's gotta pack up that office and disappear before the shit hits the fan. Thanks to you and him, our timetable just got sped up."

Ross

45

"Hey, baby. It's me. Please, please, please call me back. I know I've fucked up, and I would do anything to take that back, but I can't do anything if you don't call me. Please!" I hung up the phone, wondering if Selena would even listen to this or the other fifteen voice mail messages I'd left her since she kicked me out a few days ago. I'd already given up on texting, because that wasn't getting any response either. I picked up the phone to dial her again, but what was the point? If she didn't want to talk to me, then she didn't have to. It wasn't like I could go to her mother's house and talk to her. Tank was living there, too, ready to rip my head off if I came anywhere close to his sister.

I put down my cell and picked up my Starbucks latte out of the cup holder, staring out at the small two-story office building. I'd been sitting outside Jackson's office for an hour. I still couldn't believe a big-time agent would set up shop on a nondescript street in Queens. He would have to be getting his clients some killer deals for them to come to this rinky-dink joint when they could be with management firms in the heart of Manhattan. This location was just one of the many things about him that just didn't add up.

Now that I was no longer managing Aaron or the choir, I had plenty of time on my hands to figure out just what the fuck Jackson was up to. I didn't necessarily know what I expected to find, but I just couldn't shake the gnawing feeling that the dude was hiding something. After sitting outside his office for two hours, though, I was starting to get the feeling that this was not the way to gather information.

On the off chance that he might have some useful information, I decided to call Bentley Simpson, who had been my mentor when I first got into the entertainment business. I'd started out in Atlanta, representing some young actors trying to break into the business. An established agent, Bentley had taken a liking to me and kind of taken me under his wing. "Black folks have to stick together down here in Black Hollywood," he'd told me. I hadn't spoken to him more than once or twice since moving north to represent Aaron and the choir, but I still had major respect for Bentley. Maybe he knew something about Jackson, or could at least help me put a finger on what was off about this guy.

"Ross Parker, how the hell are you?" he said when he answered. I was happy to know he still had my name programmed into his phone. "Tell me you're calling with some good news."

"Isn't my call good news enough?" I joked. "How the hell are you doing since your retirement?"

"Hell, not as good as you. When are you gonna bring that boy out here and take over our choir, put it on the map?" he pressed me. Bentley was on the board and very involved with his church in LA. It had a celebrity-filled congregation, and photographers lined up outside the doors every Sunday to catch a glimpse of the black Atlanta elite. Bentley had been after me to convince Aaron to take over his church choir ever since.

"You know we can't leave," I said, neglecting to tell him that I was no longer managing Aaron. It would be too embarrassing to admit to Bentley, a powerhouse in the business who never would have allowed himself to be duped by someone like Jackson. "And besides, I don't trust those Atlanta tornadoes," I said with a laugh.

"You get used to them. It's just a little rocking and rolling on the road. Now, I know that Bishop Wilson runs a megachurch, but we have a *mega* megachurch. The deal we could offer you two would blow your mind," he bragged, always the super salesman.

"Listen, we just signed a deal with Johnson Morris Agency," I said, avoiding the whole truth again.

"You mean the Johnson Morris Endeavor agency? They merged a couple of years ago. Now they're bigger and better."

"Oh, yeah. That's right." I didn't want to admit I hadn't known about the merger. Alarm bells were ringing in my head, though. Jackson had presented himself as coming from Johnson Morris; never once had he mentioned Endeavor. Just one more thing about him that was suspect.

"Listen, Bentley, I was wondering if you knew an agent by the name of Jackson Young. He's in his early forties, supersmooth. I know you agents are tough, but this guy is something else." I didn't want to come out and call the guy an asshole, just in case they were close friends or something.

"Jackson Young! Whew, I haven't heard that name in a couple of years, and frankly, I'm perfectly okay with that. Talk about a shark. He gives new meaning to the phrase 'by any means necessary.' That guy will sell out his mother for the chance to make money." Okay, so now I definitely knew they weren't friends! Everything he said about Jackson squared with the impression I had of him. I guess this guy made enemies wherever he went.

"Thanks, man. That's kind of what I thought. Just wanted to make sure I wasn't jumping to conclusions."

"Anytime," he said. "Listen, I've got to run, but give me a call next time you're headed out to ATL. I'll take you and your wife out to this jazz club that just opened up. Place is jumping every night of the week."

Again, I couldn't bear to tell him the truth about me and Selena. Damn, I really had fallen far since the last time I spoke to Bentley.

"Sure thing, Bentley," I said, trying to keep the feeling of failure out of my voice. "I'll be in touch."

I was about to end the call, when Bentley spoke up. "Hey, Ross, just do me a favor, okay?"

"What's that?"

"Jackson Young is dangerous and connected, so please just stay the hell out of that white boy's way." With that, he hung up.

Still holding my phone, I stared up at the office building with Bentley's words echoing in my head. *White boy.*

Unless dude had the best tan in the world, there was no way that the man in this office in Queens was Jackson Young from Johnson Morris. This was even bigger than I'd imagined. That loudmouth motherfucker was a sham, a bragging flimflam artist. Of course, now the question was: Who the hell was he? And what did he want with Aaron and the choir?

I leaned back in my seat, running through everything I knew about this guy—what little there was. I remembered the first day he'd shown up in the bishop's office, right after Tia left Aaron at the altar. What a fucked-up time to show up and make a proposal like he did. And then to ogle the bishop's wife the way he did... That was it! This wasn't about the choir at all.

I snatched up my phone to call Aaron. He could help me make sense of all of this. Together we could make a plan to put a stop to all of this shit before it tore apart the whole church.

Aaron's cell went immediately to voice mail, which meant he'd turned it off. He usually kept that thing on and as close to him as possible. He never said it, but I knew it was because he was still hoping Tia would call him one day. Why today, of all days, had he turned it off?

A car pulled up near the spot where I'd been sitting for two hours. Two women got out, and as they passed by my car, I had to do a double take. One of them was Desiree, the new church secretary. What a weird coincidence that she was in the same neighborhood as Jackson Young's office. I wondered if she lived in one of the nearby apartments.

She was caught up in a conversation with the

other woman, so she didn't notice me. It was just as well, because I sure didn't want to explain what I was doing there.

Things got even more interesting when I watched the two of them cross the street. If I hadn't seen them up close, I would have thought the other woman was a sixteen-year-old boy, with her buzzed hair, baseball cap, and baggy jeans. The boyish one reached out and took Desiree's hand, which was intriguing enough, but I nearly lost it when they stopped on the sidewalk and she pulled Desiree in for a kiss. I'm not talking about no peck on the cheek, either. These two were going at it, tongue and all. You could not have paid me to believe that the demure church girl who worked in the bishop's office was into this kind of shit if I hadn't just seen it with my own eyes.

When I tore my eyes away from their activity, it finally dawned on me that their presence in this neighborhood was not a coincidence. Their make-out session was happening right in front of the entrance to Jackson's office.

"What the fuck is going on?" I asked myself out loud. How the hell was Desiree connected to Jackson Young? I was starting to get a really bad feeling that this whole thing was much bigger than just me losing Aaron and the choir.

I opened my phone's camera app and started

recording. They finally broke the kiss, the butch one wiping her mouth, and then they entered Jackson's office together. I didn't know yet what the connection was between them and that motherfucker, but something told me this video would prove valuable later.

Desiree

46

It was a little after nine in the morning when we climbed the stairs to Uncle Willie's office. After a long, frantic night of searching for him to no avail, we were running on pure adrenaline. We hadn't gone back to our place for fear that the cops would be out looking for Lynn. Instead, we'd fallen asleep with our clothes on in a sleazy motel, where I tossed and turned all night. My whole plan was falling apart, and now my first priority was to protect Lynn. If that meant giving Uncle Willie the money so that he would leave town, then so be it.

I had asked Lynn to wait for me at the motel, not wanting her anywhere near the office where the bishop knew she worked, but she wouldn't hear it. She wanted to protect me just as much as I wanted to protect her. She didn't say it, but I think she wanted one more chance to cuss Uncle Willie out before he left town. Those two had always had it out for each other.

Lynn pushed the door open and walked into his

office first. Willie was leaning back in his overpriced
Aeron chair, his feet propped up on the desk like
some big shot. His face broke into a grin at the sight
of the envelope I held in my hand.

"Glad to see you, girls." He glanced at his watch.
"And right at the start of business hours too. I'm
happy that you're so punctual." He laughed jovially,
as if we were there for a social visit.

"Why the fuck weren't you answering your phone
last night?" Lynn said.

Uncle Willie frowned at her. "Why is that any of
your business?" He looked at me. "In fact, this is between me and my niece. Your ass doesn't need to be
here at all."

Lynn took a step toward him, her fists clenched.
"Motherf—"

"Lynn, wait." I stopped her with an outstretched
hand. "Let's just give him the money so we can all
get out of here."

Uncle Willie nodded. "Yes, you can give me my
bonus, and then you two can get to steppin'. I need
to go buy myself a fly new suit before I go pay a visit
to Monique tonight."

"No, motherfucker, it's not gonna go down that
way," Lynn said. "She's gonna give your greedy ass
that money, but only on one condition."

"What might that be?" he asked with a conde-
scending smirk. He clearly thought he was in con-

trol of this situation, and seemed to be amused by the idea of us making any demands on him.

"You take the money and get the hell out of town."

He looked at me. "Is your girl stupid, Desiree? Didn't you explain everything to her? I'm going to get Monique; there is no way in hell I'm leaving town."

Lynn charged at his desk and got in his personal space. "Yes, you are leaving town. Some things came up, and you need to be out of this office in the next ten minutes."

Even with Lynn right up in his face, he didn't lose his cool. He took his feet off the desk and sat up, folding his hands calmly in front of him. He looked at me and asked, "What is she talking about?"

"She had a little run-in with Tia last night."

"So, what does that have to do with me? If anything, she's the one who should be getting out of town."

"It's more serious than that," I said, wishing he would stop asking questions and just get going.

"What are you not telling me?" he asked suspiciously. "How do I know y'all aren't just making up this shit to cut me out?"

I sighed, realizing it was stupid of me to ever think he would leave just because I told him to.

"Okay, it was more than a run-in. She tried to kill Tia."

He actually laughed. "Damn, girl, you have absolutely no self-control, do you? The army taught you well. You're a killing machine."

"Willie, shut up and listen for once, will you? The bishop spotted Lynn, and he knows she was working as your secretary. The cops could show up here at any time."

"Oh, now I see your dilemma, but I still don't see what that has to do with me. I'll just tell the cops I fired her. Maybe I'll even tell them she tried to attack me, and now she's going after my clients at First Jamaica Ministries."

"What the fuck is wrong with you?" Lynn yelled at him, her chest heaving up and down. She looked like she was about ready to explode.

"I've got other interests in New York, namely Monique Wilson. I'm not leaving because you fucked up."

"Look, Uncle Willie, just take the check and get the hell outta here," I pleaded. The way Lynn's temper was escalating, things could only get worse. I envisioned the cops busting in while the two of them were in the middle of a fistfight.

"I told you that he was a selfish, limp-dick motherfucker," Lynn snapped.

"And you're a stupid dike who can't do anything

right," he shot back. "I don't know how my niece can stand your ass. To tell you the truth, I was rooting for that boy Pippie to get with her."

That was it. Lynn snapped, and she was over the desk and on top of him in no time. It happened so fast I didn't have time to react. Uncle Willie reacted, though. He threw Lynn off of him, and she landed on her ass, angrier than a hornet.

Uncle Willie stood over her, laughing. "Ha! Some soldier you are. You'll be dead in no time when they deploy your ass back to the Middle East."

In a rage, Lynn jumped up from the floor, pulled a knife out of her jacket, and dove at Willie.

"Lynn, no!" I screamed, but it was too late. She had already plunged the blade into his chest.

"I *am* a motherfuckin' soldier. What you got to say about that now?" she yelled.

There was silence from Willie.

She turned around to me, a wild look in her eyes. The knife was still sticking out of Willie's chest.

"What did you just do?" I whispered as I backed away from her slowly, bumping into the wall behind me.

Lynn came toward me, holding out her hand, but I was too afraid to move. "Come on, Des. He's not a threat to you anymore," she said, still hyped up on adrenaline.

I shook my head. How the hell had everything

gone so far off the rails? I couldn't move. I just needed a minute to think.

"Come on, babe," she said. "We just have to—Oh, shit! We have to go now!" she yelled as she looked out the window behind me.

The alarm in her voice shocked me out of my stupor. "Oh my God. The cops are here?"

"No," she said, grabbing my hand and dragging me out of the office and into the ladies' room across the hall. "The bishop is coming in the building."

As we crouched down in the bathroom, we heard slow footsteps passing by the door. My breathing became more rapid; I felt like I was on the verge of a panic attack.

Lynn put her hands on my shoulders and whispered, "Des, calm down. I got this. You know I will always protect you."

She cracked open the door and peeked down the hall. "He just went in the office," she said. "We don't have much time."

I didn't know what her plan was, but I was incapable of doing anything at this point, so I had to put all my trust in her. She pulled out her cell phone and dialed 911.

In a panicky voice, she whispered, "Yes, I just saw a man with a knife go into 207-97 Street in Forest Hills, second floor, screaming and shouting like a lunatic. He said he was going to kill the man inside. Hello? Hel—"

I watched her hang up the phone in the middle of her last "hello" then pull out the battery. She turned to me, giving me a smile that was meant to reassure me: She would always take care of me.

"It's now or never. It's time to go finish what we started. Take care of the last part of your plan and get the hell out of New York."

I nodded, and she grabbed my hand. With one last look down the hall to be sure the coast was clear, we bolted out of the building.

Ross

47

I stayed outside of the office building in Queens, waiting to see what would happen next. Would the church secretary and her girlfriend come out alone, or would Jackson be with them? If the three of them were together, I would definitely be following them. I needed to gather as much information as possible to put the pieces of the puzzle together. In light of what Bentley had told me, this guy was likely an imposter, and I needed to know what was driving his game. Why was he consistently sticking his nose in church matters, always with the outcome of broken relationships? Dude was definitely up to something. I just had to figure out what it was.

To satisfy any lingering doubt, I picked up my phone and had Siri find the number for the Johnson Morris Endeavor agency in Manhattan.

A professional-sounding secretary picked up on the first ring. "Johnson Morris Endeavor. How may I direct your call?"

"Can I please speak to Jackson Young?" I said.

"I'm sorry. Mr. Young works out of our Los Angeles office. I can give you the direct number and his extension if you'd like."

"Thank you. That would be great. Oh, and can I have the number to your Queens, New York, satellite office too?"

"Sir, I'm sorry, but we don't have a Queens office."

I hung up the phone, satisfied that I was right. The guy in this building was posing as Jackson Young, and this office building was a front for something else. The first order of business was to get Aaron to destroy the contract he had signed with this fake. I hoped to God that he had read all the fine print. The choir had been winning a few competitions lately, and it would be a shame if this guy had tricked Aaron into signing something that gave away any cash prizes they received.

Unfortunately, Aaron's phone went directly to voice mail again. Next I tried the bishop's number, which rang a few times but also went to voice mail. I put away my phone and turned on the car, pulling away from the curb. I would head to the church to see if either one of them was there.

When I got to the corner, I was shocked to see the bishop's car pass by me, headed in the direction of Jackson's office. What the hell was going on? First the church secretary and now the bishop? I beeped my horn, but he didn't look in my direction. Instead, his attention was focused straight ahead; his face wore an expression of pure anger. Maybe he was putting the pieces together too—at least I hoped that's what was going on.

I circled back around the block, thinking I could catch him before he went in the building. He needed to know what I'd discovered. Maybe we could go in and confront Jackson together.

By the time I returned to the building, it appeared I was too late. I saw the bishop's car parked in the spot I had vacated, but he was nowhere in sight. I decided to find another parking space and go into the office building myself, offer the bishop some backup. It was time to face this fucking pretender and demand some answers.

I pulled into a space and turned off the car. Just as I stepped out onto the sidewalk, I spotted Desiree and her little friend coming out of the building. Unlike before, when they paused to get all lovey-dovey, this time they looked nervously up and down the block like two competitors in the Hunger Games before racing to Desiree's car. Her tires squealed when they took off, obviously in a hurry to put some distance between them and that building. I wasn't sure what the hell was going on in there, but those two sure didn't want any part of it.

As I stood on the sidewalk watching Desiree's

car round one corner, I heard another car barreling down the road from the other direction. I turned around to see an NYPD cruiser coming to a screeching halt in front of Jackson's office.

What the fuck was going on?

Two uniformed cops got out of the cruiser and ran into the building. Not long after, a second car arrived, this one an unmarked black sedan. The plainclothes cops from that car, a man and a woman, ran into the building with their guns drawn. This could not be good. All of a sudden, I was concerned for the bishop's safety. Shit had gotten deep in a hurry.

I wanted to race up the stairs behind them, but two more police cars pulled up and more cops ran into the building with their weapons in full view. My instincts as a black man in America kicked in: You do not run behind police with guns drawn unless you want to be shot by those cops.

So, I stood outside the building with a growing crowd of noisy onlookers. The fact that I didn't hear any shots was a small comfort, but I still had no idea what was happening in there. The cop standing near the crowd to keep us at a safe distance was carrying his radio. My heart sank when I heard this transmission: "Cancel the bus and send a meat wagon." I had watched enough *Law & Order* to know what that meant. They didn't need an ambulance at the scene;

they needed the coroner's truck. Someone was dead inside that building.

I started praying silently for the safety of Bishop Wilson. A short time later, my prayers were answered, but not in the way I had hoped. Bishop Wilson came out of the building on his own two feet. He wasn't dead, but he was being escorted by the two plainclothes cops...with his hands cuffed behind his back.

Bishop
48

Times like this, the only thing I had was my faith in God. I couldn't quite believe that I was sitting in a police station, my hands chained to a desk. It felt like some bad mid-'80s detective movie, except this was all too real.

I'd invoked my Miranda rights, which meant the police couldn't talk to me until my lawyer was present. That didn't mean they would stop talking *about* me, though. Every time I glanced up, I'd catch cops staring at me, huddled together in conversation. It wasn't every day that a big-time preacher from the largest black church in the borough was caught holding a murder weapon over a dead body. Considering the number of famous people who attended services at my church, this had to be pretty damn close to a celebrity arrest. The officers were clearly getting a kick out of the drama.

A young black cop walked by the gossiping group, but he didn't join in their laughter. He nodded sadly as he passed by me, and I felt a terrible wave of guilt, like I'd let that man down. I was a well-respected leader in the black community, and it must have been hard for him to see me in this position, so far fallen. Of course, I wasn't guilty of the murder, but he had no way of knowing that. And I was definitely guilty of poor judgment. Until my dying day, I would be trying to understand why I chose to go to Jackson's office instead of just calling the police after Tia's attack. My jealousy and desire for revenge against Jackson Young had turned out to be my own undoing, and now I was truly scared that it might land me behind bars.

"Bishop?"

I looked up to see Keisha Anderson coming toward me. She was a cop, but she was also a member of my church, and I could see the pain in her eyes too. I owed Keisha a lot. If she hadn't been at the murder scene, who knows if I would even be alive at the moment? Before they cuffed me, a couple of the officers seemed hell-bent on roughing me up. I didn't know if it was my elevated status in the community or my race, but they seemed to have it out for me. In their minds I was already guilty without the benefit of a trial. If Keisha hadn't stopped them, I could have been just one more name on a list of detainees abused by the police department.

"Hello, Keisha," I said, feeling happy to see her and humiliated at the same time.

She looked down at the chains that held me to the desk, giving me an apologetic look. If she didn't know for sure that I was innocent, she definitely wanted to believe it.

"Bishop, we're going to take you down to Central Booking in about ten minutes. Ross Parker would like to have a few words with you, if that's okay."

This surprised me. I hadn't been given a phone call yet, so how had Ross found me here?

I nodded, and she led me to a small room, where she chained me to another desk.

Ross came in and sat down in a chair on the other side of the desk. Keisha sat at another desk about five feet away, but she looked like she was trying her best to respect our need for privacy by busying herself with paperwork.

"Ross, I didn't do it!" I blurted out.

"I know you didn't do it, Bishop," he said firmly, and I was flooded with a wave of relief. After being in a room full of people laughing at my predicament, it felt good to know someone had total faith in me.

He leaned in closer and spoke quietly. "Bishop, I was there."

I looked at him, wide-eyed. "You were there?"

"I always knew there was something wrong with that guy. I was trying to gather information. I wanted proof that I could bring to you and Aaron, instead of some gut feeling."

I nodded. "I had that same gut feeling. I just wish I had called the police instead of taking matters into my own hands. Look where that got me," I said, glancing down at my chains.

"You weren't the only one in his office this morning," Ross said. Keisha shifted in her chair. She didn't look in our direction, but it was clear she was paying attention to everything that was being said.

"Ross, tell me what you saw," I prodded. His information might hold the key to my freedom. The fact that he had been at the scene at all today felt like divine intervention. What had led him to spy on Jackson on this of all mornings?

"Your secretary was there this morning too, with another woman."

"You saw Desiree at Jackson Young's office?" I asked. "What was she doing there?"

"First of all, his name is not Jackson Young. The guy is a fake. But I'll tell you about that later. Right now we need to figure out what happened up there and get you out of here."

I nodded. "So what was Desiree doing there?" I asked again.

He shrugged. "I don't know, but she and her

friend flew out of there in a big hurry not long after you went inside."

This confused me. If they left the building after I went in, how had I not seen them? There were still so many unanswered questions, but I prayed that at the bottom of all of this was the proof of my innocence.

"This woman that she was with—what did she look like?"

He pulled out his phone and opened up his video app. "This is them. I took it this morning when they were going in the building. I couldn't figure out what Desiree would be doing at the office, but I didn't get a good feeling." He turned the phone to show me the picture. The mystery woman was turned sideways, pressed up against Desiree, but there was no mistaking her.

"That's the woman who attacked Tia last night!" I shouted.

With that, Keisha got up from her desk and approached us. "Ross, I think you need to get the bishop a lawyer. Quick."

He nodded then looked at me. "Anyone in particular?"

"Call Monique and tell her to get in touch with John Simpkins."

"You sure?" he asked.

"Yes. He may be an arrogant ass, but he's one of

the best attorneys in the business, and right now, he's exactly what I need."

"Are you going to be all right here, Bishop?"

Keisha said to Ross, "Go take care of that now. I'll make sure the bishop is okay. And here's my number. Call me if anything comes up."

Aaron

49

The rumbling in my stomach reminded me that I hadn't eaten anything since the night before. Ever since Pippie's funeral, where Ross and I aired our differences, my creative juices had been flowing. It was a relief, because when Tia left me, I was worried that I would never feel inspired to write another song. Now I was finally in the groove again, and I'd been so wrapped up in writing this morning that I hadn't noticed how many hours had gone by. It was past noon and I was suddenly starving. I jotted down a few more notes on the paper and then put everything away in my desk in the choir room.

I decided to stop by the bishop's office to see if he wanted to grab lunch with me. We hadn't talked in a while, and I wanted to check in with him to see how he was holding up in light of his marital issues.

When I got to the church that morning, it was a little before nine, and the place was empty.

Strangely, it was now past noon and there was still no one around. Desiree was not at her desk. I knocked on the bishop's door and got no answer, so I peeked my head in his office. It was empty too.

I pulled out my phone, thinking I would try his cell. That's when I saw that a text had come through while I was working on my music. The ringer was turned off, so I hadn't heard the text alert. The name on the screen brought an instant smile to my face. I had begun to think I would never hear from her again, and as much as I'd been trying to pretend I was over her, there was nothing I wanted more than another chance with Tia. This text was the first indication that it might actually be possible.

THINKING OF YOU, was all it said, but it was enough to send my heart soaring.

I texted back: SAME HERE. I HOPE YOU ARE WELL.

I waited a few minutes to see if she would reply. If she did, I would ask her to call me so we could talk in person. I longed to hear her voice. Unlike the way I acted at the funeral, this time I would not demand answers. I would not give her a reason to run away again.

I turned the ringer back on, but unfortunately my phone remained silent. There was no response from Tia. Still, the fact that she had texted at all was a good sign. I chose to remain hopeful that she would be in touch again at some point.

In the meantime, I still needed to get something to eat. I left the bishop's office and headed toward the back exit. Tia's text had made me so happy. I really wanted to talk to someone about it, so I pulled out my phone again to call the bishop. As I stepped outside, I was looking down at the screen and almost ran right into Desiree.

"Oh, hey, Desiree. Sorry about that," I said. "You just getting here?"

She looked nothing like her usual self. Her makeup was smudged, her hair was messy, and her clothes were so wrinkled they looked like she'd slept in them. Even more unusual, though, was her demeanor. She usually had that sweet, demure Southern-girl thing going on, but now she was stiff, almost robotic.

"Aaron, do you have time to talk?" she muttered. "I have something on my mind."

To tell you the truth, she was creeping me out a little. The way I was feeling after getting that text, I didn't want anything to bring me down, and I just got the sense that that's exactly what talking to Desiree would do. She looked like she had a lot on her mind, and while it might sound coldhearted, I didn't want to be the one she unloaded on at that moment.

"Um, I was just on my way out to get something to eat," I said. "Can I stop by your desk when I get back? Once I get some food in my belly, I'll listen to everything you have to say."

"Oh, no problem." She wasn't making eye contact with me. Something over my shoulder must have caught her attention, because that's where her eyes were focused as she spoke to me.

"Yeah, so, um, I'll see you later, okay?" I said, and then left her standing there.

I got to my car and hit the remote to unlock the door. I had just reached out for the handle when I heard a click and felt someone approach me fast from behind. Immediately my body tensed up, sensing that I was in danger.

I turned around slowly to see a gun pointed at me. At first I thought it was held by a young boy in baggy jeans and a baseball cap, but then she spoke and I realized it was a woman.

"Don't move," she said.

Inside I was freaking the fuck out, but I knew that I couldn't show fear. That was one lesson I learned while in prison. Fear was the quickest way to get yourself killed.

"I really don't think you mean to point that at me." I spoke calmly. I didn't know if this woman was trying to rob me, but I wasn't going to do anything stupid.

"Yes, I do," she snapped.

I tried another approach. "Young lady, this is the house of the Lord," I said a little more sternly.

She fixed her face into a scowl. "Like I really give a shit."

"Here, you can have all of my cash." I reached into my pocket, opened my wallet, and tried to hand her the money. She knocked it out of my hand onto the ground.

She kept her gun trained on me, but turned her head to the side and spoke loudly. "You want me to do it?"

For a second I didn't know if she was a crazy person talking to herself, but then I heard a familiar voice answer, "Go ahead."

I felt a searing pain in my skull right before I hit the ground, unconscious.

Monique

50

Every time I thought about TK putting me out, I felt the veins in my neck wanting to pop. Okay, so technically he didn't walk me to the door and toss me out along with all my things, but telling me that he was through staying in his office and that I had to go was the same thing. I spent the night alone in my house, the one I'd owned before I married him. I hadn't been back there since Tia left, and let's just say that her housekeeping skills left room for improvement.

Coming back to our house the next day to gather some more of my things, I hoped TK was home. I was determined to talk him out of his desire to end our marriage. He might have forgotten it, but we were a great team, and to have his fit of jealousy and stubbornness ruin our marriage made no sense. We weren't emotional teenagers having a lovers' quarrel; TK and I were grown, and we needed to pull together and set an example for the rest of the congregation. Mature adults don't just cut and run at the first sign of trouble. Hell, as far as I was concerned, TK was one lucky man, given the fact that I remained faithful even when Jackson made it clear on several occasions that he wanted some of this good stuff. I wasn't even tempted. Unlike TK, I knew what a good thing we had.

When the house phone rang, I debated answering it. It could have been my husband, checking to see if I had left and the coast was clear. Then I realized that was ridiculous. Like I said, we were mature adults, and I would act as such. If it was TK on the line, I would tell him that he needed to get back to the house and deal with me. I was his wife, and I deserved to be treated with respect, not like some common floozy he could just kick to the curb. I picked up the phone.

"Hello." Even I could hear the tension in my voice. Damn, I had to do better than that.

"Hello, First Lady. It's Officer Jeff Watson. How are you today?"

"I'm fine, Jeff. How are you?" I slipped into my professional wife voice, the one that immediately put people at ease. I hoped that this call would be short, though, because I didn't know how long I could keep up the facade. My mind was too full of my own problems. Pretending that everything was all right when my marriage was in jeopardy was no easy task.

"Is the bishop around?" he asked.

"No, he isn't. Can I give him a message?" I reached for the pad and paper I kept handy in every room. When you're married to a man of the cloth, people call your home nonstop. There is no such thing as business hours. TK was available to his flock twenty-four hours a day.

"I told the bishop that I would give him a call if anything came up with regards to Cliff's murder."

My heart rate increased instantly. I'd been so wrapped up in my marital problems that I hadn't bothered to try to get in touch with Tia after she came to Pippie's funeral and slipped out the back. She had been in the back of my mind, though. What if Jeff was calling to say they had found evidence that implicated Tia in the murders? Suddenly I wasn't in a hurry to get him off the phone. I wanted information.

"Oh, yes. My husband is very concerned about that. Anything you can tell me to put his mind at ease, he would really appreciate."

"Well, something came up," he said, hesitant to tell me more.

"What?" I tried not to sound impatient, but I was desperate and fearful.

"Another boy was murdered. Just like the others."

I struggled to catch my breath. This was bad. Really bad. "And you think they're related?"

"This gentleman was shot in the head, same as the other three, same bloody *R* on his forehead."

I stifled a scream that threatened to escape. I was terrified for Tia. She had really gone off the deep end.

Somehow, I managed to speak. "How terrible."

"Please tell the bishop we're adding more detectives to the case. We won't rest until the killer is caught."

I squeaked out a good-bye to Jeff. "Thank you. I will make sure that TK gets your message." I hung up as quickly as I could.

I desperately wanted to talk to someone, and the first person to come to mind was Jackson. He was the only one who knew of my suspicions, the only other person who knew Tia had been at Vinnie Taylor's apartment the night he was killed. But reaching out to Jackson had gotten me into too much trouble with TK already. I didn't even want to risk his number showing up on my outgoing calls list. That would be the final nail in the coffin for our marriage.

Calling TK was not an option. He was so mad at me lately that he wouldn't even answer my phone calls. Besides, he would be furious that I hadn't come to him sooner.

The only other person I could think of was Aaron. He knew Tia better than anyone. Maybe he would know what to do—whether it was to find Tia and get her to confess, or to help her go on the run. Either way, I just knew I couldn't bear all of this news on my own.

When Aaron didn't answer his phone, I jumped in my car and headed to the church, hoping to find him there. In the church parking lot, my phone started ringing in my purse. I pulled it out, hoping to see Aaron's name on the screen. It wasn't him.

"Hello, Ross," I said, trying to keep the panic out of my voice.

Ross, on the other hand, didn't do anything to mask the anxiety in his own voice. "First Lady, we have a major problem," he said.

"Oh my goodness. What is it?" I asked in alarm. What could be worse than what Tia was doing?

"The bishop has been arrested. He needs you to call a lawyer."

"What!" I shrieked, almost dropping the phone. "Tell me what's going on, Ross. Where is TK? I need to go see him."

"First Lady, I will explain everything to you as soon as I can. Right now he needs you to call a lawyer named John Simpkins."

Three words jumped out at me: *He needs you.*

"I'm going home right now to find John's number. I'm sure TK has it in his contacts list," I said. "I'll call you as soon as I get to the house."

Throwing the car into reverse, I raced out of the church parking lot. Tia's problems would have to wait. My husband needed me.

Ross
51

After our talk, the bishop was sent down to Central Booking to be arraigned. Thankfully, I was able to get in touch with Monique, and although she was devastated, she was working on getting him a lawyer. Hopefully he wouldn't remain in lockup for too long.

Meanwhile, I headed toward the church. With Desiree and her girlfriend on the loose, the bishop asked me to meet up with Tia at the church. They'd already tried to attack her once, so he didn't want to take any chances until we figured out what the hell was going on.

"Tia!" I called out her name when I saw her going into the church. She turned at the sound of my voice, stopping to wait on the steps for me. I got out of the car, waving my hands frantically for her to come away from the church building. For all I knew, Desiree and her friend were waiting inside the door for Tia.

She came down the steps toward my car with

a confused frown on her face. "What's going on, Ross?"

"Get in." I opened the passenger door for her.

"What?" She didn't move.

"I know you're supposed to meet the bishop, but he asked me to come and get you."

"What's going on?" she asked, looking nervous. "Bishop Wilson told me to meet him here."

"Look, I can't tell you all the details right now, but there's a lot going on. It's not safe for you to be around the church. Just please get in the car."

Her eyes opened wide with fear and she climbed into the car without further protest.

When I got into the driver's seat, she put a hand on my arm to stop me from turning on the car. "Ross, please. You're really scaring me—and God knows my nerves are already shot. Please just tell me what's going on. The bishop said he was going to take care of things after my attack. Did something happen to him?"

I took my hands off the steering wheel and turned to face her. "The bishop's okay," I said, telling her a half truth. "We don't really know how it's all connected, but the woman who attacked you is involved with Desiree Jones."

"Desiree Jones? The woman who took my job?"

I nodded. "It looks like the one who attacked you is her girlfriend."

"Ross," she said, her voice full of dread. "Desiree is here. I saw her drive around the back of the church a little while ago, and I think there was someone in the passenger seat."

"Are you sure it was her?" I asked.

"Pretty sure. I mean, I never met her, but I've seen her picture on the church website."

I couldn't believe they were out in public after what happened at Jackson's office. Those were some bold bitches. "Did she see you?" I asked, even more grateful that I'd stopped Tia from going in the building.

"No. I don't think so."

"Okay, that's good." I turned on the car. "I'm going to drive around back to see if her car is still there. Getting these two might be the bishop's only chance," I said.

She whipped her head in my direction. "What do you mean, his only chance? I thought you said the bishop was okay."

I wished I could take back my words. She'd already been through so much, being attacked for God knows what reason. I didn't want her to be unnecessarily scared, but now that I'd slipped, there was no way to avoid telling her the rest.

"Okay, he's going to be fine, but right now he's in a bit of a jam."

"What kind of jam?" she pressed.

I sighed. "Some of the details are still fuzzy, but here's what I know so far: Those two women killed a man this morning, but the bishop showed up at the scene, and they arrested him for the crime. Bottom line is, unless we can prove that they did it, Bishop might be going to jail for a long time."

Tia's eyes were wet with tears. "He never would have been anywhere near them if he hadn't been protecting me."

I shook my head. "No, Tia. Don't blame yourself for this."

A blue Toyota Camry passed by us, going very fast. Tia yelled, "That's her! That's the car I saw going in the back!"

Without thinking, I put my car in drive and pulled away from the curb.

"Don't let them get away!" Tia shouted.

I followed them at a safe distance for about fifteen minutes. If they noticed me following them, they didn't react. Desiree's driving was steady and just under the speed limit the whole time. I imagine the last thing you would want to do after you've murdered someone is get caught because you're pulled over for a stupid traffic violation.

They finally backed the car into an alley in a neighborhood that I found questionable even in the light of day. There was no doubt in my mind that they were up to something, and I was determined to find out what it was.

I cruised slowly past the entrance to the alley. They were still sitting in the car, and fortunately they weren't looking toward the street as I passed by. The way Desiree was waving her arms around, it looked like they were in a heated discussion. Maybe the pressure of their crimes was getting to the two lovebirds, I thought.

A little further down the street, I parked the car. Tia reached for the door handle, but I grabbed her arm before she could jump out. "What is wrong with you? Where do you think you're going?" I said.

"I'm going to see what they're up to."

"Tia, you need to stay put. Those women are dangerous."

"You have no idea what I'm capable of when the going gets tough, Ross." I sensed there was a deeper meaning behind her words, but I still wasn't letting her go anywhere near these two killers.

"You might have nerves of steel, Tia, but you need to stay in the car. The bishop, Aaron, and a whole lot of other folks at the church would fry my ass if I let anything happen to you. So, do me a favor and keep your ass in this car," I said sternly.

She rolled her eyes, but agreed nonetheless. "Fine. I'll wait here. But if you take too long, I'm coming after you."

I got out of my car hoping that Tia would keep her word and stay put. It was already bad enough that I was running around playing detective; I didn't need to start playing Superman too.

I headed down the sidewalk, stopping at the corner of the building to peek around into the alley. The car was still parked there, but both doors were open and neither woman was inside. The trunk in the back of the car was open. I stood with my back pressed against the building, trying to decide what my next move would be. It's not like I'd ever been in a situation like this before, and my nerves were threatening to paralyze me.

The sound of a car door slamming shut startled me, and I peeked my head around the corner again.

Desiree ran to open a door at the side of the building. Her back was facing me as she held the door open for her girlfriend, whispering, "Hurry up!"

"Shut up. He's heavy, you know." With the trunk door still raised, I couldn't see what the girlfriend was doing, but she seemed to be struggling to pull something out of the car. There was a thud, and then I saw another set of feet near the back of the car. The girlfriend slammed the trunk shut, and what I saw nearly knocked the wind out of me. Aaron was standing there, blindfolded and gagged, with his arms tied behind his back.

She was pressing a gun against his head, ordering, "Move."

I couldn't get back to the car fast enough.

"You're lucky you got back here. I was just about—"

"Give me my phone!" I yelled.

She handed it to me, asking in a panicked voice, "What the hell is going on?"

"They have Aaron," I answered as I dialed Keisha Anderson's number.

Aaron

52

Having spent some time in jail, I'd been in a few scary situations in my life, but this damn sure qualified as the scariest. I'd just woken up from a blow to the temple that had my head pounding. If that wasn't bad enough, I couldn't see anything. I felt someone pulling me up, but my hands were tied behind my back and there was duct tape covering my mouth, so I couldn't fight back and I couldn't yell.

I felt a gun against my head as I was forced inside some type of building. Someone pushed me into a chair, and then I heard two female voices. They were talking too quietly for me to make out what was being said, but there was definitely tension in the air.

What the hell was going on? In my confused state, I struggled to understand. My mind wandered to the movie *Misery*, where a crazy fan holds her favorite author prisoner. Could this be a couple of deranged gospel music fans?

Suddenly, the blindfold was ripped off my face.
When my eyes adjusted to the light, I was shocked
to see the church secretary standing before me.
That's when I remembered that she was the last
person I had seen at the church before the woman
with the gun . . . It still didn't make sense to me. She
ripped the duct tape off of my mouth.

"Desiree?" I said, hoping she could help me figure
this out.

"Hello, Aaron." The smile on her face confused
me.

"What am I doing here?" I asked, still feeling
groggy. "What are *you* doing here?"

"Welcome to the beginning of the end." She
started laughing, and the fog in my brain cleared
enough for me to finally understand that she was
not here as a friend.

Without warning, another woman lunged at me,
punching me in the stomach. I keeled over, feeling
like I might throw up. She was a lot stronger than
she looked.

"Remember me?" she cackled, propping me up in
the chair to hit me again.

I did remember her. She was the one from the
church parking lot—the one with the gun.

She punched me a third time. With each blow, I
heard Desiree exclaim, "Oooh! I know that hurt!"

Though my body was throbbing, my mind was

clearer now, and I felt my anger rising. "You crazy bitch, what the hell is this all about?"

"What the fuck did you call her?" The other woman rained her fists down on me with so much force that it felt like she might have broken a rib.

"Arrrrgggggggh!" I groaned. With my hands tied, I was completely powerless. I had to find a way to stop this. "Desiree, why are you doing this?" I asked, appealing to the woman who had seemed so sweet every time I saw her in the bishop's office. Her response was filled with so much venom it felt like she was a completely different person.

"Two words, motherfucker: Bobby Taylor."

"I don't know Bobby Taylor," I said. In the last few years, especially with traveling for shows, I'd met thousands of people, most of whose names I didn't remember.

"Lynn, you hear that?" she said in an icy tone.

So, the heavy-handed one was named Lynn, I now knew.

"He doesn't remember. Ain't that some shit!" Lynn clocked me in the head.

"Fuck!" I screamed out.

"Oh, is poor Aaron hurt?" Desiree mimicked, making baby noises. No doubt about it, this bitch was crazy. I feared for my life.

I started pleading, "Look, I'm sorry. I just don't remember anyone named Bobby Taylor. Whatever

I did to him, let's just call him up and I'll apologize."

This really set Desiree off. Now she was the one swinging her fists, landing blows all over my head and torso. "You bastard! Bobby Taylor was my father, and you killed him, you evil motherfucker! You ruined my life, and now I'm going to ruin yours!"

Time seemed to stop for a second as the reality hit me. Ten years ago, I'd had a car accident. Young and dumb and foolish, I'd been drinking and driving. The driver of the other car was Robert Taylor Jr. He'd also been driving drunk, but because he died in the collision, I was found guilty of vehicular manslaughter and sentenced to five years in prison. I did my time, and I still lived with guilt, but never once had I thought about the family he left behind—the other lives that might have been destroyed by my poor choices.

"Desiree, I'm sorry. I'm really sorry."

She shook her head wildly, wiping away tears. "It's too late for sorry. Sorry won't bring him back. He was my whole life. He was the only one who understood me, and you have to pay for taking him from me."

"Please, tell me what I can do to make this right," I begged.

Lynn stepped in front of Desiree. "Why are you

even listening to this motherfucker?" she asked. "Why don't you just let me off him now? Shoot, after killing his boy Pippie and then your slick-ass uncle this morning, I'm kind of itching to do another one."

Pain shot through my heart. These two had killed Pippie because of something I did ten years ago. His blood was on my hands.

Desiree shook her head. "No, this one is mine. I want to be the one to send this piece of shit to hell for what he did to me. Give me the gun."

Lynn reached into her waistband and pulled out the weapon. She was about to hand it to Desiree when we heard a loud voice over a bullhorn.

"You, in the warehouse, my name is Lieutenant Williams with the New York City Police Department. Come out with your hands up!"

Desiree

53

"Come out with your hands up. We have you surrounded."

I looked to Lynn, my eyes wide with terror. "What are we going to do?" I'd never been so scared in all my life.

"Fuck! I don't know. How did they find us?" She stroked her hair as if there was something to pull out as she started pacing. Normally it was Lynn who kept me together, but she looked like she was about to totally lose it.

I grabbed her hand to stop her from moving around. "Lynn, think. We gotta get out of here."

"I know. I know," she said, though she didn't look like she had any more of a plan than I did.

When I rented this warehouse space a while back, we thought we'd found the perfect out-of-the-way place. The neighborhood was so run down that most of the storefronts were boarded up, and people rarely bothered to come out of their homes.

"How the hell did they find us?" I asked. Turning to look at Aaron, I felt like it was somehow his fault. This guy had killed my father, and just when I thought I was finally going to get my revenge, the cops showed up. I swear he had made some sort of deal with the devil. How else could he be allowed to live the happy life he'd had while I still suffered every day from the loss of my father?

Lynn turned my face so I didn't have to look at him anymore. She pulled me into her arms and gave me a long, deep kiss. It was the sweetest, warmest kiss I'd ever had.

"Why did that feel like good-bye?" I asked.

Tears were running down her cheeks. "I'm so sorry it turned out like this. If I hadn't fucked up and killed your uncle this morning they never would have come looking for us. We could have killed this son of a bitch and been long gone. I can't bear the thought of you going to jail, especially not for murders that I committed. I'm going to tie you up, and when we go outside, you'll tell them you were one of the hostages."

The fact that she was willing to sacrifice herself for me broke my heart in two—but I couldn't let it happen.

"No," I said. "It's not going down like that." I

turned to look at Aaron, feeling pure hate coursing through my veins. "I'm going to finish what we came here to do, and then…whatever happens, we're together to the end." I raised the gun and pointed it at Aaron.

Aaron
54

When I first heard the NYPD officer outside the building, I felt a rush of relief. Lynn and Desiree were pacing around like a couple of cornered rats, and I figured it was only a matter of time before they realized they were out of options and would surrender. But I quickly learned that I had underestimated Desiree's desire for revenge. Apparently she was willing to go out Thelma and Louise–style if she had to, as long as she finished me first. Before I knew it, I was staring down the barrel of a gun. Desiree's hand was shaking, but she stood her ground, staring me down with hate in her eyes.

"Aren't you going to beg for your life?" she hissed. "I want you to beg for your life."

"You do know we're *all* going to die in this warehouse, don't you? You kill me and they are going to kill you. Is that what your father would have wanted? For you to die in a hail of police bullets?"

"You don't know anything about my father." Tears were streaming down her face.

Lynn prodded her to toughen up. "Don't listen to him. Shoot his ass, Des."

I refused to give up. "You don't wanna do this, Desiree. Hasn't there already been enough blood-shed?"

"Not yet." She closed her eyes and pulled the trigger.

I heard the bullet whiz by my head, but I felt no pain. She had missed. There was another shot, but this time Desiree dropped to the ground. Lynn started screaming.

Before my brain could fully comprehend what had just happened, police officers broke down the door and came storming into the building. There was broken glass on the floor behind Desiree's life-less body. The shot that killed her must have come through the small window above her.

Lynn fell to her knees and grabbed Desiree, sob-bing now. Then she turned to me, full of fury, screaming, "You motherfucker! This all your fault! I'm gonna kill you!"

She dove for the gun, but barely got her hand on it before the cops opened fire, killing her instantly.

"Sir, are you okay?" I looked up to see ten emer-gency response cops surrounding me.

It took me a moment to find my voice, but finally I said, "Yeah, I'm alive."

One of the officers laughed. "And that's a good

thing, sir. Now, let's see if we can get you un-tied."

It took a few minutes for them to cut all the duct tape they'd wrapped around me, during which time I kept looking at the two dead women, wondering why it had come to this. Why had my past come back to haunt me in such a horrific way? Truth was, I might spend the rest of my life wondering about the answer to that question, but at least I was walking out of there alive. I left that building with my heart full of gratitude.

Outside on the sidewalk, Tia came rushing toward me and threw her arms around me.

"I've never wanted to hold someone so much in my life," she said.

"Me too." I pulled away and looked in her eyes, searching for answers. After all this time that she spent running away, was this really what it took to bring her back to me? Sometimes God works in mysterious ways, I guess.

"Oh my God, Aaron, I love you so much," she said, tears running down her face.

"Me too," I said as my lips fell sweetly onto hers. I had never felt so blessed and so happy to be alive.

Bishop

55

The armed guard led me in handcuffs from a small holding cell, down a long corridor, into the side entrance of the courtroom. I would be arraigned in front of Judge Warner, a man I had actually known for years. I'd had to phone him many times in the past to offer myself up as a character witness for parishioners who had gotten themselves in trouble. I had certainly never dreamed I'd enter his courtroom under these circumstances.

A quick glance to the back of the courtroom told me that I was surrounded by supporters. I saw all of the people closest to me, as well as what seemed to be half of my congregation squeezed onto the benches. Just seeing them made me feel a whole lot better—until I was led over to a chair next to my attorney and I got a look at who was sitting at the prosecution's table. Instead of some young assistant DA, it appeared I would be prosecuted by the district attorney herself. She didn't normally show up at a trial unless it was a case that could garner her lots of press. Was she here because she thought my conviction was a slam dunk? The knot in my stomach twisted itself a little tighter. If only I hadn't touched the knife when I found Jackson on the floor. Or better yet, if only I'd used good judgment and called the police instead of going over there in the first place.

I bowed my head, praying fervently as I waited for the arraignment to start.

Once things got underway, my heart was pounding so loudly in my chest that I could barely focus on what was being said. And then the district attorney spoke the words that came to me like an answered prayer, as clear as a bell:

"Your Honor, in view of the new evidence submitted to the court, we'd like to dismiss all the charges against Bishop TK Wilson."

The courtroom erupted in chaos. People were shouting "Hallelujah," "Praise Jesus," and "Amen!" The judge brought down the gavel and demanded order in the court.

"I would like to tell you, Bishop Wilson, that you are now free to leave this courtroom. Will the bailiff please remove the handcuffs?"

And just like that, the nightmare had ended. I could go home. I raised my hands to heaven in thanksgiving.

"Congratulations!" People were patting me on the back, giving hugs and prayers, as I tried to make my way out of the courtroom. Off in the distance, I saw Aaron and Tia, and they were actually holding hands. My heart swelled with joy. Monique and Ross were standing with them.

I locked eyes with my wife, and she came toward me tentatively. The people standing near me dispersed to give us a moment. She stood in front of me, hesitant for a second, and then she threw her arms around me.

"I'm sorry," she whispered in my ear.

Believe it or not, until that moment, I had almost forgotten about our marital difficulties. I felt a momentary twinge of my earlier jealousy creep back in, but this was not the place, and definitely not the time to discuss it with her.

I kissed her on the cheek and whispered back, "We'll talk later."

I untangled myself from her arms and stepped toward Aaron and Tia.

"Congratulations." Tia came into my arms, hugging me tight. This child really did feel like a daughter to me, and I was happy to have her back.

"Congratulations to you," I said, looking over at Aaron and then back to her. Yeah, prayer really could make miracles happen.

Ross came over to me and held out his hand. He

had been there to see me at my lowest point, and he never lost faith in me. I pulled him in for a hug.

"Ross, I don't know what you did or how you did it, but thank you."

"Wasn't just me," he said. "It's a long story, but Aaron deserves credit too."

"Thank you." I put an arm around Aaron's shoulders. We'd been through so much together, all of us, that we felt like family now.

Monique and I had lots of things to talk about. Coming so close to losing everything, including my freedom, I realized that I couldn't walk away from my marriage without making sure we tried everything to fix it. I asked her to come back to the house with me so we could talk.

"I still can't believe everything that's happened at First Jamaica Ministries recently," I said in the car on the way home. "And I can't believe we didn't sense anything was wrong with Desiree. I should have known."

"Don't blame yourself, TK," Monique said. "We were all fooled. She and Jackson were great actors. They set out to destroy Aaron and everyone around him, and they almost succeeded. I mean, look how bad things got between us."

I shot her a look to let her know she shouldn't be so confident that all of that was in the past. As far as

I was concerned, it wasn't. "Yes, well, they wouldn't have succeeded as well as they did if you hadn't been so easily wooed by promises of stardom. You completely disregarded my feelings about the subject in order to pursue a pipe dream. Is your job as first lady and as my wife not enough for you?"

She reached for my hand, but I moved my arm away. I wasn't ready to let her off the hook that easily.

"TK, I'm so sorry," she said. "I was a fool."

"I'm not going to argue with that."

"What are we going to do?"

"I don't know right now. I'm certainly not past this, and to tell the truth, I'm not sure that I ever will be. I'm going to have to put it in the hands of the Lord."

Aaron
56

As I entered her, I felt all of the tension leave my body, as if everything I'd been holding in for so long could be released. We'd finally reached this point, the moment I'd been dreaming of for almost two years. I had thought she was gone forever, but now I was holding the woman I loved, and I never wanted to let go of her again.

I connected with the rhythm of her hips, and we both rode that wave, our bodies closer than they'd ever been.

"I love you," she whispered, her face glowing with ecstasy.

"I love you too. I love you more than anything in this world." If someone had asked me to describe heaven, this would no doubt be it.

We made slow, sweet love for a while, until the heat became too much to contain. Tia rolled me over and climbed on top, gyrating her hips until the friction sparked an explosion. She rode me through wave after wave of pleasure, until we were both totally spent.

"Wow," she murmured as she slid off of me, lying on her back all loose-limbed and relaxed.

"Exactly." I reached over and grabbed her hand. "I always knew that it would be like this with you. It feels like coming home." I knew I sounded corny as a mofo, but it was truly how I felt. After all we'd gone through, I'd almost given up hope that this day would ever come.

"What are you thinking about?" I asked her.

"That I'm really glad we did this." She squeezed my hand.

"Me too. You wanna know what I'm thinking?" I leaned up on one elbow and kissed her face.

"What?" she asked, looking more beautiful than ever.

"That I can't wait for you to be my wife."

It felt amazing to have my life back, to know that everything that had passed would one day be a little blip on the screen of our perfect life together. We had each other, and there was nothing standing in the way of us being together anymore. The storm had passed—or so I thought.

When she didn't respond to my mention of marriage, I looked down at her and saw tension in her face. Something was bothering her.

"Tia?"

She looked into my eyes, and I saw sadness there. "This has been the most pleasurable moment of my life," she said. "It's everything I wanted to happen, but it won't ever happen again."

"Baby, what are you talking about? Once I make you my wife, I'm going to make sure you feel this loved every day."

"I have no doubt you would try, Aaron," she said, sitting up on the side of the bed with her back to me. "But I can't marry you. I can't spend every day with you knowing who you are and what you did."

I was flabbergasted. Why was this happening? Why was our perfect moment crumbling before my eyes?

I moved next to her and turned her face to mine. "Tia, are you seriously going to judge me for a mistake that happened ten years ago? I thought you understood that the accident wasn't totally my fault. Desiree's father was drunk too. And I already paid my debt to society."

She shook her head. "Aaron, I couldn't lie in bed next to you every night and pretend that what you did was okay. I can't have children and build a family with a murderer."

Tia
57

"Tia, I'm not a murderer!" he yelled desperately. "It was an accident!"

I loved this man more than anything, but it hurt my heart to see him in such denial about the truth. He was stuck on something that happened ten years ago, as if everything he'd done in the last month had never occurred.

"Aaron, this is not about the car accident. This is about you killing three men in cold blood."

He flinched as if I had slapped him in the face, then sat there quietly for a second. I assumed that in that moment he was deciding whether to come clean. "What are you talking about?" He chose the path of further deception, assuring me that I was making the right decision.

"You don't have to pretend with me anymore," I said. "I went back to Mark King's house today."

"Why would you do that?" There was a hint of anger behind his question, as if he felt I had betrayed him somehow by going there.

"I don't know. Something just didn't sit right with me, the way everything got tied up so neatly. I mean, the woman who murdered Pippie and almost killed you...why would she take it upon herself to kill the men who raped me? I couldn't stop asking myself that question."

He had a look of fear in his eyes, like I was too close to the truth that he hadn't wanted me to know. He tried to stop me from saying it, to convince me I was wrong. "Tia, why are you doing this? Pippie had a bloody *R* on his head just like the others, and you know for a fact that Lynn killed Pippie. I don't know why she killed those other men, but she was crazy. Crazy people do crazy things."

I sighed, wishing it really was that simple. "I know. I tried to convince myself that she was just crazy, but then I had to ask myself one question: Why would she have left Mark King's mother alive? If she was just killing to be killing, then why would she let one go?"

"Tia—"

I cut him off. "Aaron, stop. You can't change the truth. I spoke to Mark's mother today. She told me everything." I got up and started to put on my clothes. Aaron lay back down on the bed, sheer devastation written on his face.

"You know, I didn't go in there thinking this had anything to do with you," I said. "To tell you the truth, I didn't know what I was going to find there. Her son was a monster, but I knew that she had to be hurting because of his death, and something made me want to see her again.

"Do you know she apologized to me for mourning her son's death? She knew what he'd done to me, and she said she knew he deserved to die, but she couldn't help but still love him. That was her child.

"And then do you know what she said? She said 'You have someone who loves you that deeply, too, you know.' I had no idea what she was talking about. I thought maybe her grief made her crazy or something too. But then she said, 'The boy with the pretty smile and the dimples, he loves you that much.'"

I was crying now. "And that's when I knew it was you. She told me how it went down too. You went in there after I left, and you took things to a whole other level. All that time I thought I was losing my mind, freaking out about cars that weren't really following me…It was you, wasn't it? You were following me, and you killed the men who raped me."

"But I did it for you!" he cried out. "Those men didn't deserve to live."

"No one knows that better than me, Aaron, but it wasn't your decision to make. Don't you think I could have killed them if I wanted to? Believe me, I came close, but in the end, I realized that only God gets to decide who lives or dies. I didn't want to become a monster myself, and now I can't be married to one."

"Tia, please, don't do this."

"She's not going to tell the cops, and neither am I," I said, ignoring his plea. "I just can't marry you."

"Tia, I love you."

"I know that."

He got up and grabbed hold of my arm, begging, "Please don't leave me."

"I don't have a choice," I told him, removing myself from his grip.

"We can get past this," he insisted. "You'll see. One day it will be as if none of this ever happened."

"No, it happened, and we can't change any of it—not my rape, and not the murders—but I intend to leave it all behind. I wouldn't be able to do that if I married you. This tragedy would be at the center of our marriage forever. I will pray every day for their souls, for yours, and for mine, but I'm moving on, Aaron."

I walked toward the door, stopping to take one last look at him. "I do need to know one thing, though."

"What's that?"

"How did you do it? When you were following

me, I kept losing your tail, but you always seemed to find out where I was. How?"

"When I bought your iPhone last Christmas I added the Find My iPhone app."

What he said made sense, except for one thing. "But I changed my number."

"You never changed the phone. As long as the phone was on, I could log in and find you."

I nodded my understanding. He stood there with tears streaming down his face as I opened the door. "Good-bye, Aaron."

"I can't do this," he said. "I can't say good-bye. I won't be able to see you every day around the church and just pretend like we were never in love. I'll have to leave the church."

"Aaron, we will never be together again, but one thing will never change: I will always love you." I left him standing there, feeling at peace with my decision. Feeling like I would finally be all right.

Discussion Questions

1. Were you surprised when Tia left Aaron at the altar?

2. Did you think Tia's dream was reality?

3. Did you think Aaron was going to sleep with Desiree?

4. What were your thoughts on Jackson? Did you think he was in charge?

5. Did you realize who gave Ross an STD?

6. Who was crazier: Lynn or Desiree?

7. How did you feel when Pippie died, and did you think Tia killed him?

8. If you were the bishop, would you have left Monique?

9. Would you have taken things to the same level as Aaron if you were him?

10. Was the *Choir Director 2* what you expected? Did it live up to its predecessor?

11. What do you think is next for Aaron?

New York Times bestselling author Carl
Weber keeps readers on the edge of their
seats with his novel of love, jealousy...and murder.

Meet Darryl Graham, or as his
neighbors call him—

The Man in 3B

See the next page for a preview.

Prologue

September in New York City

It was one of those muggy Indian summer nights, where Detective Sergeant Dan Thomas of the 113th Precinct in Queens sat at his desk thinking about his latest case. He was now in his third hour of overtime, and it didn't look like he was going home anytime soon to splash around in his new pool with wife number two as he'd promised. He'd just left a horrific crime scene, where a local man had been found dead in his apartment, burned beyond recognition. Both his partner and lieutenant had already come to the conclusion that this was probably some unfortunate accident, or perhaps even a suicide, but Dan's gut told him different. It told him this was a homicide, and in all his years on the job, his instincts had never led him astray. So instead of heeding the advice of his lieutenant and letting the case go until morning, Detective Thomas sent his partner to the fire marshal's office to see if she could find out the exact cause of the fire. He also had a couple of uniformed officers bring in some of the dead man's neighbors for routine questioning. Maybe one of them would be able to shed light on the situation. Thus far, they'd only turned out to be concerned citizens, singing "Kumbaya" and praising the deceased as if he were the next messiah, but Detective Thomas wasn't convinced.

Nobody's this well loved, he thought.

"Dan," his partner, Detective Keisha Anderson, called as she entered the squad room waving a folder. She was panting, as if she'd literally run the entire way from the fire marshal's office. "I gotta give it to you, partner. Your instincts were right on as usual. Fire marshal said it was definitely not an accident. They can't tell exactly what started it right now, but someone used an accelerant to start the fire so they could contain it to one room."

Thomas nodded his approval. "Nice work, Anderson. Those idiots over at the fire marshal's office usually take two weeks to get us anything relevant. What'd you do, promise to sleep with one of them?" Thomas laughed.

"Nope, promised you would," his partner replied with a laugh of her own. "Big, burly guy named Sullivan. He said he likes to be on top, so you're catching tonight, not pitching." Thomas gave her the finger, and she shot back, "Hey, just thought you might wanna be prepared."

Anderson handed Thomas the file, then sat on the arm of a nearby chair as she waited for him to read it. When he finished, Thomas looked up, trying to hide a vindicated smile that spread across his thin lips. He'd call the wife and tell her the pool would have to wait. Once again, his intuition had been spot-on.

He looked over at his partner.

"So where do we go from here?" she asked as Thomas got up from his chair.

Thomas didn't say a word. He gestured for Anderson to follow him as he headed toward another room. Once inside, he pulled back a curtain that revealed a large picture window, which served as a two-way mirror.

"You wanna know where we go from here, Anderson?" Thomas asked as he stared at the five people sitting on the other side of the glass. "For starters, we're going to drill each one of them until we find out who the murderer is."

Walking away from the glass, Thomas retrieved a small notepad from his suit jacket and began flipping through pages. His partner watched the five suspects. They were all eating fried chicken from Popeyes and drinking soda and coffee ordered by the lieutenant and paid for by New York City taxpayers.

"I don't know, Dan. They all look like one big, happy family." She shrugged. "What makes you think one of them is a murderer? I mean, there's still the possibility of suicide."

"Possible, but not probable. This guy didn't kill himself, and my gut tells me one of them did the job for him."

Thomas walked back over to the window next to Anderson, and they observed the group on the other side.

"What do you mean? What do you see that I don't? To me they all look pretty normal, more like the guy or girl next door than killers." Anderson's eyes went from the group to Thomas and then back to the two-way mirror again.

"Maybe, but you've been on the job long enough to know that looks can be deceiving. I see five people who are hiding something."

"Hiding something like what? They all look content."

"If you had just lost a member of your 'big, happy family,' as you put it, would you still be sitting here, smiling and laughing while enjoying your food? Or would you be genuinely broken up about it?"

She scanned the group again. "Yeah, I guess you're right. I never thought of it like that. The only one remotely upset is the kid."

"Mm-hmm," Thomas said. "It's like when the

troublemaker of the family dies. Everyone shows up at the funeral for protocol. Do you see any tears being shed for that man in there, Anderson?"

"Nope, I haven't seen anything more than a few crocodile tears. All I see is a bunch of people getting fat on the city's dime." She folded her arms. "So, who do you think looks good for it? They can't all be in on it."

"No, but my guess is that it's one of the two ladies. A gruesome murder like this could only be a crime of passion. It's not an easy thing to light a person on fire and burn them to a crisp. Not unless you really hate them."

Anderson nodded her agreement. "Which one?"

"Take your choice." Thomas glanced down at his notepad, then at the very scantily clad woman at the end of the table. "The neighborhood gossip said the deceased had a history with them both. Word is the pretty young thing over there is a schoolteacher, but I ain't never had a teacher who looked like that."

"Me neither. What was her connection to the deceased?"

"From what I'm hearing, jilted lover."

"Now that, my friend, would give her motive," Anderson reasoned. "But if that's the case, why are you even looking at the other one?"

"You mean the fat ass?" Thomas said without missing a beat.

"Dan!" Anderson snapped at his lack of political correctness, then added under her breath, "Although she does have one hell of a donkey butt."

"No, I'm not saying she's a fat ass. That's what the deceased called her in front of the entire neighborhood this morning."

"Damn. I'd kill a motherfucker for that shit myself."

This time Anderson managed to get a laugh out of Thomas. "Exactly my point."

Anderson shook her head and then moved on to the next suspect. "If I had to put my money on somebody, I'd put it on him." She pointed at the handsome man sitting next to a young college-aged kid. "You do realize that Cliff Huxtable over there is a fireman. And who would know more about setting a controlled fire than him?"

"Nobody, except maybe a fireman's son." They both turned toward the boy.

"Isn't he like some straight-A genius or something like that?"

"Mm-hmm, and so was the Craigslist Killer. That same gossip I spoke to said that he and the deceased spent a lot of time together in the deceased's apartment—until they had a falling out."

"What about him?" Anderson pointed to a thin, light-skinned man in his late twenties wearing a well-tailored suit and a silk tie. He had a plateful of chicken in front of him but never took a bite. "Why does Mr. Shirt and Tie look so nervous?"

"Him? Not sure, but he's the jilted lover's current boyfriend, and I hear him and our victim had a lot of beef over the girlfriend."

"Ohhhh. I've handled more than my share of love triangle cases. He could easily turn out to be our number one suspect." She shook her head uncertainly. "I just don't know, though..."

"What's there to know?" He looked his partner in the eye. "Like I said, one of those people in that room is a murderer. Now all we have to do is figure out which one."